No Marriage of Convenience for a Cowboy

Escape to Cowboy Crossing, Volume 4

Alexa Verde

Published by Alexa Verde, 2023.

No Marriage of Convenience for a Cowboy

Book 4 in the Escape to Cowboy Crossing series
By Alexa Verde

About the book

An elusive woman with secrets, a quiet cowboy, a precocious child and a rebellious teenager, and a marriage of convenience that hides real feelings...

.

Arianna Montemayor is so far from her comfort zone that it's not even on the same planet when this eternal nomad and former runaway considers becoming an instant mom. To win custody of her niece and nephew, she needs a stable job, a house, and a husband, not necessarily in that order. For help, she turns to a local cowboy and the most responsible man she's ever met, Kieran O'Neill. But once scarred in many senses by men she trusted, dare she trust again?

.

Kieran would never refuse someone in need, especially orphaned children or the woman whose affection he's been trying unsuccessfully to win. He's drawn to her even if she keeps everything about herself a secret. But if he marries her, it wouldn't be a marriage of convenience for him, but a real one. Then he discovers the children have scary secrets, as well, ones they don't realize themselves.

.

When danger strikes, will Arianna have to sacrifice her new life to keep Kieran and the children safe?

~

Escape to Cowboy Crossing
Women scarred by their painful pasts, bonded like sisters by the secrets they share. Cowboys able to see the hurting hearts behind the tough facades. And someone willing to kill to get what they want...

Dedication

This book is dedicated to Sharon Dean, with heartfelt thanks for her help and support.

Chapter One

"I HAVE A HALF SISTER?" Arianna stared at the police officer. She wasn't surprised often in life, but this news nearly rendered her speechless.

"Had. She was your father's child. She died after an accident. I'm very sorry for your loss. But you do have a nephew and a niece."

Now there wasn't anything nearly about it. Arianna was speechless. As she did her best to comprehend it, her mouth slackened until she surely resembled a fish thrown out of the water, gasping for air.

Granted, she'd cut all ties to her family after parental rights had been taken from her parents and she'd been placed in the foster system. The half sister must've been born after that.

Someone she'd never known and now never would. The sense of loss was strong, considering the woman was a stranger, someone Arianna would've passed on the street without recognizing. And those poor children...

Her gaze moved to the short-haired woman in a strict navy suit who'd introduced herself as a social worker, and Arianna's mind whirled. The reason for her presence here...

No, hopefully not.

"Is the children's father going to take care of them?" Arianna licked her dry lips.

"The children's father or fathers are unknown," the social worker said, her voice weary.

What about Arianna's father?

Right. She shuddered and placed the memory deep where it belonged, in a far corner of her mind that should have three locks and an alarm system to get to it. Even if her father was still living, he wouldn't qualify to take care of children. She wouldn't trust him with a rat. Though a rat might've recognized a kindred spirit in her dad.

Then it registered. *Hold on.* Was she expected to take in the children?

"Will you consider adopting the children?" the social worker asked.

Arianna shook her head so violently long hair slapped her cheeks. There had been a reason she'd avoided romantic entanglements all these years.

Avoided getting attached, except to her foster sisters, and even there she'd set boundaries. Kept secrets.

Including one that was going to haunt her forever. Pain sliced through her.

Something had broken inside her. Something very necessary to form a family. To survive, she'd numbed her feelings. To become what she was now. There was no way back from that.

She shook her head again. "I can't. I can't! I… I travel a lot. I don't have a permanent home." It didn't make sense to have one with all her travels. She'd just received a new assignment for a remote location in Asia. A risky one, but that was her favorite thing about the assignment. Happily married now, Madeline didn't need her help any longer with the mystery behind her assault solved and another threat eliminated. After her wonderful wedding, Madeline had moved into Brandon's ranch house. It was a pity to leave the large lodge empty, but some things couldn't be helped. Arianna had stayed in one place long enough and had the unmistakable itch to move again.

She'd learned early that it was much more difficult to catch a person who was moving fast.

Guilt stabbed her. The children… No. It would be better if someone else stepped in. Children needed someone warm and cuddly. Someone with a safe profession and no emotional and physical scars. She was anything but.

"Isn't there anyone else who can take care of them?" Unfamiliar-to-her desperation sounded in her voice. She cringed. She'd promised herself she'd never be desperate again.

The social worker frowned. "There's one more option. Your cousin. He's married now, so it might be a better option."

Everything inside Arianna shuddered, and her heart did a one-eighty. He'd never gotten punished because she hadn't any proof.

Her world upside down now, she leveled her gaze on her visitors, then shocked herself by saying, "No. No! He can't have them. That's not going to happen."

"It's better than letting them go into the foster system."

Right. Right! And she'd just refused to take the children in. Because she wasn't fit to be a mother, among other reasons. And one of her previous assignments hadn't ended well. If she was tracked down, could it put her in danger? Much worse, could it put the children in danger? She was sure she'd covered her tracks well, but life had no guarantees.

She was as far from a good mother figure as Asia was from the Show Me state.

But the alternative... She suppressed another shudder. She couldn't let that happen. She raised her chin and heard herself saying, "I'll take care of the children. What do I need to do to win custody?"

The sudden decision affected her like a bucket of cold water. But she couldn't change it. She wouldn't let innocent children go through what happened to her. Pain knifed her, dragging her into the abyss of memories, but she held onto the edge of the cliff. She'd survived before, but barely.

The social worker blinked while the police officer studied Arianna. She could understand their confusion. Moments ago, she'd been reluctant to become an instant mom.

The officer's eyes narrowed. "This is not a competition, ma'am. The children's welfare is at stake."

How come nobody cared about her welfare when she'd been a child? Arianna squared her shoulders. No point in being bitter. She'd rather draw compassion from her experience. She softened her voice and rearranged her facial features. "I understand. I'm asking for your help."

The social worker came through. "You need to show that you can provide a stable environment for them. You just stated you travel a lot and don't have a permanent home."

She certainly did. Argh. "I'll get a house and a stable job. In fact, this lodge is available. I know my friend will gladly let us stay here. You can see for yourselves it has plenty of room for the children and a spacious fenced-in yard for them to play in. I can get a slide installed. The security is state-of-the-art here." Maybe she shouldn't have stated the latter. But she knew all too well how important security was. "I have a clean record." She'd walked on the edge of the law sometimes, but they didn't need to know that. "I'm financially secure."

The social worker looked away as if she didn't want to state the obvious. "Your cousin would have an advantage because he's married."

Arianna's mind whirled. Okay. Okay. She needed a permanent job and a respectable husband, not necessarily in that order.

The first one was doable. The second one?

Why did Kieran pop into her mind? He was as respectable as they come with a great reputation in the community. He was as stable as she was... fluid. *And* he seemed to have a crush on her.

Tall, muscular, and surprisingly caring, he was also the first man who'd made her heart race in years, though she'd done her best not to show it. With her lifestyle and messed-up past, she hadn't considered a romance with him.

Could she consider a marriage of convenience?

She'd done a lot of reckless things in her life. But could she marry a man she barely knew for the sake of children she'd never met?

Kieran walked to the office after turning the animals out to the pasture. He preferred working outdoors to taking care of paperwork, but his eldest brother, Brandon, who usually managed the ranch, was a newlywed. It wasn't fair to expect him to still do his many duties.

Kieran didn't mind stepping in. He *did* mind his little brother dogging his footsteps and not lifting a finger to help, never mind that he was only home on vacation. With Sean away helping their widowed aunt on her ranch, the outdoor work kept everyone else busy. "You could pitch in, you know."

"With the horses maybe, not with the office work." Declan shrugged, flashing the cheeky grin he usually reserved for the cameras. That grin and the many fascinating places Declan had visited must be a great combination because his channel was popular. "You'd never be able to clean up the mess I made. What's up with you anyway? You'd think you and our formerly grouchy brother switched places."

Kieran snorted. "Getting hitched somehow branded Brandon with a permanent smile."

Declan was right, though.

Kieran had to remember to iron out his frown. "Doesn't it bother you that three of our brothers married in such rapid succession—and we're not even dating?" He didn't begrudge his brothers their happiness. On the contrary, he was thrilled for them. But a place somewhere deep inside him felt... was it empty?

"Who says I'm not dating? And who wants to get married?" Declan shut the door behind them, closing them into the small office, then sat on a corner of Kieran's cluttered desk and picked up Kieran's favorite pen. Declan didn't even seem to mind that the pen was a bit chewed on the corner. "I won't deny it's weird how fast it happened or how their wives just happen to be foster sisters. But our brothers couldn't have found better women. I'm happy for them. I suspect you are, too. So what's really eating you?"

Trust meddlesome Declan, always sticking his nose where it wasn't wanted, to get into mischief. Kieran snatched the pen back before his brother could mess with it. Chewed tip or not, Kieran loved that pen. It could be refilled and still wrote great. Yes, he held onto people, places, and things. And he liked it that way.

Unlike his flaky brother who'd rarely spent the night at the same place, unless it was his vacation at the ranch.

"Yep. Like I said—grouchy." Declan swung his leg, the heel of his fancy loafer thudding against the desk leg.

Sure, those shoes worked jetting around the world after the next big story, but who wore such ridiculous things on a ranch? Their slick surfaces were already dull with mud, mud Declan's leg-swinging action was crumbling onto Kieran's already not-so-clean floor.

Declan smirked. "That sunny disposition wouldn't have anything to do with the fact that Arianna's leaving soon, would it?"

Frowning again—Kieran could allow himself to frown in his own office where he should be alone—he powered up the laptop. He didn't know why that news had hit like he'd fallen from a horse.

Everyone in Cowboy Crossing knew she wasn't going to stay for long. She'd come here to help her foster sister Madeline, who'd had amnesia after being hit on the head, and once the threat had passed, Arianna would have no reason to stay.

"She's never paid attention to me, so why should it matter that she's leaving?" He clicked open a file on feed and farm supplies. "One can't lose something one didn't have in the first place."

Saying that... *hurt*. He stared at the spreadsheet without the numbers registering.

"Not sure why you're so drawn to her, bro. Of the five foster sisters who've become part of our family, she's gotta be the most mysterious. The most elusive. I won't deny she's piqued my curiosity." Declan held up a hand when Kieran's head jerked up. "Just my *curiosity*. If you want to pursue her, you won't be tripping over me."

Which was good. Not that Kieran planned to pursue her, but Declan had a certain reputation with the ladies Kieran wasn't sure he could stand up against. Arianna was the most mysterious and most elusive, yes. And Kieran and his brothers—present company excluded—were simple men who worked hard and liked simplicity and certainty. Everyone—present company *included*—said the truth in his family, and there were no secrets.

"Even if she's a sister-in-law, we know nearly nothing about her." Declan's voice had grown soft, speculative. "From what I've heard, the town gossiped about the foster sisters from Houston a lot. But they couldn't even speculate about Arianna, though many people tried. Huh. Even Mom, whom everyone credits as *the* best local source of gossip—ahem, *information*—admitted defeat in Arianna's case. And that's saying something since I get my fascination for stories and quest for truth from Mom."

Again, Declan was right—not that Kieran expected any less than an accurate and quick assessment of the facts from a world-renown reporter. And Mom had talked to her daughters-in-law and Arianna's other foster sisters and still had gotten little on her life. Arianna didn't say much about herself even to the people closest to her.

He should've taken the hint and stayed away. Instead, he cataloged the things he did know. He rocked back in his chair.

And Declan snagged the pen again, clicking the back of it as if the familiar feel of a pen in his hand steadied him. Made sense. Kieran had rarely seen Declan without one. "Unlike her foster sisters, she entered the system when she was already a teen after her parents lost parental rights."

Compassion unraveled as Declan spoke. Something awful must've happened for social services to interfere that way.

"She speaks Spanish fluently and has a working knowledge of several other languages. She doesn't maintain any contact with her biological family. She loves her foster sisters but keeps her distance from anyone else. She received a GED, but again, unlike her foster sisters, she didn't continue her education."

Whoa. Had Declan been digging into her life?

Kieran wasn't sure how he felt about that, but he added what he knew. "She likes the color black—clothes, boots, eyeliners, you name it. Like she's in mourning." For what, he ached to know. "She always seems to be on guard, even when her posture appears relaxed." For what, he also ached to know.

His heart jolting in his chest, Kieran continued, instead of reading the numbers on the spreadsheet. "And she has gorgeous chocolate-hued hair and the most amazing green eyes I've ever seen. They seem to change their color upon her mood, which is the only way to even attempt to read her."

Declan slapped the desk. "I knew it. You *are* serious about her. I can look into her more if you want. I have... connections."

Kieran shook his head—so quick it whipped his neck. They should give her privacy. He wouldn't like it if someone started digging into his life. Though frankly, he had nothing to hide.

Did she?

"Got ya." Declan released the pen. It rolled along the massive scratched oak table and rocked against more stacks of papers than Kieran liked to see.

Kieran reached over to steady it. "I *know* I need to let this ridiculous attraction go." And why was he confiding in Declan? His most irresponsible and mischievous brother was sure to prank him with this, if not spread the story far and wide.

After a sad glance at the laptop, Kieran stood and walked to the window that opened to a spectacular view of sprawling emerald-hued hills spotted with cows. Then he strode back to the desk. "I gave up on romance years ago when the woman I loved traded me for big city lights. I don't need to have my heart ripped out again for the same reason. I don't know if she's a believer, either, and that should be important to me."

"Tell yourself that all you want, *mope* all you want—or *do* something about it, bro. She's not sticking around unless you do something to make her stay. It's been my experience that women can change their minds fast with a little sweet talk." And with that, Declan pushed off Kieran's desk and sauntered across the room, his silly city-slicker shoes making squishy sounds rather than rapping on the wooden floors the way a good pair of work boots would. Kieran would have to buy him some real men's boots.

The door clicked shut behind his brother, and Kieran sank back against his chair, spreadsheets forgotten.

At the knock on the door, he got up, welcoming the distraction. He wasn't getting much work done anyway. Weird. This must be someone new. Everyone on the ranch knew they didn't lock doors.

As he opened the office door, he blinked. Did his thoughts conjure up her image?

Arianna was standing there, dressed in black jeans and a black top with long sleeves and matching combat boots. A faux-leather bracelet wrapped her wrist twice, and heavy eyeliner and mascara outlined her eyes. With her head in a familiar defiant tilt, she didn't look like she'd made an effort to be appealing, and yet his pulse skyrocketed. Go figure.

Yet... something was different in her posture. Caution? Well, she always looked cautious, even at dinner at his parents' place where everyone was super relaxed. But this was a different kind of caution. Maybe mixed with uncertainty. What was going on?

Did she come to say goodbye?

While profound sadness stirred inside, that could signify he meant something to her. *Yeah, talk about being just pathetic.*

She shrugged. "We can talk like this. I guess."

Oh. He was standing there, gawking. He gestured for her to come in, and she stepped inside, making him wish he'd picked up the papers strewn around. And when was the last time anyone dusted around here? It wasn't like someone could write in the dust on the shelf, but it wouldn't be long before they could.

"What do you need?" he asked gruffer than he'd intended.

Just great. That'd be an efficient way to make her like him. Not!

She moved her hands from her pockets and ran them through her hair. "A job."

Okay. O–okay. "And you came to *me* for that?"

Really, where were his manners? He cringed. Probably ran away with his good nature. He waved for her to take a seat, but she remained standing.

So he would, as well, and leaned against the desk.

She stepped closer, invading his space. He took a moment to place her scent. It was that subtle. Sandalwood. Something was unusual about that scent. Exotic, maybe? And why did it make his heart go even faster?

"You're the de facto manager of this ranch while Brandon and my sister are on their honeymoon, correct?" She ran her fingers through that rich mahogany-hued long hair again, making him want to do the same.

Hold on. Was she nervous? That didn't look like her.

"Do you plan on sticking around?" And why did that idea give him a burst of joy?

She studied the hardwood floor, worn-out by generations and displaying its scuff marks proudly. Then she looked up. "Maybe."

His heart rate kicked up. Had his family rubbed off on her? His parents and brothers had that effect on people. Or was she immune to it? "For how long?"

She shrugged. "A while."

If this was a job interview, it wasn't going great. "Do you have any work experience on a ranch?" He studied her. Okay, let's be honest. He just couldn't look away.

Her eyes dulled, dimming to the color of a swamp. "I've never even seen a cow up close." At least, she was upfront about it. He'd met people who exaggerated their education and experience on their applications.

"I guess that's a no." Then he had an idea. "Tell me, what skills *do* you have?"

"I can shoot, fight, track people, and speak several languages, though none of those languages would help me communicate with farm animals." Her chin rose higher, and a challenge girded her voice.

How exactly could he have her apply those skills at the ranch? Maybe that was the reason for the challenge.

He shouldn't want her to stay. But he did. "Maybe apply to the police department in Springfield?" Surely, her foster sister, who already worked there, would put in a good word for her.

Her eyes dulled further. She shoved her hands into her pockets again as if shutting an invisible door. "No vacancies. Besides, I don't want to go anywhere close to the police."

And why was that? No, he didn't want to know. This woman was trouble, and he'd do best to stay away from her.

"It's okay." She pivoted toward the door, her long hair swishing along her back. "It wasn't a good idea, anyway."

Wait!

He placed a hand on her shoulder, then jerked his hand back when she flinched. "Do you know how to cook?" So much for staying away from her.

Her lips tipped up as she slowly turned around, drawing his attention to her mouth. Not a good idea. "Better than I know how to—what exactly do you do with cows?"

Oh boy. That didn't sound promising. Cowhands usually had tough stomachs, but Kieran wasn't sure they were *that* tough.

Chapter Two

Kieran knew showing up at the lodge where Arianna was staying wasn't a good idea. But Madeline—not Arianna!—had shared about Arianna's orphaned niece and nephew she'd agreed to take in. He told himself he was doing it for the children who were about to arrive in the small town. Not because he was helplessly, hopelessly attracted to Arianna.

He could list many reasons not to succumb to that attraction, including that technically he'd just become her boss. Not that he could imagine her letting anyone boss her around. He'd never imagined such stubbornness and defiance could be appealing, either.

Until he'd met her.

But here he was, on the lodge porch, a bucket of paint in one hand and paintbrushes in the other. Arianna had already buzzed him through the gate, though she'd sounded surprised.

Well, *color* him surprised, too. He glanced at the bucket. No pun intended.

She opened the door, and his heart did that little jolt it always did in her presence. Her luscious mahogany hair was pulled back in a low ponytail, exposing her high cheekbones and incredible green eyes. A man could get lost in those eyes and never find his way back. Wouldn't want to.

"Hello, Kieran." She cleared her throat.

Right, he'd been staring at her. He seemed to do it a lot in her presence. He lifted the paint bucket, his flimsy excuse for being here. "I thought it would make sense to prepare the rooms for the children. You know, to make them feel welcome. Then maybe we could go shopping for age-appropriate furniture."

The house's owner, Kieran's sister-in-law and Arianna's foster sister, now lived in Germany where his military brother was stationed. But she'd made it clear Arianna had carte blanche to change the house any way she wanted.

Arianna's lips parted slightly, drawing his attention to her well-defined mouth. Again. Was the temperature rising outside, or was it his own? "Right. Good idea." She stepped aside. "Come on in."

He walked in, close enough to breathe in her signature sandalwood scent. It smelled of faraway lands and something... forbidden. His heart gave another jolt. Why did she affect him so much? Why did he have to come back to her?

She didn't let any man get close to her. And she'd eventually take the children and return to Houston. Strange that she was going to bring them here in the first place instead of letting them stay in their familiar environment. Especially considering she was from there and had grown up there. Did she have her reasons?

"That was thoughtful of you." She led him to a smaller room that must be next to her own. The fully furnished lodge offered plenty of rooms to choose from. "What color did you bring?"

"Pink. I mean, I didn't want to follow stereotypes, but the little girl at the neighboring ranch likes pink."

While, based on her clothing choices, Arianna preferred black. He was yet to see her in anything different. Maybe he picked the wrong paint.

"Sounds good." The corners of her lips tipped up a tiny bit. Not a smile, but the beginning of one. Why did it feel so important to coax a smile out of her?

He placed the materials on the carpet. "We'll need to cover the floor first. I have everything necessary in the truck. I'll bring the tray and tray lining, too. Do you have a cap and goggles? If not, I've got extras."

She tilted her head. "I have a cap, but I could use a pair of goggles. But aren't you busy at the ranch?"

He looked away. "I, um, took some time off." For the first time in years. Like several of his brothers, he'd made the ranch his life and always had a lot of work there.

Something unreadable flashed in her eyes, making them olive green. "Thank you. Madeline is back from her honeymoon. So she and Jessie were going to come over this evening to prepare the house. But your help will speed up the process. Besides, I feel guilty taking them away from their husbands."

Was that a note of wistfulness, or was it *his* wishful thinking?

"You're very welcome. I'll be right back." He hurried outside to his truck and returned with the rest of the things. Besides her subtle sandalwood scent, another scent drifted to him. A homey scent he'd never associate with Arianna. A pie, maybe?

"Let me change. I'll be right back, too." She returned fast indeed, now dressed in worn-out black jeans with rips from wear, not fashion, and a black T-shirt. This was the first time he saw her in something short-sleeved, and a tattoo—black, what else?— marked her arm.

A large letter *E*. Clearly someone's initial. Jealousy stabbed him. Was it a tribute to someone she loved?

Her gaze followed his, and her eyes became tender like the first leaves in spring as she looked at her tattoo. Whoa. He'd never seen them that way before. Then she turned away. When she looked back, those eyes were unreadable again. He must be right in his guess. She must've loved the person the tattoo was dedicated to. Loved them very much.

Covering their hair with caps and their face with goggles could change a person's appearance. But there was no mistaking her guarded posture or those long legs he shouldn't be paying attention to.

For some time, they worked together in silence protecting the floor, then taping over the moldings. Their hands touched a few times, and she jerked back every time while something akin to an electric current passed through him.

He'd never experienced anything like this, even with his first love who'd broken his heart. Why did it have to be with a secretive woman who never intended to stay?

Lord, why?

She handed him disposable nitrile gloves. Well, that would cure the hand-touching reaction. And much easier to peel off gloves than to scrub off paint.

He put rollers on the holders, and they started painting.

"I never had my room painted the way I wanted. Didn't even realize I could ask," she said so quietly he wasn't sure he heard it.

He didn't know what to say, so he didn't say anything. He'd often wondered what her childhood was like to shape her character the way it was. But he suspected it would be something he wouldn't like.

Teens rarely ran away from happy homes, and there had to be a serious reason for her parents to lose parental rights. Arianna was a survivor, but he wished he could spare her the things she'd had to survive.

"Dad never wanted a girl. He wanted a son. He didn't have any use for a girl. Well, except to bring him dinner if Mom wasn't at home. Or to fetch him cigarettes. Or slippers."

Slippers. Like a dog. Arianna didn't say it, but she didn't need to.

"I'm sorry to hear that." She'd probably never told this to anyone, and he felt honored and at the same time hurt on her behalf.

"It's okay. It wasn't that bad. Unless he got angry. I learned to avoid anything that made him angry. Including appearing in front of him unless he needed me to."

"That must've been horrible." A vise squeezed his heart. His childhood was so filled with love that he couldn't even imagine what hers was like. He stopped painting. Stopped moving. Nearly stopped breathing.

Her brushstrokes were even, her movements calm as if she weren't sharing a heart-wrenching story she'd lived through. "It's okay. It's in the past." Her voice grew stronger, every word enunciated with a hard edge now.

He nearly exploded. "It's *not* okay. It shouldn't have happened." He ached to hug her, to comfort her, but she'd push him away, wouldn't she?

"But it did. It wasn't the worst, actually. More like a prelude for the things to come." She paused, paint dripping from her roller as she stood there. "I just wanted you to know I'm damaged. A lot. And I wouldn't want my sharp pieces to cut anyone else."

He flinched. He'd hoped that she'd opened up to him. That her words, as painful as they were, were a show of trust. But was this all a warning?

A warning not to get close. Not to fall for her. How could he tell her he wanted to do everything to help her heal? "Arianna, I—"

She stopped him with an upraised hand. "Enough about me. Let's talk about something nice."

And she wasn't?

Before he could protest, she continued. "Tell me about *your* childhood."

Warmth spread through him as he kept painting. "To say my childhood was nice is an understatement." Oh no. He didn't mean to rub it in. He froze, then moved the roller before the paint could drip.

But she nodded, so he kept going about his mischief with his brothers, mornings and afternoons taking care of horses and cows, Sunday afternoon barbecues, and Friday evenings making the world's best s'mores at a campfire. There'd been a lot of work involved, and as a child, he'd sometimes envied the children in town who didn't have ranch chores to drag them out of bed with the dawn. As one of the more responsible boys in the family who seemed to mature earlier than the others did, he'd sometimes frowned on the mischief his brothers got into, especially Declan.

Now Kieran had a new appreciation for those days and missed them. There were lots of differences in the way he and Arianna had grown up, but the biggest one seemed to be that he was loved while she'd never been.

It was difficult to accept love and affection when one didn't know what it was. Not that... that he was in love with her. But he was *in like* with her. No doubt about that.

Once they finished painting, she eyed the walls. "We can put up decorations when it's dry, right? Do you think she'd like flowers? Or bunnies? Or puppies? Or kittens?" She grimaced. "Yeah, yeah. I should know what my niece likes."

He didn't ask what she'd preferred when she was little, because that seemed like putting salt in her wound. And it looked like she already had more salt there than all the oceans combined.

Compassion stirred, but he schooled his features so she wouldn't see it and mistake it for pity. "Why don't we ask her when she's here?"

She nodded. "Well, I doubt her brother will like pink, so we'll leave the color of his room for him to decide."

Did she say *we* by accident? Either way, he liked how it sounded. Way too much.

"We'll have to go to Springfield for furniture," he said. "Cowboy Crossing is too small a town to have a decent selection. Would you like to take your car or follow me?" Well, actually... Arianna seemed like a person who preferred to be in the driver's seat. And if she didn't get a chance to do things alone, she'd want to lead. He was comfortable and confident enough for that. "Or I'll follow you."

The beginning of a smile became a half smile. Progress. "No sense taking two vehicles. But we'll need a truck to haul heavy pieces. We can go in yours."

She surprised him again, and he liked it. He appreciated the predictability in his life. If something new happened, it often meant there was a problem. But he enjoyed discovering new layers of Arianna. Fine, more than that, she fascinated him.

She peeled off her pink-paint-spattered gloves, then her goggles, giving him an unobstructed view of her spectacular eyes, and his entire being responded with longing for things that couldn't be.

"I can wait while you change." He had a few flamingo-hued droplets on his jeans but nothing major, while she had lots of stains on her pants.

"I'm fine like this." She took off her cap and shook out her hair.

For a moment, he didn't know how to breathe. The urge to run his fingers through that luxurious hair and feel its silkiness became almost irresistible.

She was right. She *was* fine, even without makeup except for the eyeliner and mascara and dressed in a worn outfit covered in drying paint.

Huh. Unlike Madeline, her foster sister who'd just married his eldest brother, Arianna didn't seem to care what people thought of her. He should've guessed as much since she didn't seem to pay attention to all the rumors about her reasons for always wearing black.

"But we both do need to wash our faces and arms." She walked to the hall and gestured to the right. "Guest bathroom is that way."

After some efficient scrubbing, he met her in the hall. She wore laced-up combat boots and carried a small rectangular purse that, of course, matched the rest of her outfit.

As he opened his truck's passenger door for her, he belatedly realized how many things were crammed into his vehicle. "Sorry about the mess. Um, please, move the dirty boots aside. And the cowboy hat can go on the back seat. And the floor might be muddy." At least, he didn't have any food wrappers inside. He hoped.

She rolled her eyes before climbing into the cab. "Don't worry about it. Really. I'd be fine in the truck bed. I'm not picky."

Maybe not. But, to him, she was like royalty, and he wanted her treated that way. With respect and admiration.

He drove off, grateful the scent of french fries and hamburgers he'd bought yesterday didn't linger in his truck. Though sadly the scent of onion rings had persisted.

As he turned on the familiar road he'd traveled so many times, he relaxed, and his thoughts drifted off. She didn't seem much of a talker, but neither was he, and he'd never liked empty chatter.

He'd thought it ironic and more than a little inconvenient that three of his brothers, who'd wanted families, had fallen in love with foster sisters who shied away from commitments. He'd even told his brothers at the time they should maybe choose someone different to fall in love with.

Well, the joke was on him now. Because he could be falling for the foster sister who was the most secretive and commitment reluctant of them all.

Children. He was helping her because of her nephew and niece. It didn't matter that he'd never met them.

Neither had she, and she'd uprooted her entire life for them. He admired that. As careless and aloof as she strove to look, she had a good heart. Why she tried so hard to hide it, he couldn't comprehend.

Well, maybe he'd started to, after what she'd told him about her family.

Sprawling emerald-hued hills dotted with cattle herds passed beyond the window, a view dear to him. His heart shifted. Could she love this place, too? Several of her foster sisters seemed to. But Arianna was different from them, and even more different from anyone he'd ever met in his home state. She was truly unique.

"Do you think I'm insane?" she interrupted the purr of the motor.

His fingers tightened around the steering wheel. Unique, yes. Insane? Never. "No." He stole a glance at her. "Why would you say that?"

She stared straight ahead. "I mean, does it make me insane to believe someone like me can become an instant mom?"

"It doesn't make you insane. It makes you kind."

She grimaced. "It's too late for the latter."

He shook his head as he slowed around a curve. "It's never too late to be kind."

Chapter Three

"You're not my mom!" Jackson shouted at Arianna and whirled around, his shoulder-length raven-hued hair flipping in the air and separating them by an invisible curtain. Then the door slammed in her face. "I don't want breakfast! I'd rather die than be here!" The boy's heated words filtered through the door right after the lock clicked.

Her heart sank as she stared at the barrier between them, or one of them, really. It wouldn't be difficult to pick the lock and open the door, but it seemed close to impossible to gain her rebellious nephew's trust. She lifted a fist to knock but thought better of it.

She understood his anger. She did. He was grieving, and she'd taken him out of a familiar atmosphere and dragged him across several states to an unfamiliar small town where he didn't know anyone.

So much for the welcome-home banner and balloons Kieran, Madeline, and Jessie had helped her make and display in the lodge. After she'd flown them in yesterday, Jackson had gone to sleep without talking to her, except for occasional grunts. This morning, when she'd knocked on his bedroom door to ask what he wanted for breakfast, it hadn't gone much better.

He'd stayed the night with his sister, though Arianna had offered him his room, but by the morning, he'd gone to his room. The alarm would warn her if he tried to sneak out of the lodge. Yet she'd spent a sleepless night worrying he'd be able to disable it somehow and checking the cameras a hundred times.

Argh. She rubbed her temples, considering her options. Should she take her nephew and niece back to Houston? She knew people there. She could rent a house and find a stable job in the megalopolis without much effort.

But she didn't want the children anywhere near *that* family. She shuddered. Yes, people could change, but she wouldn't take that risk. Pangs jabbed her insides. What could she have done differently? Well, no use dwelling on the past.

Besides, there was a reason she'd wanted to remove Jackson from that environment. Some quick research and help from Jessie, her foster sister who used to work as a cop in Houston, revealed his friends were up to no good.

No, it was best to stay here. Jessie and her cop husband could be a good influence on him. Arianna's other foster sister Madeline, a newlywed, had cautiously volunteered to babysit Isabella. A local program in place for troubled teens already offered counselors, lessons, and assistance if Jackson agreed to go to it.

Sadly, with his record, he'd qualify. He'd regularly gotten in trouble at school, instigating fights and talking back to teachers. That was when he'd bothered to go to school because he'd skipped school a lot.

But then, what did Arianna expect, with his mother working most of the time and no father figure in his life? Not that she could provide him with a father figure here.

Unless...

Kieran's image flashed in front of her eyes.

No.

Guilt stung. Arianna didn't even qualify to be a mother. She resisted the urge to gnash her teeth. What was she thinking? Good foster parents could take in Jackson and Isabella. People who, unlike Arianna, knew what they were doing.

She sank down the smooth wall to the hardwood floor that wasn't exactly cold at the end of summer but was hard by definition and wasn't welcoming. Then she drew her knees to her chest and hid her face against them as if she could hide from the world.

Fine, Kieran being here factored into her decision. She'd never expected herself to think that, but apparently, she might need a husband. To keep the children. And while she was far from wife or mother material, he'd make a perfect husband and father.

When she'd stepped into his office and he'd asked what she needed, she'd nearly answered "a husband." But it was best to ease into that slower. After a few days of being nice.

Arianna snorted. She had no clue how to be nice. Or how to flirt, for that matter. If she tried on some of Madeline's high-heeled shoes, Arianna would most likely stumble into the nearest wall.

Yes, she'd caught Kieran's interest, but she had no idea how to keep it. How could she ask him to commit to a marriage of convenience when all the convenience would be on her side and none on his?

What could she offer him, really? With two traumatized children in tow?

Her heart skipped a beat. She couldn't deny being drawn to him. But she wasn't in love. Would never allow herself to be. This would never work. But at least she had a permanent job. Sort of. She could cook, but her skills were nowhere near Genevieve's or Madeline's. Genevieve would make a great mother, too. After all, being the eldest of the foster sisters, she'd mothered them all while their foster parents hadn't done that great a job.

Quiet footfalls made Arianna bolt to her feet, her arms shooting up to protect her vital organs and ready to strike.

Her blonde hair adorably tousled, Isabella blinked up at her, barefoot and still in her pajamas adorned with princesses, and her lower lip quivered. "Are you mad at us?"

Arianna cringed. Her heart twisted. She'd further managed to scare a child who was already scared. She unfisted her fingers and rearranged her facial features into a smile. "Of course not, sweetie."

Isabella blinked again and didn't look like she believed Arianna. Her baby blues watered. Was she... was she going to cry?

Uh-oh.

"Jackson said you were mean to bring us here. *Are* you mean?"

Arianna hadn't panicked when she'd had a gun to her head or a knife to her throat. But here, with a rebellious teenager and a traumatized child, she panicked. She was so far out of her comfort zone that they weren't even on the same planet.

What now?

"I'm not mean." Well, except for when she'd had to be. But that wasn't really *mean*, was it?

She knelt near Isabella so they would be on the same level. The wisps of blonde hair tugged at Arianna's heart. So much innocence in those naïve blue eyes. At Isabella's age, Arianna had been naïve and innocent, too. But that hadn't lasted for much longer.

She stilled herself against the shiver inside. She couldn't allow Isabella to see despair or hurt on her face. "I'm not mean," she said again. But neither was she kind. Not anymore. "You probably shouldn't be standing barefoot on the floor. How about piggybacking to your room and finding your slippers?" Arianna turned so her niece could climb onto her back.

Isabella didn't move. Then she climbed on and wrapped her tiny hands around Arianna's neck.

Arianna's heart made a strange movement in her chest as she straightened up.

Then a call on the intercom made her flinch. She didn't expect any visitors. Her foster sisters had agreed to give her time to bond with the children before overwhelming them with more unfamiliar faces.

So far, that bonding wasn't going great. She pulled up the camera feed on her phone.

Kieran was at the gate. Her heart reacted, but she steeled herself against it and buzzed him in. Was he here to talk to her about the job? It was Saturday, and she was supposed to start on Monday. Or did he want to fire her already?

She nearly groaned. How was she supposed to handle childcare and a job, even a part-time one? How did single parents around the world manage?

Kieran had told her that for dinner the cowboys used lunch meat or cold cuts for sandwiches or leftovers from lunch, so once she cleaned up after lunch, she could go home.

But what about before then? She couldn't rely on Madeline to babysit Isabella every day. Daycare? Arianna didn't want the child to feel she'd been passed to someone else, though passing her to Madeline wasn't much better. But no matter what, Arianna didn't want Isabella to feel unwanted.

Summer vacation had already ended, but Jackson was expelled from school, anyway. It would be a miracle to get him enrolled here—and another miracle to persuade him to go. She could try to homeschool him, but she couldn't even get him to open the door to her. Her communication skills were pathetic in ideal situations and nonexistent in a situation like this. She needed Kieran's help, and she knew it.

Marching through the hall, she clenched her teeth, then unclenched them for Isabella's sake. She checked the peephole, then opened the door for Kieran. She didn't *like* needing help. She'd been on her own since she'd been a teen. She'd survived by learning to rely only on herself. With time, she'd learned she could rely on her foster sisters, but doing so hadn't come easily.

She checked the cameras, especially the ones outside Jackson's room. He had a reputation as a runaway, and he clearly didn't care for being here. Not that she blamed him. She'd run away from home—if one could call it *home*—many times before being placed in foster care.

Then she opened the front door, and Kieran tipped his brown cowboy hat to her, a warm smile on his face that only brightened when he saw Isabella. Unlike the day she'd visited the office, his leather cowboy boots were clean and a bit on the shiny side. That day, he'd worn a shirt that had been threadbare at the edges. The Wrangler's shirt now hugging his muscular torso in a way that should be appreciated looked brand new. Did he dress up for her?

The scent of cedar and hay drifted to her.

Excitement bubbled with a surprising dosage of relief. She was... glad to see Kieran here. She shouldn't be.

She waved him inside.

Isabella squealed on Arianna's back. Not so much because of the man but because of the large teddy bear in his arms. The toy was about half of Isabella's size. If the way to a man's heart could be through his stomach—Arianna had never bothered to find out whether that was true—the way to a child's heart could be through a teddy bear.

Or so she wished. If only things could be so simple, but then, in her life, they never were.

"Auntie, can I have the teddy bear? *Pwetty* please?" Isabella couldn't roll her *R*s yet, and Arianna found it adorable.

Or should she worry and take the child to a speech therapist? She had no clue and needed to do research. "Of course, sweetie."

Jackson opened the door and poked his head out. "They just want to buy you with that teddy bear, Cricket. Your auntie never cared about us before. Never even showed up to see us." Then his accusatory dark eyes narrowed at Arianna. "Already bringing a guy over, huh? You're just like..." He clammed up as if realizing he said too much. "Never mind." He slammed the door again with such force that it shook.

She swallowed hard. *You're just like... who?* Another thing she was supposed to know if she'd been a proper aunt. He seemed to be protective over his sister at first, and he'd taken good care of her on the flight here. But those protective instincts somehow disappeared once they'd reached the lodge.

Kieran's eyes hardened as he stepped inside. "Want me to talk to him?"

Arianna shook her head. She did want him to talk to Jackson, but the teen might think they were ganging up on him.

"Down!" Isabella pummeled her little fists on Arianna's back.

So much for bonding. Arianna let the girl slide to the floor, and Isabella ran to her room without a second glance at the teddy bear. Arianna sent Kieran an apologetic grimace and followed the girl. Did she take her brother's words to heart?

Isabella climbed into her brand-new ballerina-slipper-hued bed, scooted into the furthest part of it, and drew the blanket over her head as if she didn't want to face the real world.

"Isabella." Arianna spoke as softly as she could.

She'd never felt this helpless. A shiver traveled down her spine, and her hand flew to her stomach. Her fingers stroked over her T-shirt's smooth fabric where it hid the deep lines she'd been marked with forever. Okay, yes, *she had*, when she'd been a teen, but she'd promised herself she'd never be helpless ever again.

However, this wasn't about her but about a sad little girl.

Now what?

Kieran placed the teddy bear on the carpet near other plush toys they'd bought together. "I guess we'd better leave Isabella alone."

Right. Arianna nearly snorted. Like that would solve the problem.

But then, these children were her responsibility, not his. He'd helped a lot already by painting the girl's room, buying age-appropriate furniture and then assembling it when she couldn't figure out what to put where, and getting numerous toys and insisting on helping pay for them. He'd even constructed a dollhouse for Isabella and suggested building a treehouse, but they'd run out of time.

He leaned against the small white desk. "Arianna, you know what I'm going to do today? I'll check on the ponies."

And Arianna needed to know that information because? She blinked. Unless feeding ponies would be part of her new job.

He continued, a mischievous twinkle in his amber eyes. "Oh, did I tell you we had a newborn calf? He's adorable."

The word *adorable* sounded weird coming from this manly man, but she caught on to what he was doing because Isabella's blanket slid down a bit and one curious blue eye poked out.

"We might get another calf today. Oh, do you know what I'd like for breakfast?"

Arianna better do something besides standing there. Kieran had done most of the heavy lifting already, including yesterday when he'd carried the furniture. Not that she'd minded the sight of his bulging muscles.

Uh-oh. What was she thinking?

Her cheeks flamed up when she muttered, "*What* would you like for breakfast?" It wasn't much of a contribution.

"Pancakes!" He grinned. "With smiley faces on them."

Now the entire face appeared from under the blanket. "*I* wanna eat pancakes, too. With a smiley face. And I wanna see a pony. And a calf." The girl's voice was small as she sat up. "*Pwetty, pwetty* please?"

Something inside Arianna changed. She'd worried whether she'd truly be able to love these children. But it wouldn't take much for this little girl to crawl into her heart. Even without "*pwetty, pwetty* please."

And maybe Arianna was wrong before. Maybe the way to a child's heart wasn't through a teddy bear or even pancakes and ponies and newborn farm animals, but through a lot of love and genuine care. Was a damaged person like Arianna, who'd never known much love and care, capable of giving it?

A lump formed in her throat, and she couldn't utter a word.

Isabella must've misinterpreted Arianna's silence because she said, "I'm *sowwy*. I'll be a *vewy* good girl. I *pwomise*. I'll sit in the closet quiet-quiet."

Arianna froze. What kind of things had happened in that house? "Of course, you can have pancakes. And we'll go see the ponies and calf." Maybe Jackson would have the decency to tag along for his sister's sake.

Isabella tilted her face. "With a smiley face?"

Arianna chuckled, relieved. "With a smiley face." That seemed important to Isabella. She probably didn't have many of those in her life. Arianna hadn't at her age, either. People surrounding her mostly frowned and yelled at each other then. And the one person who'd smiled at her...

"*Mi mariposa bonita.*"

My beautiful butterfly.

A shiver ran down her spine. Better not to remember. Ever.

Then she leaned forward, trying to choose her words carefully. "Sweetie, why would you need to stay in the closet quietly?"

"Mommy told me to." Isabella scooted to the edge of the bed.

Arianna exchanged glances with Kieran who looked as worried as she felt.

"To play hide and seek with your brother?" Arianna doubted it was for hide and seek, but she hoped it could have some innocent explanation. Even as she tensed inside, she kept her voice soft and tender and her expression the same. Her acting skills came in handy not only in her job.

Isabella leaped from her bed, making her blonde curls jump. "No, silly. Mommy told me to hide so bad guys wouldn't find me."

Kieran flinched. Arianna's only reaction was that her eyes widened slightly.

"Did you *see* the bad guys?" Arianna asked carefully. Her voice didn't change, still warm and sweet as the syrup she was going to slather pancakes with, though inside she went on full alert. When the social worker had mentioned the accident, Arianna hadn't questioned it. But she should've asked for details. Was Isabella in some kind of danger, with *bad guys* after her?

Arianna would have to ask Jessie to look into it. And find a way to talk to Jackson. He could have important reasons to run away from home.

Hopefully, not as important as Arianna had. Her stomach clenched.

Sending blonde curls flying, Isabella shook her head. "Of course not. I was hiding, *wememba*? I hid good." Then her hands slipped under the blanket. "Can I take my toy, please?"

Arianna's heart just about stopped as she stared at an azure-blue toy butterfly that appeared in the girl's little hands. "Did... did your mom buy you this?" She could hope, right?

Isabella shook her head again. "No. My uncle Ric. He got me a dress with wings, too. He said I was *pwetty* like a *buttafly*."

Arianna's world tilted on its axis, and for a moment, everything disappeared, except for a soft whisper in her ears from decades ago.

Mi mariposa bonita.

"Let's find your slippers." Kieran's voice was strained as he moved closer, grounding Arianna and returning her to the present.

Chapter Four

Later, Arianna entered the kitchen, examining it with a critical eye. With Kieran's help, she'd gone through the house doing her best to make it childproof. But the lodge renovations hadn't been done with children in mind.

And the place had to be teen-proof, too. All weapons were tucked away in safes. It would be difficult for anyone to guess the codes to open them. But not impossible.

Doubts crept in. They must've reflected on her face as she forgot to school her expression because Kieran squeezed her forearm. "It's going to be alright."

The physical contact sent a jolt of awareness through her. At least, she didn't flinch when he touched her this time like she'd done from any touch or even an unexpected noise during her first years in the foster home. She'd learned to accept hugs from her foster sisters because they were nonthreatening, but not any signs of affection.

It had taken falling in love for the first time to tolerate a touch. From one man only. She swallowed hard. That hadn't worked well, had it?

What would've happened if she hadn't gotten out? Most likely, she wouldn't be alive.

Frankly, the most physical contact she had with people these days was in combat. She suppressed a sigh. This decision to become an instant mother was going to be a disaster.

She shifted away from Kieran, which caused his hand to drop. "Let's get started."

If her moving away offended him, he didn't show it—unlike a few of her suitors who'd been angry when she'd turned away from their signs of affection. Instead, he went to the pantry to get the ingredients while she retrieved bowls and measuring cups. She'd learned fast not to start any romance at all. That way, nobody's feelings got hurt.

"I wanna help!" Isabella rushed to the fridge and snatched eggs.

Uh-oh.

But before Arianna could react—and she usually had a fast reaction—Kieran was near the girl. "That's great. Here." He handed her a small milk carton. "Please help me bring milk to the counter. I'll help you with the eggs."

"Okay." Isabella released the egg carton, but not before Kieran caught it.

Frankly, Arianna didn't mind a messy kitchen. Madeline had kept it spotless before moving in with her new husband, as perfect as everything was around her. Well, Madeline wasn't perfect, no matter what her beautiful appearance projected. Deep inside, she was nearly as damaged as Arianna was but still found marital bliss.

Arianna stole a glance at Kieran. Was there hope for her, too?

He pressed on Isabella's cute upturned nose playfully, and the girl giggled.

Arianna stilled, cherishing the sound. It wasn't outright laughter, but it was the closest to it since she'd met this child. And he was the reason for Isabella's joy.

"Thank you," Arianna mouthed to him as she dug out mixing spoons and spatulas.

He shrugged as if it were no big deal.

But to her, it was a big deal. A huge deal, even. Very few people in her life stepped up to the plate, people she could rely on. And none of them yet were a man.

But as he interacted with Isabella, Arianna went gooey inside. She closed her eyes, then opened them. She couldn't allow herself to become soft. Couldn't let herself get attracted to him.

Too late for that. A hot wave rushed through her when their gazes met and held.

Okay, she *was* attracted to him already, but under no circumstances could she let herself fall for him. And he couldn't know about her attraction. Giving him hope would be cruel. She broke eye contact, using breaking eggs into a bowl as an excuse. The whip of her wooden spoon in the eggs gave her a momentary respite to compose herself. Usually, she could compose herself in a flash. It was another essential part of her survival. But when it came to Kieran, it was different.

The next time she looked at him, his eyes dimmed, and guilt stung her.

"We'll need flour," she told him.

Instead, Isabella dashed to the pantry. Arianna tensed, but the girl brought the pack to the counter without an incident.

"Thank you, sweetie." Arianna reached for the flour to add to the batter.

Isabella screamed. "I wanna do it!"

"Sure." Kieran lifted the girl.

Whack! Most of the flour ended up on the counter and some of it on the hardwood floor.

An angry voice from her past rang in her ears.

"Did you drop the flour?"

Smack!

"That's how you treat food I worked hard to earn?"

Her cheek burned as if it had been slapped recently and not decades ago.

"Are you okay?" Kieran's concerned voice pulled her back to the present again.

She pushed the memories away. What was wrong with her? She'd managed to avoid her memories for a long time, yes, with occasional dreams and thoughts, but not the barrage she'd had today. But, of course, she also never thought of her past or her family, and having the children in her life brought back that part of her—and resurrected fresh fears for them. "Yeah. Of course."

"Oh. *Sowwy*." Isabella put the mostly empty sack on the counter, and her lower lip trembled again.

"That's totally fine." Arianna cleaned the counter, then the hardwood floor, hoping nobody would notice a slight tremble in her hands. "See? All good."

Kieran placed the girl on the floor, eyed Arianna, and cleared his throat. "Um, you have a speck of flour on your face."

Arianna wasn't much for appearances, but that was before she'd met Kieran. Self-consciously, she reached for her cheek. "Here?"

His neck reddened. "No, to the right. Also, on your nose."

She rubbed the tip of her nose, then swiped her fingers to the right. "Here?"

"No, silly." Isabella giggled again, a little louder this time. "Mr. *Kiewan*, show my auntie. I'm too small to."

Arianna froze like a deer in headlights, though normally she wouldn't associate herself with that cliché. She wasn't prey. Neither was she a fragile butterfly with wings so easy to destroy.

Not any longer. Not for decades.

"Um, okay." The blush on his neck spread higher as he stepped closer.

Quite endearing that this large, bulky man could blush. The sense of feminine power was intoxicating. Almost as intoxicating as his scent, cedarwood and hay.

With a stove behind her, she didn't have space to back away, and neither did she want to. Her heartbeat kicked up as she stared into his eyes. He was close enough for her to see tiny honey dots in them. Close enough to kiss...

Excitement pooled in her belly. What was she thinking? More importantly, was he thinking the same?

His finger brushed over her skin, and she flinched. Nonthreatening. *Remember*. His touch was nonthreatening. Why was it so difficult for her body to comprehend?

His jaw hardened, and his arm dropped. "All gone."

So was the moment of tenderness between them.

Maybe her giving him the cold shoulder doused the fire of his attraction. Or maybe he was simply kind to her and Isabella. She heard some men were simply kind. She wouldn't know, of course, but her foster sisters testified that the men in the O'Neill family had morals and good hearts, as well as great physiques.

It was for the better to pull away, but disappointment still ripped through her. Disappointment was a familiar territory, though, frequented so often she should have streets with her name on them there. Tenderness from a guy, on the other hand, was an unfamiliar land, more like a mirage in the desert of her affection.

She washed her hands, then placed one on Isabella's shoulder to remind herself where her priority was now. No sense in wishing for things that couldn't be. She'd learned that lesson the hard way at fourteen.

His grin was unexpected and all the more welcome. "You looked cute with a white nose."

Arianna didn't remember the last time someone called her cute, if ever. She didn't smile often, at least not sincerely, but this time, she couldn't help grinning back. "Thank you."

Isabella looked up. "I wanna white nose, too."

Arianna chuckled, then dipped her fingers into flour and touched Isabella's nose. "You look cute, too."

Then the smile slipped off the child's face. She sighed. "I miss home. And Mommy."

Arianna's heart ached. Doubt wormed in, too. Had she done the right thing by jerking the children out of their familiar environment? Just because horrible things had happened to her didn't mean they would happen to them, as well, or particularly to Isabella.

Had she made an unforgivable mistake?

Or was her subconscious giving her convenient excuses to get out of a very inconvenient situation?

Right now, she had no clue how to comfort the child. Nobody had comforted Arianna, except her grandmother, but that hadn't lasted long. Well, her foster sisters had tried, but by the time Arianna had arrived at the foster home, she'd been too broken for someone to pick up the pieces and glue them together.

Kieran's look was as worried as she felt. He must've had little experience with children, especially traumatized ones. On the other hand, he'd had a lot of experience with being loved. She knew that from seeing his family dynamics during dinners at his parents' place and from stories shared by her foster siblings who'd married into the family and been embraced with much love.

Then he brightened as he leaned to Isabella and extended his hand. "Would you like to dance, little lady?"

Arianna blinked, then blinked again. How in the world was this logical?

Isabella seemed to think the same. Her mouth moved in a funny way as she gave it a thought. Then she shook her head. "I wanna, but I'm too small to dance with you."

"How about this?" He picked the child up and whirled around the kitchen, singing some tune Arianna didn't recognize. Out of tune, but that mattered little here. Actually, wrong, it mattered a lot that he couldn't sing well but still did it to comfort the child.

Isabella's lips kicked up, and Arianna could breathe easier. This wouldn't make Isabella less homesick, but it was a good distraction. One she couldn't come up with, or execute, for that matter.

Gratitude warmed her, and then a tiny burst of envy bumped it. She could imagine herself dancing in his arms way too easily. The force with which she wanted it was disturbing. The temperature seemed to rise in the kitchen, even without the stove being on.

As if reading her thoughts, he gestured for her to join in. She hesitated, then shook her head. While her heart was about to leap out of her chest to join him, the rest of her body was scared.

Huh.

She'd only seen the serious side of him before, the responsible brother ready to take care of the entire ranch, if needed. This spontaneous part of his character appealed to her on several levels.

No. Thinking. Like. That.

Her phone beeped with an incoming text in her pocket, and she ignored it. If it was her girls, she'd call them later. And if it was a new assignment? She suppressed a grimace. She'd have to refuse it. The children came first.

Was it selfish to wish she'd come first for someone at least once in her life?

She finished the batter and stole a glance at Kieran. She even knew who that someone was. Maybe it wasn't selfish. But it was unrealistic. She'd learned early on that dreams didn't exist for girls like her. That her fairy tale couldn't have a happy ending.

"Down!" Isabella finally demanded. "I wanna eat. So I can go see the pony."

Kieran placed her on the floor.

Breakfast was delayed, but they set the table. Isabella helped, though it cost them a plate. Arianna didn't mind. She could buy more plates. The jagged pieces of the broken one went into the trash. It was the jagged pieces of her soul that she didn't know what to do with.

Arianna glanced at the hall, then at Isabella. "Sweetie, would you please invite your brother to breakfast?"

Argh. Arianna was passing along an unpleasant task she should be doing. But Isabella had way better chances of bringing Jackson to the table than Arianna did.

"Okay!" Isabella darted to Jackson's room.

Kieran seemed to read her mind again. "He'll come around—eventually."

Her eyes widened, but she managed a half nod, though she wasn't sure Jackson would ever come around.

How could Kieran be so in tune with her thoughts? She'd prided herself on being able to hide her thoughts and intentions. But with him, her defenses seemed to be stripped bare.

And that could be dangerous.

Because if one day he truly saw through her, he'd pity her. She couldn't endure that.

"You'll like it. We made *gooood bweakfast.*" Isabella's innocent voice tripped into Arianna's thoughts.

Frowning and lips tight, his long hair more disheveled than usual, Jackson made it obvious he didn't want to be here, but he allowed Isabella to drag him to the dining room. Once again, Arianna's eyes narrowed as she studied the dynamics between them, their facial expressions and body language. Just because people were blood-related didn't mean they cared about each other, and she knew too well that a more mature, stronger male could take advantage of a younger and naïve female.

Jackson's posture was tense, and his mouth tight, exhibiting defiance. But that defiance was aimed at Arianna, and she didn't feel a threat toward Isabella. The girl looked up at him with complete trust. Surely, she was young enough she hadn't learned how to pretend.

His ripped gray jeans hung low on his hips and pooled up over his bare feet, and his black T-shirt carried the same inscription as the sign he hung outside his room—Keep Out.

He obviously meant it, at least regarding Arianna. His sulky expression softened as he looked back at his sister. He allowed her to drag him, though he could've easily resisted.

Arianna relaxed a tad. She'd also bathed Isabella yesterday before bed, and hadn't seen any bruises or suspicious wounds. The girl's words about hiding in the closet and bad guys still created unease in her stomach. But no bruises or cuts were a good sign.

She swallowed hard.

Her mother must have seen bruises on Arianna's little body and later scars after her cousin stayed over. How come she'd never questioned it? Why hadn't her mother protected her?

She'd taken her husband's side, her husband who loved his nephew way more than he loved his daughter. Even decades later, the answer left a bitter taste in Arianna's mouth. She resisted the urge to touch a scar on her arm, covered skillfully with a tattoo.

Back to the present.

Physically, Isabella seemed to be okay, though Arianna intended to take her to the doctor to make sure. A child psychologist, maybe? So far so good, but she wouldn't let her guard down. And the issue remained—the girl had been locked up while bad guys were in the house. What bad guys? Why had Arianna's half sister allowed them in, instead of calling the police? Why hadn't she tried to move into a safer place?

If Arianna hadn't gone no contact with her family, she might know the answers to those questions. Might even have helped the half sister she'd never even known about. A weight pressed on her shoulders.

"I don't care for breakfast," Jackson said.

"That's sad because your sister helped make it." Not Arianna's proudest moment, but she had to use whatever was at her disposal.

Isabella's lower lip quivered as she looked up at her brother. "You not gonna eat the pancakes we made?"

His dark eyes softened as he patted his sister's hair. "Of course, I will, Cricket." He sat at the table. "I hate you," he muttered in Arianna's direction.

"I know." She shrugged, nonplussed, then gave a tiny headshake to Kieran who seemed to want to jump to her defense.

Her phone pinged with an incoming text. She'd check it later, but intuition told her to do it now. She fished it out of her pocket and read the text.

The person in question called and asked about you. Be careful.

Her insides went cold, and for long moments she stared at the screen as if that could make the letters disappear.

Chapter Five

Two days later, Arianna swallowed around a lump in her throat as she stood in the ranch's spacious kitchen, the wide windows overlooking rolling pastures. It gave the place a feeling as open and free as the land around it. Still, she hadn't been this nervous when she'd gone on dangerous missions in faraway countries. So why now?

Yes, she needed this job, but there had to be more to it. Was it because her boss's attentive gaze unnerved her? The coffee aroma spread through the small place from the pot she'd just made, but that wasn't much of an accomplishment. Kieran had refused coffee, so she didn't pour herself one, either.

"Here we have plates and cups." He opened the oak cabinets to show her around.

"Thanks. Are you sure your mother won't mind watching Isabella?" She rested her hands on the girl's shoulders protectively, reluctant to let her go. "Madeline volunteered to do it."

His mother walked into the kitchen. "He is sure." She leaned to the girl. "Hello, darling. I'm Mrs. O'Neill, but you can call me Grandma."

"But you aren't *my* grandma." Isabella studied the older woman.

"That might change one day," Mrs. O'Neill said thoughtfully. "Let's go see some animals."

"I wanna see the little calf again!" Isabella slid her tiny hand into Kieran's mother's larger and wrinkled one with too much trust for Arianna's liking.

"Sure thing." The woman was about to lead the girl away, leaving Arianna with a sense of loss.

Was Arianna getting this attached already? Nah, couldn't be. "Thank you so much for this." Jackson had his first day at school—by some miracle, the local school had accepted him. She had a strong suspicion that the miracle was something of Kieran's doing. But Isabella was too young for school, and Arianna didn't want to place her in daycare unless she had to.

His mother nodded. "No problem, hon." Then she lowered her voice as she glanced at her son. "I'll enjoy this little one, especially considering my sons aren't in a hurry to give me grandchildren."

Kieran groaned. "You have married sons, and I'm not even married."

"Exactly. What are you waiting for?" She led the little girl out of the kitchen.

"The right woman, maybe?" he muttered, throwing a half-apologetic and half-frustrated glance Arianna's way.

Despite the slight bickering, this family clearly loved each other. She'd never known that kind of love in hers. Wistfulness unraveled in her belly.

She couldn't let it show on her face, so she busied herself following him as he showed her where the utensils and pots and pans were. Her body moved in his direction, and his scents of cedarwood and hay affected her senses, so she shifted back.

Argh. She didn't need this infatuation with her boss, of all people, but she needed to help the children survive.

"Are scrambled eggs, bacon, and toast okay?" Cooking a late breakfast after dropping Jackson off at school gave her the chance to get to know the kitchen before cooking lunch for the entire team. She put on a marmalade-hued apron—they didn't have black ones in the local store—and tied the strings.

"Sure." He leaned his large frame against the counter, watching her.

Warmth uncurled inside her at his attention. But then she reminded herself why people watched others. It wasn't the case here, but she ground her teeth and washed her hands with lavender-scented soap. "Don't you have to go, um, mend fences, feed horses, or milk cows or something?"

When she faced him, the hurt in his eyes sent a stab of guilt through her. But it was best to send the message loud and clear even if an important part of her protested.

"The horses are in the pasture, grazing, and so are the cattle. Did you say *milk* cows?"

She blinked. "Well, yeah." She was a city girl, but even she knew where milk came from. And she'd seen plenty of cows out in the fields here.

A mischievous twinkle appeared in his eyes. "We might need your help milking cows."

Her jaw slackened. "What?"

Brandon, Kieran's brother and Madeline's husband, entered the kitchen, and Arianna greeted him with her hand while still gaping at Kieran.

"And would you mind getting eggs from under the chickens, too?" Kieran grinned. "Fair warning, some of them might get feisty and peck you. And if a chicken has difficulty delivering, help her."

Her jaw dropped. *What* did she sign up for? "Delivering what and help her how?"

"Well, you know."

Delivering eggs. She soooo did not want to imagine that picture, much less, um, help in the process.

Brandon rolled his eyes. "Bro, seriously?" He jammed his hands on his hips and rocked back on his toes. "My brother is joking. Eggs are in the fridge. And our cows were bred for meat, not for milk. Even if we had milk cows, you wouldn't have to do it by hand."

Arianna's eyes narrowed at Kieran, throwing daggers. "I should be grateful you didn't tell me to get a pig for bacon. Or to take wheat from the fields to a windmill to make flour for the toast."

"Of course not." He spread his hands. "We don't grow wheat or raise pigs on this ranch."

"Unless you count my brother this morning." Brandon chuckled. Then he sobered up. "Don't mind Kieran. He's usually respectful and even shy."

Kieran gave his sibling a playful punch on the shoulder. "Thanks, bro."

She came to her senses, then turned to Brandon. She had a high respect for the guy in general, but most of all because he made Madeline happy. And Madeline deserved to be happy. "Would you like some coffee? I just brewed a fresh pot. Sorry, breakfast isn't ready yet."

"I'll get it. No problem." He eyed Kieran, then her, and grinned about something. Minutes later, Brandon took the steaming mug with him.

She'd better start on that breakfast. She opened the fridge door and was met with a gust of cold air.

"Let me help you with the eggs." Kieran closed the space between them, cornering her.

Close enough, she could reach out and touch him. Close enough, she could see tiny brown dots in his amber eyes. Close enough, she could lift on her tiptoes and kiss him....

A hot wave rushed through her. What was she thinking? Just because her foster sisters had fallen in love and married these irresistible cowboy brothers with Irish blood didn't mean she had to follow their example.

She had a million reasons not to, but now, she couldn't remember even one. "Thanks, but I can do it myself." She'd done it since she'd been little. She snatched a carton of forty-eight eggs.

In her haste, it wobbled out of her hands. They hurried to catch it at the same time, and their hands met each other instead of the carton that landed on the white tile. Irrational fear sent a shiver through her.

"Oh no." She squatted near the mess.

"Are you wasting food again?"

The angry scream of her memories made her yelp and lift her arms as if to defend herself. It had been no use then, and her little body had hit the wall. It had been a mystery only the eggs had been broken that day and not her bones.

Why was she remembering it now?

Breathe.

Deeply.

You're safe. You're safe. You're safe.

"That's one way to make scrambled eggs." Kieran didn't sound irritated. "It's okay. Don't worry about it. We have plenty more."

Her mind must've been scrambled, too, because she usually had a much better reaction than this.

She'd been punished harshly for much less when she'd been little, and she blanched again.

"No food should be wasted!"

The words etched in her memory just as much as later scars etched into her skin. "I... I'll clean it up." While she hated the way her voice trembled, at least she'd kept the tremble from her hands this time. She'd thought she'd put her past behind her a long time ago. Apparently, not.

He picked up the sloppy carton. "It's no big deal, really." Why did concern sound in his voice?

She watered some paper towels and scrubbed the floor before throwing them away and washing her hands again.

"I'll start on the bacon." He walked to the fridge. He must be afraid that, if he left her to her own devices, they'd be eating bacon off the floor.

"I appreciate it." Accepting his help grated. But she didn't have a choice here unless she let his family and ranch hands starve, and she wouldn't do that.

Okay. Okay. She pulled herself together.

Her first day at work was turning into a disaster, and she hadn't even started cooking yet. The second flat of eggs made it to the counter without issues, and she soon had them in a bowl, then added milk she thankfully didn't have to get herself from a cow.

"Does your family like onions, peppers, or ham with eggs?" Her voice sounded even now. Indifferent. Good.

"What you have is great already." He turned on the stove and let the pan warm up, then lined the strips up in the pan. "We're a bit late today, so I'll just fry them. But tomorrow, I'll show you a neat way to cook them in the oven. They come out super crispy and don't make a mess or splatter the cook with hot grease."

"Okay." Grandma had taught her how to cook many things, but bacon was panfried, not baked, in her experience.

The yummy aroma spread through the kitchen, making her stomach rumble. She'd been moving the spatula in the largest pan she'd ever seen when her phone rang in her pocket.

She grimaced. "I should've turned it off, but it's Jackson's first day of school. The phone is on in case the school administration calls if he gets in trouble."

Oops. She shouldn't sound so resigned. As if she'd expected him to mess up. He deserved her giving him the benefit of the doubt, especially considering she hadn't received much of the latter when she'd been in a similar situation. Her reputation in school at his age hadn't been much better than his.

"Please feel free to answer it." Kieran moved to take the spatula to keep the eggs from sticking to the pan. "But do you expect him to get in trouble on the first day of school?"

His proximity sent a jolt to her heart.

Huh. Was she judgmental? Was she used to not expecting much from people to keep herself from getting hurt later?

"I wouldn't expect anything less from my nephew." The words slipped from her tongue before she could stop them. She slid the phone from her pocket and frowned at the unknown number. Could it be a marketer?

Then she swiped it to answer and pressed it to her ear. "Hello."

"I've missed you." The familiar male baritone, smooth like velvet, used to stir undercurrents in her belly.

Until, on one assignment, she'd been so much in love that she'd missed the danger signs. She'd been wounded and added to her scar collection. He'd nearly been killed. While his health and career had rebounded, she'd been blacklisted for those kinds of assignments ever since. Overridden with guilt, she'd stayed by his side until he'd fully recovered. Once he had, she'd left and hadn't seen him again. She'd been sure he hated her for all the damage she'd brought him.

"I... I can't talk right now." She didn't want to sound dismissive. But she had other priorities.

"I'll be quick, then." Victor's voice went serious. "This might interest you. I have a new assignment, and I want you to go with me. If successful, we'll receive fifty each in a week."

Thousand. She resisted the urge to whistle.

Kieran worked both pans as if he'd done it for years, and maybe he had. She enjoyed the view, which she shouldn't have. But then, she'd done plenty of things she shouldn't have, and one of them was talking to Victor now. Strangely, imagining his movie-star looks with chiseled features didn't cause the usual fire in her belly.

Even if she could go, which she couldn't, she doubted she'd be hired. "I don't think the client would agree to me taking on this job."

"The client *requested* you. One mistake doesn't make many years of great work disappear." He sounded like he meant it, but one could never know with him. He knew how to control his voice even better than she did her own.

How could he forgive her when she couldn't?

Kieran emptied the pan filled with eggs and vegetables onto a gigantic shamrock-green platter and started on a new batch. But he was waiting to use the eggbeater until she was done with her conversation.

She wasn't paid to talk on the phone with her long-lost love. "I can't go. And sorry, I'm at work now."

His voice sharpened. "You're on an assignment I don't know about?"

Did he monitor her? Why? Maybe he just couldn't forget her. It would've given her great pleasure at other times. But not now. "Listen, I've got to go. I'm, um, cooking."

"You're cooking?" Victor laughed. "Okay, I need to answer the client in three hours. Please think about my offer. I... I'd love to see you again."

She hesitated and nearly said the same. But for some reason, she couldn't. So she just said, "I'll talk to you soon."

Then she disconnected and hurried back to the counter. "I can take over from here." She grabbed the eggbeater.

Kieran sent her a curious glance. "I'm not in any hurry."

After churning the eggs and milk into a froth, she poured them into the pan. Hmm. She didn't want him to think she'd been lollygagging while he'd been doing her work, so she blurted out, "It was a job offer. I mean, an assignment for a week."

A muscle jerked in his cheek. "We can help with the children if you want to go."

Really? Did he have to be that unselfish? Or was he just playing a role like many people in her life?

She did her best to keep from accidentally touching him, which was a challenge in the confined space. "The guy who called and who'd be going on the assignment with me... We have a history together. It's complicated."

"A history?" His eyebrows rose.

Why had she started down this slippery slope again? She reduced the fire underneath the eggs and brought a loaf of bread to the counter. Kieran and his family were open and honest, so they might not like their employee hiding something. Well, too late for that. She popped slices of bread down in the toaster. "We were involved. Then I nearly got him killed."

Kieran whistled, then layered paper towels on another matching platter, and transferred the bacon from the pan onto the plate. "That's complicated indeed."

"Yep."

Once the food was done, Kieran and Brandon helped her set the table and helped her clear it after the meal.

She was putting dishes in the dishwasher when her phone rang. Was it Victor again? She couldn't even untangle what she felt for him any longer. He was the only man who'd broken down some of her defenses, but even with him, she'd kept an emotional distance.

Well, there was certainly guilt. But what else? It had been affection and the fire of passion once, but she'd ruined it, dousing it in a cold river of her mistakes. Even before her colossal, unforgivable failure, he'd complained she'd been too distant, never let him in. No doubt, it would be the same with Kieran.

How could she ask him for a marriage of convenience?

She ignored the call, but then it started ringing again.

"Please feel free to answer it." Kieran stepped outside the kitchen as if to give her privacy.

She answered the phone reluctantly. Local number. Huh.

"Hello, may I speak with Ms. Montemayor?"

Her stomach tightened at the gruff female voice. "This is she."

"This is Principal Dowell, and this is about your nephew Jackson. Would you be able to come to school, please?"

Great. Now, Arianna would have to leave before finishing the dishes. Then she bit into the side of her cheek, clamping down on the guilt. "What happened? Is he okay?"

"He initiated a fight. I understand he has difficult circumstances, but we don't tolerate that kind of behavior in our school."

Chapter Six

Kieran pressed on the gas pedal as he drove Arianna to school—he'd volunteered because he was in good standing with the principal, unlike her nephew. Not because Kieran got lost in Arianna's spectacular green eyes every time he looked at her.

She'd reluctantly accepted the help, clearly for the boy's sake, and now was sulking in the passenger seat, staring out the window. Why was it so difficult for her to understand that in his family they helped each other? And as his employee, she was part of his family. Sort of. That was what he'd told her.

The issue was, he shouldn't be feeling toward an employee what he felt toward her. An attraction. And...

Turning to the school's street, he frowned at the unfamiliar feeling now burning him like acid in his underbelly.

Jealousy.

It gripped him the moment she mentioned having a history with the caller who wanted to go with her on some mysterious assignment who knew where.

Her eyes had softened to the hue of green moss when she'd heard that guy's voice. Regret, guilt, and something else flashed there. Was it love? It had gutted Kieran like a fish.

The fact that she'd nearly gotten the guy killed and there might not be a way back from that was somewhat of a consolation. Kieran flinched. Seriously? What was he thinking?

He parked near the school. Thankfully, it wasn't any time close to the pickup hour, so the place wasn't crowded yet. She jumped out of the truck before he had a chance to walk around and open the door for her.

Oh well.

He caught up fast. "Our small town is friendly. I wonder why Jackson got into a fight."

Her stride was purposeful, and her shoulders rose. As if realizing the latter, she pulled them back. "It's friendly to *you* because you grew up nearby. We're new here. Outsiders."

Huh. She put herself on the other line from him.

He opened the massive front door. Then he walked the same halls he'd walked as a youth. A teen who should've been in class rushed by, her eyes rounding at the sight of Arianna.

Arianna grimaced. "The way I look... It's going to complicate Jackson's chances for the principal to go easy on him, isn't it?"

Yeah, clomping along in tall black combat boots and a black outfit, with gobs of mascara on her eyelashes and a large tattoo on her arm, she wasn't a typical soccer mom. But he needed to encourage her as he guided her to the office.

"I think the way you look is great." Heat crept up his neck. "I mean... I think... I hope you don't think I'm flirting with you." Especially at such an inopportune time. He was so not great with women.

She rolled her eyes, increasing her pace. "I don't think that."

"Good." He nodded.

Or... Maybe not so good?

The moment she spotted Jackson outside the principal's office, she rushed to him.

Kieran reserved judgment about the boy for now. He might be hurt and lashing out at someone. But the people he'd taken his anger out on—as well as their parents—wouldn't be as understanding.

"Are you okay?" She leaned toward the boy.

He lifted his face with a large shiner and shrugged. "Like you'd care."

Her lips set in a firm line. "I do. What happened?"

Ducking his head again, he said nothing. His long raven-hued hair hid his face.

She rubbed her forehead. "I'd rather hear your version before I hear anyone else's. Honestly. I'm on your side."

Kieran wanted to step in, but he held back. They didn't need the boy to think they ganged up on him.

Jackson looked up at her and opened his mouth.

But the secretary, Ms. Bennett, stepped out and frowned at Arianna. Her leather skirt was short for working at a principal's office, so she must be pushing her privilege of being the principal's niece. And seriously, what was up with those nails? He'd never understood why women displayed long fake fingernails that could poke an eye out. Yet he shouldn't be judgmental. It was none of his business, really.

"You're Jackson's aunt, I presume?" Ms. Bennett asked. "Let me check whether the principal is ready for you."

Arianna glanced at her nephew, but he'd clammed up. So she raised her chin. "Yes, I'm Arianna Montemayor. Thank you."

Ms. Bennett's frown became a smile as her gaze switched to Kieran. "Well, what a pleasure to see you again, Kieran. What can I help you with?"

"I'm here to accompany Ms. Montemayor," he said, and that megawatt smile dimmed. "Considering she's new in town and all."

Ms. Bennett and Arianna glared at him. Huh. What did he say to cause a hostile reaction from both of them? He'd never understand women.

Jackson didn't look too pleased to hear Kieran, either, but with that permanent scowl, it was difficult to tell.

Ms. Bennett stepped into the principal's office and returned fast, then waved Kieran and Arianna inside. Principal Dowell's eyebrows drew together when they entered the office. Not a good sign. Kieran made introductions while the women faced off like bulls in a pen.

"Please take a seat." Principal Dowell gestured at the chairs before a sturdy maple desk that dwarfed the room.

The desk was new, but he remembered the large windows overlooking the schoolyard. She hadn't been the principal during his time. She'd taken the position a year ago when their principal had retired, and people said Principal Dowell ruled with an iron fist.

Her salt-and-pepper hair was tied into a low knot, not a single strand daring to be out of place, and small glasses perched on an extremely long nose that drew associations with a stork. She was rumored to have a collection of gray suits because some had to end up in the laundry eventually, right? She looked the same as a year ago, only a few more wrinkles had showed up uninvited like disobedient students since the last time he'd seen her.

Mrs. Dowell leveled her disapproving gaze on Arianna, zeroing in on her tattoo. Then her gaze turned surprised when it moved to Kieran, as if she couldn't understand why he'd associate with this woman.

He shifted closer to Arianna, hoping to shield her from hostility, and pulled out the chair for her, scraping the carpet with an irritating noise.

They took their seats.

The principal lowered herself into a chair, her back straight as if a rod was tied to it. "I sympathize with Jackson's situation and the tragedy of his family. But we can't condone aggression toward other students, so—"

"Why did the fight start?" Arianna interrupted her.

Uh-oh. He should've warned her interrupting Mrs. Dowell wasn't a good idea.

"The boys refused to tell us." The principal pushed up the glasses that decidedly had a long way to travel before falling off. "It doesn't matter. Violence isn't tolerated at our school."

Arianna leaped to her feet, and the chair clattered behind her. "It doesn't matter? It doesn't matter? How can you say that? What if he was bullied? What if he tried to defend himself?"

Mrs. Dowell's jaw slackened. Nobody talked to her like that in a while, if ever. "Then he should've told an adult, a teacher, instead of throwing a punch. And if you're going to be talking like that—"

"Some children aren't tattletales. Besides, adults don't always believe children, even if the child tells the truth." Her lower lip trembled as if the matter was personal to her. "So you have to survive whatever way you can. Defend yourself."

"It's never justified to—"

"Oh no? Let me show you something." She lifted her black T-shirt. "Do you see these scars? I was twelve years old when someone started doing this to me. For *years*. Do you think I wasn't justified to defend myself, either?"

Kieran was speechless, and so was the principal, probably for the first time in her life. They both just gawked.

Shock and compassion mingled into a bundle of feelings he couldn't untangle. What she'd gone through was incomprehensible, and the scars were probably the tip of the iceberg of pain. He knew, of course, that her foster sisters had experienced difficult childhoods, and he'd suspected hers was far from rosy, too.

But he'd never imagined... this.

How had she even survived?

Wide-eyed, Arianna looked around as if coming to her senses, then groaned. "I shouldn't have said that."

He should be supportive instead of sitting there with his jaw on the worn-out carpet. "Arianna, I—" He had no clue what to say, but before he could figure it out, she bolted to the door.

The moment she jerked it open, Jackson fell through. She caught him before his face could meet the grayish carpet.

"Are you okay?" She steadied her nephew.

"Yeah. Oops." He avoided her gaze as he jerked free.

"Were you eavesdropping?" Mrs. Dowell's voice grew stern.

The secretary must've stepped out somewhere, which—niece or not—might earn her a lecture.

"I, um, I'll wait outside." Jackson studied the gray carpet.

"No, young man, too late for that." The principal raised her nose. "You'll have to stay in my office. Take a seat."

Totally out of place, Kieran wondered if her parents had spared her reading about Pinocchio when she'd been little.

Jackson grimaced as if saying "Do I have to?" But he dragged his feet to the chair the principal pointed at. He sank into the seat, his shoulders hunched and head ducked, his long hair hiding his face again. His scuffed shoes that had seen better times were still positioned toward the door as if he'd bolt at the first opportunity. Then, as if it were the most fascinating thing in the world, he picked on one of many loose threads in his jeans from more rips than Kieran could count. Despite Arianna buying him new clothes, he'd worn the ones he'd arrived with.

He clearly didn't expect any mercy, and something in Kieran softened. His own life had been filled with hard work and responsibilities, but he'd never had to raise his defenses like that. He knew his parents always had his back. The boy might think nobody had his back now.

Kieran's body leaned toward Jackson, but he stopped himself from interfering. It would only make matters worse. Arianna sat beside her nephew, her expression concerned.

A quick knock at the door made them all glance in that direction.

"Yes?" the principal snapped.

The secretary's blonde head popped in. "Noah and his father are here. May they come in?"

Mrs. Dowell nodded. "Please let them in."

While Jackson was sulking and wrapping his arms around his middle as if to protect his vital organs, the other boy strode inside, sporting expensive clothes and brand-name sneakers, a superior air, and a smug smile. There were probably two reasons for that. First, it had already been reported that Jackson had thrown the first punch. Second, Noah's father, Calvin Hearn, was wealthy and helped buy school equipment.

Besides being way better dressed, Noah was stockier than Jackson was, and his beefy neck resembled his father's, though on a smaller scale. Kieran's eyes narrowed, and he exchanged glances with Arianna. Wasn't it strange Jackson had assaulted a stronger boy who must have friends in school to join him while Jackson had none? Suspicion flashed in her eyes, too, as if she thought the same.

Doing his best to wipe out his immediate animosity against the father and son, Kieran moved toward Arianna and Jackson as if they were his family to protect. A ridiculous notion, of course.

Calvin marched forward. "I demand you punish the other boy. He hurt my son. I expect nothing less than justice from this school. Bullying won't be tolerated. That other boy should be expelled or penalized—such as made to wash dishes in the cafeteria for weeks."

Jackson sank even lower in his seat like he wanted to disappear.

Arianna clenched her fingers into her palms as if trying to stop her anger as she jumped to her feet. "Let me introduce myself. I'm Arianna Montemayor, Jackson's aunt. The 'other boy' has a name. Jackson Montemayor. And nothing will happen to my nephew until I have a clear picture of what occurred. Even if I have to interview every teacher, student, and mouse in this school."

Noah deflated a bit.

Jackson looked up, more confidence in his dark eyes now. "I don't think there are mice here, though I heard someone brought a hamster once."

The principal's eyes narrowed. "Let's wrap this up. I don't want to see any fighting again. For now, Jackson and Noah both will get detention. Next time, the punishment will be more severe."

Jackson perked up and straightened in his chair. He mustn't be a stranger to detention and must've expected worse.

But Noah's eyes popped wider. "Why? He hit me first! And unlike *him*, I have friends in class! I wanna hang out with them, not this trash."

Arianna's entire posture went rigid. "What did you just say?"

But the boy was on a roll already. "I didn't even say anything that bad. Just that we didn't need the new trash to roll into town and make things worse for us."

Kieran reached his patience limit. "Noah, you don't ever talk about your fellow students like that."

"I didn't talk about Jackson." Noah shrugged and pointed at Arianna. "I talked about *her*."

Now Kieran reached his boiling point, and he was an even-tempered person. But Arianna's laugh stopped him from lashing out.

What? She was *laughing*?

She flattened her smile. "Okay, that was inappropriate. But... Jackson, you were defending *me*? Was this what the fight was about?" Her gaze incredulous, she gaped. "Why? You don't even like me."

"What a family," Noah's dad muttered.

"I don't *like* you. But nobody offends my relatives," Jackson grumbled without lifting his head.

"Thank you, but there are other ways to do it. We'll talk about this later." She eyed Noah. "That phrase sounded like something an adult would say. Where did you hear it?"

The boy's look at his dad was a telltale.

Calvin's thick neck exploded in red splotches above the collar of his ironed white shirt, and he tugged at his fancy tie. Then he took off his jacket as if the atmosphere was getting too hot for him here. "I didn't mean anything by it. It was just words."

"Often, words result in hurts, both physical and emotional. I don't care anymore when people insult me. I've experienced much worse things. But what if I said anyone who hurts my family would be hurt back? Would you consider that *just words*?"

Calvin Hearn visibly swallowed. Sweat beaded on his bald head, and he loosened the tie that now hung crooked. Even his suit didn't look as impeccable.

"Enough!" The principal raised a hand, her eyes intense behind her thick round glasses. "While I don't condone name-calling and it'd better stop, it doesn't change the fact that Jackson physically assaulted Noah. That's a much worse offense."

Noah's lips widened again, though the smile wasn't as smug.

Jackson lifted a hand to rake his fingers through his long black hair, a contrast to his sister's blonde strands. His dark eyes, again a color different from his sister's baby blues, narrowed. As his arm rose, his sleeve rolled down to reveal a bruise. It looked fresh. Just like the shiner.

Kieran flinched. "When and where did you get that bruise?"

Jackson didn't say anything. But Noah's gaze became furtive, and he looked away. He shifted away, too, as if wanting to put distance between himself and Kieran.

Kieran leaned toward him, holding eye contact and enunciating carefully. "You hit Jackson this morning, didn't you? You hit him and walked away, probably while your friends cheered you on. If he didn't retaliate when you insulted his aunt later, he'd look like a weakling."

"He's a new kid! He has to prove his worth! And we didn't invite the likes of him here."

Kieran's gaze narrowed. "'The likes of him'?"

"Troublemakers!" Beefy hands fisted, Noah stared into the carpeted floor, his previous smugness gone now.

"Why didn't you say something?" Arianna asked, her voice unusually soft with a tint of sadness.

"Because I'm not a snitch!" Jackson muttered.

What he hadn't said was he probably didn't expect the adults to believe him anyway. Just like they hadn't believed Arianna, based on her outburst that still had Kieran reeling. Jackson had a certain reputation in his previous place, and the students must've found out about it here.

Kieran leveled his gaze on Calvin Hearn, who had the decency to blush which spread to his head where sweat now shone almost as much as that diamond horseshoe ring on his pinkie. A faint odor reached Kieran, and the armpits of Calvin's once pristine, expensive white shirt now showed dark stains.

"Calvin, you insisted bullying wouldn't be tolerated," Kieran said. "Would you dish out the same punishment to your son as you dished out to mine—ahem, my employee's nephew?"

Noah stepped back, his mouth agape. "I'm not washing dishes for three weeks in the school cafeteria!"

Kieran pulled back his shoulders. "That might not be such a bad idea." He smiled at Mrs. Dowell. "How about community service at our ranch? We could always use help with the animals." He let a mischievous smile escape. "Especially removing manure."

"Doing what?" Noah screeched.

The corners of the principal's mouth lifted a tad. "I like this idea, Mr. O'Neill. Two weeks of community service after school at your ranch under your supervision. For both boys. And now we're done."

Noah's eyes were huge. Meanwhile, Jackson's shoulders straightened, and relief softened his taut face.

"Thank you, Principal Dowell." Arianna's features were relieved, too. She got up and muttered in her nephew's direction. "If I threw punches every time I got offended, there'd be too many people unable to get up."

Calvin Hearn laughed. "Yeah, right."

Arianna looked at the principal. "With your permission? I believe this might serve educational purposes."

Mrs. Dowell gaped at Arianna as if she'd never seen anyone like her. Kieran could relate.

Arianna seemed to take the principal's silence for agreement. She walked to Calvin. "You don't have any injuries or physical disabilities, I hope?"

"No, why?"

Kieran wasn't sure what happened, but the next moment, Calvin was thrown to the carpet. Kieran managed to maintain a straight face as he helped the embarrassed man up.

Arianna flipped some dust from her shoulder. "Please note, I went easy on you."

"Wow!" Her nephew gaped. "Can you teach me that?"

"Depending on how you do at school and the ranch, I can give you lessons. Then, if anyone bullies you, they'll have to do it at their own risk." She sent a glance Noah's way, but he'd already scurried out of the office without waiting for his dad.

Then she turned to the principal. "Thank you for giving us a second chance."

The woman nodded. "I should've warned you, if Mr. Hearn shed any blood from your, ahem, educational demonstration, you'd have to pay for carpet cleaning."

Huh. Kieran started warming up to the principal.

Arianna didn't smile, but her eyes crinkled at the corners just a bit. "Gladly." Then she turned to Calvin. "I don't care any longer what people call me. But as this reflects on my nephew by association, let me explain something to you. Why is it that you consider people like us inferior to the people like you and your son? Is it because you can write a big check?" She whipped out a checkbook from her purse, sat, and wrote something. Then she handed it to the principal. "Here's a donation for gym equipment and other school needs."

Mrs. Dowell's eyes became about the size of her glasses. "That's... that's very generous. We've never seen a single donation like that before."

Calvin's nostrils flared, and he wiped his shiny head with a handkerchief again. "I, um, I didn't mean to..."

Arianna grimaced. "Okay, that probably wasn't the right move. The ability to write a large check doesn't make me better than anyone else. And I didn't mean for it to look like I'm buying a better attitude to Jackson here."

The guy blushed.

"Listen, I don't wear fancy clothes or shoes or drive an expensive car. But I speak several languages and have traveled the world. I can name five generations of my ancestors. I know where I come from, and it's not trash." She raised her chin.

Jackson's lips widened, but it was difficult to say whether it was a scowl or a hint of a smile.

She placed her hand on her nephew's shoulder protectively. "Please, next time, don't make assumptions about people you don't even know. And Jackson might be an outsider here, but he has a family who'll stand up for him."

Kieran took his place nearby. "That's right."

Chapter Seven

Arianna couldn't believe she'd allowed herself that outburst in front of Kieran—and the principal, no less! She'd let her temper get the best of her sometimes, but rarely. And not like that. Never like that.

Had Jackson heard what she'd said? He'd been eavesdropping. Had he figured that all out?

Her insides went cold despite the heat coming from the stove at Kieran's family ranch house.

She whirled around the kitchen, doing her best to make up for lost time. She couldn't be late with lunch on her first day. Seasoned steaks were in the pans already, spreading a mouthwatering aroma, and she'd been working on a mountain of coleslaw. That mountain required lots of cabbage and fast slicing.

Alone in the kitchen, she'd expected to appreciate the solitude. She'd been a loner her whole life. She'd had to be, except for the time spent with her foster sisters. Instead, she missed Kieran's presence and even his gentle teasing.

She peeled another carrot and shredded it to add to the coleslaw. She wasn't too proud to admit he'd saved the situation today in the principal's office while she'd nearly ruined it. His calm confidence was the antidote to her bruised temper.

He'd unearthed the truth and found the culprit. Then he'd come up with the best solution for everyone, except for himself. Her heart shifted. As much as she tried to be indifferent to him, it was difficult not to admire the man.

Admire the man...

Her hand stilled above the pan as she'd been checking on the steaks. Uh-oh.

She'd never replied to Victor. And she'd put her phone on silent mode before going into the principal's office.

Grimacing, she wiped her hands on a paper towel and fished the phone out of her pants.

Wow. Fifteen missed calls from Victor. But only one text.

I guess I got my answer.

Disappointment should've twisted her gut. Kieran lived in a world so different from hers he was not only on another planet but also in another universe. But Victor was from a world she could relate to. With a traumatic childhood, he'd built himself into something from the ground up, and he was nearly as guarded as she was. Keeping people away was as much his mechanism as it was hers.

Memories flooded as she diminished the fire under the pans and rattled a gigantic tray loaded with biscuits into the oven. Then she returned to the coleslaw. After this, she'd be seeing cabbage in her dreams at night.

She'd seen Victor in her dreams when she'd fallen in love with him.

In a rare moment of openness, he'd told her about his disastrous childhood. She could relate. He hadn't stayed in one place for a long time. She could relate. He'd avoided relationships. She could relate. He was rough around the edges and unapologetic. She could relate.

Before she'd made a huge error, she'd hoped they could form a reluctant alliance, even if for survival rather than joy. They could understand each other because, when they looked at each other, they nearly looked into a mirror. Not appearance-wise, of course. Emotion-wise.

Neither Arianna nor Victor were wholesome, solid, and open like Kieran and his brothers. Several of her foster sisters had found happiness with the O'Neills. But each of her sisters had a far higher degree of wholesomeness than she'd ever had.

Not only had she been cut into pieces, but those jagged pieces could slice open anyone who tried to get close to her.

Even Kieran.

Especially Kieran.

Then why did her heart stutter any time she thought about him?

Well, her heart would have to catch up with her mind, and her mind said an attraction to him was a no-no.

The biscuits' aroma lifted to her nostrils. She was used to exotic locations and the thrill of the search, not... this at-homeness. She'd thought that, like a shark, she always needed to be on the move. If she slowed down, then she might remember too much. Then the pain would be too much to bear.

Bear. Her gaze fell on a mug with a teddy bear holding a heart. A bear. With a heart. On a mug.

Nobody had ever given her such cute things.

"Need any help?" Kieran's voice made her whirl around, the knife still in her hand. "It smells good in here."

"I'm fine. Didn't break anything this time." She glanced at the mug precariously close to the counter's edge and pushed it deeper. "Yet."

"Unless Kieran's heart counts." Declan strode into the kitchen, the reporter brother who traveled the world but came to the ranch for periodic visits between trips.

She blinked. What did he just say?

"He's joking." Kieran shoved his younger brother's shoulder playfully.

She'd done her best to avoid breaking anyone's heart, including her own.

"Here." Kieran clattered a stack of plates into his brother's hand. "Might as well help set the table as long as you're here anyway."

"Right." Declan grinned. "You need your privacy."

Kieran shook his head as if in disbelief while Declan walked to the dining room.

Envy over the sibling relationship stung Arianna. Yes, they teased each other, but they could rely on each other, as well.

She'd often wondered how different her life might've turned out if her grandmother had lived longer. Her insides filled with a mixture of warmth and ache. Her grandmother had cooked enough enchiladas and rice and beans to feed the entire neighborhood, and she was all about *comunidad* and *la familia*. She'd become a widow young and never remarried, carrying her love through her entire life.

That said, she adored her granddaughter and took care of lots of friends' children. She'd been incredibly creative not just with food but also with making clay vases and sewing clothes. If Arianna closed her eyes, she could still smell the yummy scent of Grandma's empanadas, still hear the gentle voice as she told the children gathered around her *cuentos de hadas*, or fairy tales.

While Arianna's father was a bad apple, her grandmother was the true representative of their culture with her enormous heart and sense of family.

Then Arianna's heart twisted. It was her fault her grandmother died from a heart attack. Tears burned behind her eyes, and she blinked furiously.

Or how would her life be if she'd joined her foster sisters earlier? Their foster parents hadn't been much, but the sisters had raised each other, with the oldest of them, Genevieve, doing the biggest part. Would Arianna be able to let people into her life then? Would she still have this constant itch to run?

She'd never know, and the not knowing knotted her stomach.

"You look as if you're miles away." At the oven's beep, Kieran removed the biscuit tray from the oven, then plopped the golden things into two bread baskets. "By the way, if it's okay to ask, what did you decide about that assignment?"

Declan entered the kitchen, and Kieran handed him the bread baskets. Declan rolled his eyes and stomped back to the dining room.

Figuring it would be easier than explaining, she showed him the phone screen, then scooped sauce onto the shredded cabbage in its huge bowl and mixed it up.

His eyes dimmed as he sliced baked potatoes and added butter and sour cream in the middle. "Are you upset?"

"No." The answer came fast and sincere. She handed Declan the coleslaw bowl the moment he returned to the kitchen, and this time, he didn't even roll his eyes before marching out to the dining room. Smart guy. She liked that brother.

Though not nearly as much as she liked Kieran.

"I don't even understand it myself." She flipped the finished steaks onto platters with the already done ones and turned off the stove. "Normally, I'd want to go. I wouldn't hesitate. It's a great opportunity, and it's the kind of work I like. The company would be great, too. But now... It's like I want to stay, and not just because my nephew and niece are worth the sacrifice."

Or maybe she was staring at one of those reasons she hadn't gone on the assignment, a reason she didn't want to admit to. Then it hit her. "Oh, my niece! I didn't even check on her. What kind of aunt does that make me?"

"A busy one. Cut yourself some slack. I already checked on Isabella. She's doing fine with my mom. And I wanted to tell you—"

She didn't get a chance to find out what he wanted to tell her because a crowd of cowboys filed into the kitchen and piled their plates with steaks and baked potatoes.

Kieran let everyone go first, and so had she, beaming under their praise. Now she just hoped nobody got indigestion. At least, they wouldn't throw the plate in her face like her dad had done.

Then people left for the dining room, and Kieran shifted closer, giving her a whiff of his cedarwood-and-hay scent that somehow sent her heart racing. "We should join everyone."

"We should." Once she looked into his eyes, she had difficulty looking away. Her breathing went shallow.

"Let me help you remove this apron."

She nearly said she could do it herself perfectly well, but then... she didn't. She was so used to doing everything herself. Having someone help her felt more pleasant than she wanted to admit.

She lifted her long ponytail. His fingertips brushed against her neck by accident as he untied the strings, and her skin tingled in their wake. Had she turned off the oven? Because it felt way too hot in here.

Then his fingers lingered on her skin, and she knew it wasn't by accident. Fire erupted in her belly, and she closed her eyes.

"Auntie! I had so much fun!" Isabella's voice made Arianna fling her eyelids open.

She jerked away from him as guilt stabbed her. She was losing sight of her priorities. Heat crept up her neck. Her cheeks must be the color of tomatoes or maybe even beetroots by now.

She leaned toward the little girl and avoided looking at Kieran. "I'm glad, sweetie. I'd love to hear all about what you did. Let's wash your hands and go eat lunch." She sent Kieran's mother a grateful glance. "Thank you so much for taking care of my niece."

The woman waved her off. "No trouble at all. I enjoyed her. I'm sure the animals did, too."

Hold on.

Arianna's eyes widened. She hadn't flinched from Kieran's touch. Hadn't moved away. She'd enjoyed it. What did that mean?

Things that came easily to other people had taken an enormous effort for her. Hugs, especially if from a male. Friendly chatter—or friendships, for that matter—outside of the circle of her sisters. Any kind of touch, especially, again, from a male. Trust. The list was huge.

Arianna's lips twitched up on their own accord. The scene was so... peaceful. But her life had never been peaceful. And if there was a lull at some moment, it only meant a storm was brewing.

Kieran shook his head as he helped Arianna clear the table and place dishes in the dishwasher.

Why was he behaving like this? Unlike Declan, for example, who was spontaneous, impulsive, and adventurous, Kieran was responsible and thought through things before doing them. He'd worked hard at the ranch and was proud of providing food for people. Things beyond the horizon or out of his reach had never beckoned him.

He'd only followed his impulses with one person many years ago and had a heartache to show for it.

Now, instead of working in the field or at least in the office as he'd normally do at this time, he was lingering in the kitchen as if tied to Arianna by her apron strings. The ones he'd tried to untie so clumsily he'd touched her. And then he'd touched her olive skin again, unable to resist the fire in his belly that had nothing to do with the stove.

He nearly groaned as he stacked more dishes in the dishwasher while Arianna scrubbed the pans, spreading around the scent of lavender soap. Who was he kidding? He wanted to touch her, and he had. And it had only made things worse. It had been wrong of him. While he'd seen some of his friends go through rebellious stages as teenagers, even a couple of his brothers, Kieran had never desired the forbidden. Yet he'd been drawn to her like she was an enormous magnet.

He hurried back into the dining room and returned with more plates and a sense of regret because they were the last stack. He wouldn't have an excuse to stay around her longer.

Argh. As his feet padded a familiar path along his mom's hooked rugs, he nearly ground his teeth. Arianna was an employee and, therefore, off-limits. She kept people at arm's length. How many times would he have to remind himself to make his heart stop longing for her?

She'd tied her long hair in a bun this time, but a strand sneaked out and fell on her face. With her hands in soapy yellow rubber gloves, she blew that rebellious hair out of her way.

His pulse went into a canter, and it took all his willpower and then some to stop himself from reaching out and tucking that strand behind her ear. He stacked the last dishes and utensils in the dishwasher and straightened.

He'd dreamed of running his fingers through that luscious hair that smelled of sandalwood and *forbidden* when she'd let it drape her shoulders. But the bun wasn't helping him, either, because it exposed her graceful neck. That elegant line and a tiny birthmark where her neck met her shoulder were going to be his undoing.

Warmth spread through him. She looked up from the sink, and their eyes met.

Great. Now he was caught staring. He flushed.

As always, her dark eyes were unreadable while all his attraction must be spilling out of his eyes. He'd never learned to control his facial expressions. Never had to.

She didn't look away and didn't look down. She wasn't the type to. But he didn't expect her full lips to part—not that he should be looking at them. Didn't expect her to take off those rubber gloves and turn toward him.

His pulse went into a full gallop. He needed to stop that rapid heartbeat but couldn't look away from her, from the gentle oval of her lovely face, from the darkness of her forest-green irises where her pupils dilated.

Could he hope his attraction wasn't one-sided? Not that it should matter because it didn't change the circumstances. But somehow, it mattered more than taking his next breath.

A jolt of joy reminded him she'd sort of refused her mysterious assignment and stayed at the ranch. Of course, it wasn't because of him but because of her nephew and niece but still...

The strand of hair fell on her face again, and this time, she made no effort to move it. He tucked it behind her ear, trying not to touch her tender skin and trying *to* touch it at the same time. Her breath hitched, sending a heated response through his bloodstream.

She fascinated him. Not just those soulful impossible-to-decipher eyes or the long neck or that tiny birthmark. Everything in her called to him on a level he'd never known existed, from her ferocious loyalty to the children she'd never even met before she'd taken them in, to her readiness to drop everything for her foster sisters, to her guarding the secrets of her past.

He didn't know how to heal her. Probably nobody could, except God. He winced. He didn't think she was a Christian, so he shouldn't be attracted to her. But why did he have the feeling that God had led him to her, as well as Isabella and Jackson? The children had needed her, but they seemed to need him, too. So how could he turn his back on them?

Kieran shouldn't look at his employee—especially a nonbeliever—in this way. But he wanted to believe God had put this woman in his path for a reason.

That reason couldn't be to break his heart, right?

His mind spun when she leaned toward him. A little more, and their breaths could mix. A little more, and their lips could touch. Could their lives touch, as well?

"Auntie! Auntie! I wanna you paint my face!" Her niece bolted into the room.

Arianna jerked back, her cheeks going pink, and that affected him like a cold shower. What had he been thinking?

Oh, right. He wasn't.

His mother sent him a guilty glance as she followed the little girl into the kitchen. "I offered to do it, but she wanted *you* to paint her face."

Isabella grinned. "Yes, Auntie. *Pwetty* please."

Arianna blinked rapidly, her smile wobbly as she rested a hand atop the girl's head. "Sweetie, I'm at work. I'm sorry. But I'd be glad to do it in the evening."

The smile slipped off Isabella's face, and she ducked her head, catching strands of hair on Arianna's fingers and wisping them out of place in her pigtails. "*Sowwy*, Auntie. Did I make your boss upset with you? Was I bad?"

Okay, it was time to step in. "The boss isn't upset." Well, maybe a tiny bit about a kiss that had never happened, but it not happening had to be for the best. He tried to ignore the disappointment that soured the food in his belly. "The cleanup is almost done. The boss thinks your auntie can leave early today."

Yeah. Maybe he shouldn't be using the word *boss* so much. Besides emphasizing the unwanted dynamics between them, it was as if he wanted to show his superiority, which wasn't the case at all. Plus, Arianna didn't look like a woman who appreciated being ordered around.

Thankfully, she didn't seem to think it was the case at all. She brightened. "Great. We can do the face painting now." Then she blinked again. "I need to buy things to use for it, right?"

"I can borrow them from neighbors. They have lots of children. And more on the way, probably." His mother looked pointedly at Kieran. "So many blessings."

Seriously? Again? "Mom, I'm not even married!"

"My point exactly. Hopefully, someday my prayers will be answered." Mom disappeared from the kitchen, leaving behind that *friendly* reminder again.

"Auntie, I'm a child. Am I a blessing?" Isabella lifted a thoughtful gaze.

Arianna leaned to her, smoothing back the mussed blonde hair, her expression so tender it almost pained him to see it. "Of course, sweetie."

The girl sighed. "Mom used to say I was her punishment."

Arianna's eyes flashed, but only for a moment. She hesitated, then sank to the floor beside Isabella, and hugged her. "You're never a punishment. You're my joy, and I want you to remember it—always."

The girl grinned from ear to ear. "Okay, Auntie. I'll *wememba*."

The face painting was fun until Isabella asked Arianna to paint a butterfly on her cheek. Arianna dropped the brush. Her fingers trembled. That was weird. Did something about butterflies cause her such a strong reaction? But why?

Kieran's gut tightened as he picked up the brush as if nothing happened. "What color would you like?"

"Blue." Isabella lifted her adorable face to him.

Arianna stared into space before mouthing a thank you his way.

"Don't mention it," he mouthed back and dipped the brush in azure-blue paint. Unlike Brandon, Kieran wasn't a great artist, but he hoped it did look like a butterfly when he was finished.

Later in the afternoon as Arianna made sandwiches for the cowboys' dinner in the kitchen while Isabella was drawing ponies in the living room with Madeline, Arianna's phone beeped in her pocket. He stopped spreading mayonnaise on the bread—yes, he was suddenly in the mood for a brisket and mayo sandwich—and sent her a quiet look. She blanched as she read the text on her phone.

Alarm shot through him, and Kieran blurted out. "Is it something bad?"

"It was from my cousin Ric. He..." Her breath faltered. "He said he's going to get the children."

Kieran's stomach clenched, and he shifted closer, going into protective mode. "Was it a threat?"

"It was a promise." She closed her eyes and reopened them, and for the first time, he could read the expression there clearly because it was stark despair.

"We can hire lawyers." His heart went out to her.

Her eyes widened at his use of the word *we*, but she didn't correct him. "My chances still wouldn't be great. Considering my history, I'm not a mother role model. Whereas, he has a great reputation in the community, a surgeon's job with a high income, and a ready-made family with three sons who are doing fantastic in school and a wife that sounds ideal. He can argue the children would be better off with them, considering she can stay at home and take care of them."

Kieran should be able to do something, say something, or come up with something. He was the problem-solver in the family. Even if right now he was baffled about how to solve this one. "Is there anything, anything at all, my family and I can do to help you?"

Her gaze unmoving, she stared at the wall behind him. "Yes, you can." Her chin trembled. "But it's too much to ask. I don't have the right to."

Did she think so little of herself? Or was it him? That he wouldn't step in when the well-being of two innocent children was on the line?

He cupped his hands on her shoulders. "Go ahead. Try me."

She looked him in the eye. "Would you marry me?"

His jaw dropped, and so did his hands.

Chapter Eight

Had she pushed him too far? Of all the skills Arianna had accumulated, communication wasn't one of them. She could be too direct sometimes, too abrasive.

She'd suggested a walk outside because Kieran had nearly gasped for air in the kitchen. Plus, standing in the shadow of the large tree might help hide the emotions even she couldn't conceal. She took a deep breath for courage.

Her lungs filled with the scents of grass and earth and something... homey. A foreign feeling to her.

Or was it?

She'd known the sense of home once at her grandmother's place, but it wasn't for long. Her complete opposite, Kieran was all about the sense of home and family. One of the many reasons her offer was unfair to him.

In a marriage of convenience, she'd be the one gaining while what would he have to gain? She knew all too well that people only agreed to something if they stood to gain something and often only if they stood to gain a *lot*.

She stumbled over her words as she flattened her palm on the rough bark, leaning against it because her knees went weak. "It would be in name only. Separate bedrooms. I'll sign a prenup. I'll take care of the children."

How she'd do that while working, she wasn't sure, but she'd do her best. She had a new respect for working mothers. And thankfully, she had a circle of support in her foster sisters and in Kieran's mother. Jessie had offered to babysit, and Genevieve had said she'd fly from Houston if needed, but Arianna didn't want Genevieve to take off in the middle of the school year.

Her words tumbled on, stopping Kieran from speaking.

"The ceremony would be simple. No expenses on your part. I'll pay for everything. Then... after I hopefully get the children, I'm asking for a year. Two, max, so it's not a sudden change for them all over again. I'll cook. Better than I did today. I'll clean the house. I—"

"The answer is yes." His eyes probed hers. "And you don't have to clean the house or pay for the wedding or sign any prenup."

Her world spun. As everything whirled, she focused on him, like a child spotting something to keep from getting dizzy on a merry-go-round. She leaned her back against the tree and caught her breath. Behind him, the tranquil blue sky mocked her turmoil.

Was it that simple? "B–but my nephew is a handful. And then there's the mystery of bad guys Isabella mentioned—"

"I'll do it. Did you expect anything different?" His gaze was as open as the sky above.

While hers, she'd purposefully hidden by shadows from the foliage. Among the green leaves, a few were turning golden. Change of seasons. But it was winter in her heart forever. "I–I didn't know what to expect."

He'd do it for the children. Not for her, because he didn't even wince when she'd said the marriage would be in name only. She should be euphoric. Maybe a part of her was, but a different part, a part she kept hidden from everyone, usually even herself, was sliced with disappointment.

He was a noble, kind man who'd stepped up when needed. Yet she'd even nearly managed to destroy Victor, a man who wasn't that noble and not that kind. Sort of like she was.

She'd have to work hard to hide her growing feelings for Kieran and keep the marriage "in name only." A near-kiss like the one in the kitchen could never happen.

Her gut tightened.

When the arrangement expired, she needed to leave Kieran the same way she'd found him. Unhurt by her.

Her bun had come undone, and the wind whipped her hair around her face. She hadn't even thanked him. "Thank you. I know it's not much—"

"It's more than enough." His amber eyes searched hers. Then he swiped her hair away from her face and tipped her chin.

Her breath caught in her throat, and she wanted to lean into his touch—oh how she wanted to. Which was already a miracle. Since she'd run away at fourteen, he was the only man she'd allowed to touch her without her shrinking away in fear. On the contrary, a pleasant wave spread through her at his nearness. But she had to make herself move away. "I can't..."

His eyes darkened, and his hand dropped to his side. He stepped back. "My apologies. I wouldn't push you into anything you didn't want."

She did her best to calm her racing heart. Usually, she liked an adrenaline spike, but it was different now. Everything was different now. She'd navigated unfamiliar territories easily in the geographical sense, but she had no clue how to navigate this unfamiliar territory.

Not wanting to wasn't a problem, quite the opposite. Of course, she couldn't tell him that. But she should tell him something else. "Things in my past... They could come back to haunt me."

It was only fair for him to know.

His features didn't change, and he didn't look surprised. "All the more reason for me to marry you. I know you're extremely capable of defending yourself, but one more person wouldn't hurt."

Especially when children were involved. He didn't say it, but he didn't need to. Was she an unfit mother? She'd consider backing off if the alternative for them wasn't so horrifying. Or was she simply projecting her trauma onto them? So what if Isabella was the only girl in the family? So what if she was the same age now as Arianna had been when Ric started coming to visit?

But he'd said Isabella was pretty like a butterfly, just as he had with...

Arianna flinched.

No, she couldn't take even a minuscule risk. Isabella's life was too important.

Arianna stepped away from the safety of the tree and out into the open. She'd been to many places, many of them gorgeous, but something about the majestic sweep of the emerald fields, the tranquility of the lolling cows, and the endlessness of the azure sky spoke to her.

If she was capable of putting down roots, would this be the place? Would this be the man?

Or was she painting illusions in her mind like she'd painted the flowers on her niece's cheeks, only for them to disappear with the first wash?

"What about you being my boss?" She grimaced. This could get awkward fast. "In some workplaces, work romance between a supervisor and an employee is not allowed."

He shrugged. "We're not those places. But you have a point. What do you think about my mother being your supervisor from now on? Not that you need any supervision."

Arianna had heard plenty of jokes about mothers-in-law, but according to her foster sisters, Mrs. O'Neill was the best mother-in-law in the world. A blessing they thanked God for almost as much as they thanked Him for their husbands. This place, where people cared about each other, felt mystical.

Arianna just hoped she wouldn't bring disaster to their doorstep in return for all that kindness. Her hand moved to smooth the fabric over her stomach, fabric that hid hideous scars. If she could pray, she'd pray for these people.

She couldn't pray. Her frozen heart didn't believe in kindness from above just as it stopped believing in kindness on earth.

But didn't she have to believe in Kieran's kindness, for her nephew and niece's sake?

She tilted her head. "Sounds good to me."

"You won't regret it." He stood there, legs wide apart, as solid as that tree whose species she didn't even know, rooted in this land.

Meanwhile, she was as unsettled as a lonely leaf, shriveling in on herself, and carried by the wind. She wasn't scared she'd regret it. She was worried he would. But she didn't say it out loud. The agreement was too precarious to ruin it.

She shifted toward him without realizing it. She was drawn to him. There was no denying it.

Now she'd be spending even more time in his presence. How was she going to do it without falling for him? He was what the children needed, a father figure who'd take care of them instead of abusing them.

But *she* wasn't what *he* needed. The wind threw her hair into her face again, and she swept it away. If only she could sweep away her thoughts as easily.

Had she made the biggest mistake of her life? Had *he*?

The wedding ceremony was simple indeed.

While that had been what Arianna asked for and promised, Kieran didn't feel it was right.

Growing up with brothers, he didn't know much about girls. But wasn't it common knowledge that all girls wanted the wedding of their dreams with a gorgeous white dress and long veil, a sea of flowers, and a multilayered wedding cake and whatnot? There was a reason weddings were such a huge industry.

Granted, his brothers' weddings to Arianna's foster sisters had been done in a way less spendy and far less grand scale. They could even be called hasty, like Paisley & Cormac's wedding, when his brother had to leave for the military base in Germany.

But Arianna took simplicity to a new level. His parents—especially his mother—were so thrilled with the proposal they'd immediately agreed to host the ceremony and reception in the backyard.

Despite his protests, Arianna had spent the evening before the wedding prepping sandwiches for the reception, and her foster sisters had baked a cake and helped with a variety of finger foods.

Today, Isabella was an excited flower girl in a fluffy powder-blue dress with butterfly wings who flitted down the aisle and diligently covered everyone in sight in rose petals. Behind her, Jackson was a rain cloud, ready to burst on her parade as he carried the rings along with his stormy scowl. At least, he'd grudgingly worn slacks beneath his black *unripped* T-shirt.

"How are you holding up?" Brandon, who'd been through the ceremony most recently, stood beside Kieran by the wedding arch—a trellis his brothers had built and fixed gold and silver balloons to while his sisters-in-law strung it with autumn-hued ribbons. "That frown won't look so good in the pictures, bro."

Right. "Says the family grouch."

"I haven't frowned since my sweetie said yes—you shouldn't be frowning, either. What's eating you, anyway?"

"Nothing." Kieran stopped craning his neck. "I'm just trying to see if Jackson brought the rings. Earlier, well... I saw him patting Madeline's dog and holding the ring box very close to Rusty's lolling pink tongue."

Brandon let out a guffaw that surely drew onlookers' attention. "The boy will be fine. The dog and rings, too. You're cheating, you know, gaining a full family and being the first to give Mom grandkids. I'm kidding, of course. But Mom hasn't stopped smiling since the moment she heard about this wedding."

Before Kieran could respond, Arianna appeared. He'd prepped himself for her to come down the makeshift aisle in black jeans and a matching T-shirt if that was her preference, but...

"Wow," Brandon whispered. "She did it. Madeline *actually* did it. She said she'd loan Arianna that shimmering silvery dress. But I never believed she could talk Arianna into wearing it—figured that was asking too much of her matron-of-honor duties. Guess I should know by now not to be surprised by anything my wife does."

Kieran let his brother's ramblings drift into the background as his focus narrowed on Arianna, a true vision. His heart nearly stopped beating, then somehow seemed to match its tempo to each step she took as she paced toward him, supported by Madeline, who now lived at the ranch with his brother, and Genevieve, who'd flown in from Houston for the occasion.

Arianna's silver-gray dress held no decorations, and black combat boots peeped out underneath it. With no veil, no tiara, and no flowers in it, her mahogany hair flowed over her shoulders, a mantle all its own, and she carried a spectacular wedding bouquet of golden-hued maple leaves as unapologetically unconventional—and stunning—as she was. No jewelry, though soon she'd be wearing a wedding ring.

She wore no blush and no lipstick, yet her face shone with a natural beauty even the heavy mascara layers and thick eyeliner couldn't obscure. Beyond those embellishments, her beautiful eyes drew him in, locked with his, and spoke a silent vow.

He'd never seen a bride like this, and surely, none of the guests had, either.

Yet he couldn't look away from his autumn bride. She was like a river in the moonlight, mysterious and utterly gorgeous.

Then his heart nearly stopped beating for a different reason. She stumbled twice as the dress was too long for her and she kept stepping on its hem. At one point, he nearly thought he heard fabric ripping beneath the clomp of those boots. He almost rushed forward each time, but she caught herself by then with the help of her foster sisters.

"Don't worry, bro. Nobody even blinked," Brandon whispered, hopefully low enough no one else heard him.

"At this point, people are used to stumbling brides in this family," Jessie joined in from further down.

"I heard Madeline had her hair set on fire when she was a bridesmaid at Cormac and Paisley's wedding," Declan, who'd missed that event, added quietly. "After that, everyone agrees—if nothing's burning, then everything's great."

And it was. Kieran couldn't ask for a better day. The sky was clear with not a cloud in sight and not a threat of a single raindrop—though, from his mother's sniffles, there was a threat of *tear*drops behind her sunny expression. He breathed the scents of grass and sun-warmed earth, grateful for the joy and beauty of the most important day in his life.

He gave thanks to the Lord, prayed for Arianna and her nephew and niece, and asked to be the best husband he could be to her, and the best father and friend to the children.

The guests turned their heads when she passed, and he didn't blame them. She was... incredible, and he still couldn't wrap his mind around the fact she was about to become his wife. Even if it was in name only. That was the only part of this wedding he wasn't fond of. The chairs were mismatched, and Arianna had asked not to decorate them with flowers. But nobody seemed to mind.

Did *she* mind that nearly all the guests were from his side? She only had her foster sisters, Genevieve's daughter, and Jackson with Isabella attending for her. All her sisters were bridesmaids. Their dresses didn't match the way bridesmaids' dresses usually did, but he'd be fine if they'd shown up in T-shirts and jeans.

He'd never been one for appearances and wasn't about to start now.

Because the most important and precious thing was that Arianna was walking toward him, now only inches away. When she took her place, she smiled up at him, her smile a rare treat and a treasure, and his heart turned in his chest. He had to remind himself this was just an arrangement.

It felt real. Too real.

She was marrying him for the children's sake. He was marrying her because... well, yes, to help her and the children, but it was more than that.

Because he wanted to.

Because the woman beside him occupied all his thoughts and dreams.

Because, even if nothing else happened, he craved to have her beside him. Too bad she didn't feel the same way.

He stifled a cringe as he listened to the priest. Was Kieran taking advantage of the situation? He'd have to keep those thoughts of attraction and those desires to himself, no matter how difficult it was going to be.

To him, marriage was for life, the way his parents' marriage had been. But when the time came and she decided to leave, he'd have to set her free. His gaze slipped to the little girl and the way her face had scrunched when she'd said days ago how someone had cut her butterfly's wings.

He'd never cut Arianna's wings. She'd be free to leave whenever she wanted. Even if it broke his heart a second time.

Chapter Nine

Arianna still couldn't adjust to married life even over a week later. She'd probably never adjust to it.

Early in the morning, she tiptoed into the lodge kitchen to avoid waking anyone, passing rustic décor that somehow suited her, its rough edges complementing her equally rough ones. On Saturday, people deserved to sleep in, though Kieran had already left to feed the animals and check on them. Weekend or not, his job needed to get done, and he'd done it without complaint. Thinking about him sent warmth straight to her heart, and she stifled it fast.

But the cowboys had a day off, and therefore, so did she.

Besides, his parents had told Kieran and Arianna to take some time off, being newlyweds and all.

Arianna snorted as she poured water into the coffeepot and lined the filter in it. Her, a newlywed. The word felt stranger than extra-spicy Indian food on her tongue, even spicier than the flavors she'd grown up with. She added a hefty dose of coffee and turned the pot on, then brought eggs from the fridge to the counter, and slowed at a twinge of nostalgia over her first day working at the ranch.

She started making an omelet, the scene still surreal as if she was an actress playing a role. She and domestic bliss existed in parallel universes, never to cross.

Yet here she was, cooking breakfast for her children and waiting for her *husband*—wow!—with a longing she didn't want to push aside. She warmed the pan and sautéed onions the way her nephew liked—something she'd learned from Isabella—then poured in the mixture of eggs and milk.

Her phone beeped with an incoming text, and she winced, reluctant to look at the screen. Threats had started the day after the wedding. Always from an unknown number. At least once a day. Sometimes twice.

Always telling her she was going to pay.

A shiver traveled down her spine, despite the heat coming from the stove, but she kept her chin up. Her hand, cutting ham with a knife for the omelet, didn't shake.

A pressure squeezed the air out of her lungs. She didn't mind danger in her life so much. It even added a certain flavor. But bringing danger to others tied her empty stomach in a knot.

She slid the cubes of ham from the cutting board into the pan and reduced the fire under it. A warm coffee aroma spread through the room and mixed with the scent of bread as the slice she'd placed in the toaster popped out.

"Did you burn my toast again?" Her father had bellowed when she'd been eight and cowered in the farthest kitchen corner, knowing any moment he'd yank her out of there.

The scent of burned toast appeared in her nostrils, even though the one in her hand was just right.

If her mother hadn't worked night shifts… If her father had been kinder… If her grandmother hadn't died when Arianna was still little… Would she have been such easy prey for an unscrupulous relative when she'd become a teen?

She poured herself a cup and buttered a slice of toast. She needed the energy to figure the current threat out.

But first things first. She fished out her phone from her pocket and opened the text.

Yup.

Another threat.

She wasn't one to share her thoughts or problems, but with the phone in hand, she found her thumb hovering over the call button. She pressed the quick-dial for Genevieve. If she was going to talk to someone, it'd be someone too far away to interfere. Someone who knew about the possible danger. Someone who'd always been there for Arianna and their foster sisters. Arianna still had trouble imagining this world had people as caring and giving—and forgiving—as Genevieve.

She answered on the second ring.

Arianna grimaced, then turned off the stove as the omelet was ready and covered the pan with a lid to keep it warm. "I got another threat." She spoke before Genevieve could say anything, before Arianna could change her mind about sharing her problems.

"Oh, Arianna…" Just the softness of Genevieve's voice was as comforting as a hug. Not that Arianna had indulged in Genevieve's hugs often. "Have you told anyone other than me?"

"I showed the threats to Jessie." Their foster sister who was a cop. "The result was the same as last time."

"Burner phones?"

"Yep. In Texas."

"So that could mean..."

"Exactly," Arianna filled in as Genevieve's voice trailed off. "They could be connected to my so-called family."

"*Or* your previous jobs. Maybe even what you've done for Paisley."

Arianna ground her teeth. "I keep checking the children through the night. I mean, yeah, I'd do that anyway, but after these texts, I've increased the check-ins. At least, the text said *you* will pay. One small consolation."

"I know you can take care of yourself." A soft sigh whispered through the speakers before the next words came in a rush. "But I wouldn't count on them meaning *just you* you. What if it means you as in plural? As in 'the family'?"

Pressure squeezed the air out of Arianna's lungs. "I've never minded some danger in life. It even added a certain flavor. But bringing danger to others..."

Just the thought tied her stomach in a knot, and she couldn't finish saying it. Falling silent, she carried hot black coffee and lonely buttered toast to the round knotty pine table, munching on the toast on the way. She was used to eating fast to avoid being seen by her father. If he'd been in the living room, she'd stayed in her room unless called by him. And later, as a runaway, she'd had to survive on scraps people had thrown away. Even those she'd had to fight for. She was no stranger to an empty demanding stomach or cold seeping into her bones.

Her fingers wrapped around the warm cup as if she still needed to warm up. *Think.*

"If this isn't connected to my darling family, why would anyone threaten me now? It's been a month since my last job."

"Do you think some people found out your... secrets?"

"Maybe." Sadly, she couldn't tell her girls any specifics and put them on the trail, but Genevieve, who was working on her English PhD, could probably pick up on clues faster than the rest of them. "I can't say anything to you, client confidentiality and all. But I can put out some feelers among my former coworkers."

"Do you think this could be connected to your project with Paisley? You helped her a lot, after all."

Paisley now lived in Germany with her military husband, but before that, Arianna had been helping her support and relocate abused people escaping their circumstances, and the abusers hadn't been happy about that. Paisley even had a price on her head for some time.

Sipping her coffee and welcoming the clarity it brought, Arianna sighed. "I'd better make a mental list of the abusers she and I helped people hide from in the last year."

"Good plan."

"Jessie can follow up on those and trace through gas stations and grocery store cameras to see whether any of them have showed up in Cowboy Crossing."

"Of course, some of those people were affluent and could hire out help instead of doing the dirty work themselves." The tightness in Genevieve's voice made Arianna shiver. Genevieve knew what rich people could get away with, what they could do or pay to have done. She'd spent almost her whole life under the shadow of that knowledge. "I'll ask Paisley to see what she can find out online."

A computer expert, Paisley was proficient at uncovering information from the dark web. Although with her cotton-candy pink-and-blue hair Paisley appeared as fragile and colorful as the butterflies she loved—oh, the irony for Arianna, who'd prefer tarantulas to the constant reminder of butterflies—she sometimes suspected Paisley was the strongest of their foster sisters. But Arianna could never understand how her perky foster sister managed to delve into the underworld while remaining untouched in her cheerful outlook.

Arianna took another bite of toast but had lost her appetite. She chewed more for the sustenance than for the taste. A body required nutrition to survive. Besides, childhood beatings had taught her that one didn't waste food.

Ever.

She winced and didn't let her memory go there, concentrating on the current task, another survival technique she'd learned the hard way. "I've been careful, very careful."

"Of course, but information can leak." Genevieve sounded worried.

"Yes."

"People can come after you."

"Also a yes." Arianna groaned as she took another sip of the scalding coffee. "With my lifestyle, with my history, why did I think I could take in two children and risk them being vulnerable because of me?"

"Don't go there, Arianna. You're going to do a great job as a mom." Said the woman who, despite their nearness in ages, had been as close to a loving mom as Arianna had ever known. Not to mention the woman who was the only one of their sisters who'd actually become a mother. "Those kids are better off with whatever dangers you could bring near them than they would be with—"

"Right," Arianna cut her friend off. Not even wanting to think about the alternative. Her phone beeped a notification. "Kieran just entered through the gates. I've got to go. Call me later?"

"Sure. Keep me posted. If you need me there, just say the word. I'll pray for you."

"Thanks." Arianna wasn't sure what the point of praying was because she wasn't sure God existed, but a part of her envied her foster sisters who believed in a God who cared.

Then, as she hung up, her heart squeezed for a different reason. Anticipation, attraction, and yes, that longing she was so unused to and had no clue what to do about all gripped her with a ferocious force.

How had it happened that this great guy was her husband?

Pretty much by emotional blackmail.

Cringing, she hung her head.

Yet her legs carried her along the hardwood flooring to a hall rug depicting untamed wildlife. As she stepped onto a prowling wolf's image to meet Kieran, his face lit up, his joy so clear she forgot everything she'd just thought. Instead of acting aloof, she rushed to him and threw her arms around his neck. "Welcome back home."

Huh. Since she'd turned twelve, she'd never initiated a hug with a male. Not even Victor.

Kieran's eyes crinkled at their corners, and his soft laugh ruffled her hair. "Thanks."

Then he drew her close. He smelled of leather, grass, outdoors, and hope. The latter scent was the most unfamiliar one because it had rarely made an appearance in her life. She surprised herself by leaning into his broad chest.

Her heart stuttered, and a pleasant wave spread through her, her head spinning in a delicious way.

Then footfalls behind her made her withdraw and whirl around.

"Ew," her darling nephew said by the way of a morning greeting before schlepping into the bathroom, his gray pants hanging low on his hips.

"Good morning to you, too." Kieran seemed unaffected by the boy's reaction.

But Arianna was. She stepped back, heat rising along her neck.

What was she doing? Her excited greeting and embrace were so idyllic they only underscored how much they didn't belong in her life. And one would think Kieran was gone for a month instead of hours by the way she'd clung to him like a vine to a tree, desperate for support and nourishment.

That wouldn't do, especially considering the latest developments.

She couldn't leave Jackson and Isabella because they needed her, and yet, she needed to run again because she might be bringing danger to them and Kieran. How was she going to untangle this mess? Things were simple before.

Do what needs to be done. Disappear far away. Rinse and repeat.

She couldn't live like that now. "Um, breakfast is ready. Coffee, too." She shifted from one foot to the other.

He grinned at her. "It's wonderful to come home to a warm embrace and hot coffee and breakfast. Let me take a quick shower and change, and I'll help you set the table. Just give me a few minutes."

Then she was left there standing in the hall, those wolves on the rug nipping at her heels, foreign emotions nipping at her heart—and every bit of her yearning to snuggle into his embrace again.

Ridiculous. Truly ridiculous.

Okay, she was forgetting something. Right. Wake up Isabella.

Some parent, she was. She needed to help Isabella change from her pajamas into day clothes, most likely something with butterflies printed on it, and make sure she brushed her teeth. Amazing how many times the child had said she'd brushed her teeth, but her toothbrush bristles were still dry.

Arianna had thought nobody was fond of butterflies like Paisley. Arianna had been wrong. But she'd never told either one why even a butterfly picture sent shivers down her spine.

Mi mariposa bonita.

She'd had butterfly wings like Isabella's, lovingly made by Grandma, and had kept them like a treasure. Then she'd cut them into tiny pieces when she'd turned thirteen.

Stop.

She hurried to the girl's room where colorful cutouts of pink and azure butterflies mocked her from the wall. "Good morning, sweetie. Time to wake up."

Isabella opened her eyes, blinked a few times, then covered her head with a blanket. "I don't *waaaanna* get up."

Yup. And yesterday, she didn't want to go to bed. For hours, she'd needed a bedtime story, a glass of water, then milk, then orange juice, then to use the restroom (naturally), then a bedtime story again, then the restroom, and so on. How people did this every day was beyond Arianna.

Bath time was a challenge, too. First, Isabella didn't want to take a bath. Kieran had helped by unearthing rubber butterflies somewhere because Arianna had been about to hit her head against the bathtub. Then the sweet child didn't want to get out of the bathtub, even when most of the water had already ended up on the floor and Arianna's clothes and hair.

But what worried Arianna the most were Isabella's nightmares. Nightmares had woken up Isabella twice last night, leaving her screaming. Arianna had held the little girl for hours until Isabella calmed down and fell asleep. Arianna didn't know what to do about that except take her to a child psychologist. So she'd scheduled an appointment.

"I made us a yummy breakfast," Arianna finally said.

The ruffly blanket didn't move even an inch. Arianna suppressed a sigh. What was she supposed to do?

Kieran popped his head in the doorframe. "How about we go for a picnic later? We might even catch some butterflies."

Curious blue eyes appeared from under the blanket embroidered with—what else?—butterflies. Maybe Isabella and Paisley were related, not Isabella and Arianna. Paisley would know what to say to the child. Arianna had no clue.

The blanket flew to the floor, and Isabella leaped from her little pink bed. "I don't wanna catch *buttaflies*. I don't wanna hurt them. I just wanna look at them. They are *pwetty*. Like you, Auntie."

"You're right about that." Kieran lifted the girl in the air, making her squeal, then placed her on his shoulders, locking her in place. "Your auntie is very pretty."

Arianna's jaw slackened. She'd been called pretty before, but that had been when she'd put in an effort for her assignments, using a dress, an assortment of makeup, and a wig as disguises and plastering on a smile as a necessity. That was part of her job, like the uniform people in other professions put on before showing up to work.

And when she'd caught appreciative glances, it had been more a nuisance than a triumph because she didn't want to attract attention. Victor had never complimented her appearance because such things weren't discussed between them. Though he'd complimented her professional skills. Little good those skills had done him when he'd been shot. She suppressed the wince.

But now... now her heart perked up at Kieran's words, even if he'd simply agreed with the little girl. A part of herself she denied wanted to be pretty for Kieran, just for him, and that part awakened hungry for attention.

Some time—and lots of wasted toothpaste—later, they all gathered at the table.

"Would you mind if I say grace?" Kieran asked.

"Of course not. I mean, I don't mind," Arianna added hastily.

Jackson rolled his eyes, and she sent him a stern look.

They'd gone through this at every meal. And every time, she cringed over being unable to join Kieran. But she wasn't a believer. How could she believe in a kind God after what had happened to her?

Working with Paisley on her project, Arianna had seen enough suffering to cement her nonbelief. Because, even if she could persuade herself she didn't deserve God's kindness for some reason, that couldn't be true for those abused people.

Isabella didn't seem to have the same issue, thankfully. "Amen," she called out, then bounced in her seat. "I'm *hungwy*!"

Arianna scooped a large helping of omelet onto the girl's plate, this time tenderness constricting her heart. If one looked at Isabella now, it would be difficult to believe she'd screamed and cried just hours ago. Was the loss of her mother the reason for her nightmares? Or was something more sinister behind them?

Arianna cringed. She hadn't asked the girl yet about hiding in the closet and "bad men," but she'd have to soon. She'd asked Jackson, but he'd just scoffed and walked away. She'd spoken with Jessie to help research Arianna's half sister's accident and her life, and Jessie had talked to her former colleagues in Houston. So far, Jessie hadn't come up with anything suspicious. Arianna's half sister had seemed to change her relationships with men often, which wasn't good for children, but it wasn't a crime. Jessie had said she'd continue digging.

"I'll get the orange juice." Kieran got up and crossed to the kitchen, then returned with a carafe.

When she nodded, he poured her a glass, then did the same for Isabella while Jackson shook his head.

The scene was so mundane that it felt surreal. Arianna rarely had such meals as a child, except at her grandmother's. Saturday mornings had started with screams, and Saturday nights ended with shouts, too. Sometimes with the clatter of broken dishes. Her parents had loved each other passionately. They'd put some of that passion into the fights, as well.

This was a borrowed family. The children could be yanked from her at any time. Even as the thought stabbed her, another needled behind it. Kieran wouldn't have a reason—or rather, *obligation*—to stay with her then. She could lose all of them. A fist grasped her heart and squeezed painfully.

But at that moment, it felt like her family, more real than any she'd ever had. Well, her foster sisters had tried to become her family, but she hadn't been ready then and pushed them away. How they'd stuck around her for the rest of their lives was beyond her.

Her gaze caught Kieran's, and she basked in its warm amber glow.

Granted, her foster sisters were wonderful, but she'd joined their makeshift family too late, and by the time she'd dropped her guard, she'd spent too little time with them. She'd been too broken by then.

Was she too broken for this new family, too?

She plucked one of the last two slices of buttery toast from the plate in the center of the table, then paused, hesitating when Jackson eyed her. "Did you want one?"

He muttered something unintelligible, then grabbed the last slice.

Right. She shouldn't expect decent conversation from him yet. "There's more bread if you want to toast another slice or two." She spread jam on hers, then pointed the butter knife his way. "Just don't go running off after you eat. It's your turn to wash dishes."

That earned her a glare. Which oddly made her smile. But was she making another mistake? He was already hostile to her, though at least he hadn't been in any more fights at school. Isabella's nightmares and words about hiding still sent a shiver through Arianna.

Then there was Kieran....

She sipped her orange juice, the cold tangy taste lingering, and studied him over the rim of the glass. His smile was open and sincere, and it tugged the corners of her mouth up, as well. Her fingers disentangled from the smooth glass and moved in his direction but stopped midair.

She hid her gaffe by leaning toward her niece and rearranging her pigtails. "Can I get you more omelet?"

Isabella shook her head, sending those adorable pigtails flying. "My tummy is full!"

Only a person who'd grown up starved knew how important it was to fill a child's tummy. It was so simple, really. Until Jackson and Isabella had entered her life, Arianna thought she lacked a maternal instinct. But even she realized children needed to be fed as well as nourished with love—and kept safe. Why hadn't her parents realized that? Well, her mother had tried for some time. Until...

Still, what Arianna was doing wasn't enough. How could she help a traumatized child and a rebellious teenager?

Kieran caught her gaze and mouthed, "You're doing great."

Once again, she basked in his support and mere presence.

How long would this last, though? Her fingers slipped into her pocket to the cold metal of the phone that housed a new threat.

Not long at all. She could only hope that, when her world fell apart, she'd be the only one falling with it.

Chapter Ten

In the afternoon, Kieran leaned back on the blanket and stared at the endless cerulean sky, his heart—and okay, his stomach—full.

He'd thought his life was fine as it was, but he'd never before had this feeling like his heart was about to burst. He turned to his side and propped himself on an elbow. The scents of moist life-giving earth mixed with that of bread and deli meat and ripe tomato still lingered in the air.

Giggling, Isabella ran, whirling around and dancing with blue and orange butterflies. Her tangerine-hued dress with a black belt and dark lace on the cuffs reminded him of the monarch butterflies now floating through the field. Had Arianna chosen that dress for Isabella on purpose?

A butterfly landed right on Arianna's nose, and she blinked as if unsure what to do. She froze, and something unreadable flashed in her eyes.

He suppressed laughter to avoid scaring the beautiful creature and committed the image to the memory for when... His mood dampened. No, it was best not to think about it.

Jackson was sitting on a tree stump, deeply engrossed in his phone, his entire posture showing what he thought about this picnic idea. But he'd shown up. Even if for his sister's sake, that was something.

"Auntie, she thinks you're a *flowaa*!" Isabella squealed as she ran to them.

The butterfly fluttered its gorgeous wings and took off into the sky.

"What's its name?" Arianna bid her farewell with a gaze.

A longing for things as fragile as butterfly wings, as ephemeral as clouds, unraveled inside him.

Was she comparing herself to the butterfly, never to stay in one place for long? Was keeping her at the ranch like pinning a butterfly under glass? And was he selfish to hope it wasn't?

Isabella giggled again as she plopped on the blanket near her aunt. "*Buttaflies* aren't people, silly. They don't have names like we do."

This time, he couldn't help chuckling. "I think your aunt meant what kind of butterfly it was. A monarch. They look like viceroys, but the shape of their wings is different."

"*Monaach* is like a king, right? Aaaah." The girl pointed to a butterfly with turquoise wings that landed on a dandelion. "What about that one?"

"It's a red-spotted purple."

The girl's lower lip stuck out. "Why *puwple* if it's blue?"

He didn't know the answer. But he did know red-spotted purple adult butterflies only lived six to fourteen days. A lot of beautiful things weren't meant to last.

Was his fleeting happiness with Arianna and her niece and nephew one of them? Something clogged his throat.

The girl tilted her head. "Don't be sad. It's okay not to know."

Was it, though? He knew close to nothing about his—wow!—*wife*. Not the tragedies of her childhood, not the dreams of her heart, not even the jobs of her choosing.

Her being an enigma might've been a part of the attraction. But considering that someone had been threatening her, he needed to know the secrets of her past to protect her and their future.

Hadn't she realized that?

Her gaze moved around, and she was shifty. Maybe bringing her and the children out in the open wasn't his best idea. He winced. Open fields were a familiar area where he thrived, but it was different for her. Just like how his life was open for everyone to see, while hers was locked behind many rooms and many doors.

Closed off, even to her husband. A churning burned like acid in his previously contented stomach. He had no reason to complain, though. She'd warned him the marriage would be in name only, so he knew what he was signing up for.

And he was ruining this wonderful gift he should be grateful to God for.

"Auntie, *bwaid* my hair." The girl shifted closer to Arianna.

Good thing she didn't ask *him* because he'd have no clue how to do that.

"One braid or two?" Arianna took out a brush from her black purse and started combing the girl's curly blonde hair.

"Two." The girl sighed, and her tiny shoulders slumped forward. "Like Mom used to do."

Arianna's hand froze midair. Then she continued as if nothing happened, the only difference the unmistakable sorrow in her eyes. "Okay. Would you like me to weave you a wreath of flowers, too?"

"Yay!" Isabella perked up, then blinked. "*Buttaflies* won't miss *flowaas*, will they? They use *flowaas* for food, you know."

Amusement crinkled the edges of Arianna's eyes. "I'll just take a few flowers, and the butterflies will have the rest of the fields for themselves. That ought to be enough for breakfast, lunch, and dinner for a long time."

The girl nodded. "Okay. You said nobody should go *hungwy*. That should include animals."

How could anyone not love this sweet girl? His heart swelled.

Arianna's eyes widened. "That's right."

How could one not fall in love with this mysterious woman? But he had to resist.

For a few blissful moments, Arianna braided the girl's hair, and he couldn't look away. Was anything more beautiful than an image of a mother and her daughter? And though Arianna and Isabella looked different, from their hair hue to eye color, and Kieran knew they weren't mother and daughter, the picture gave him that tugging-at-the-heartstrings vibe.

Arianna's expression, so often guarded, softened as her hands worked on Isabella's golden hair and she looked at the little girl, and a warm smile widened her lips. Her upraised shoulders slid back, and the angles rounded, smoothed out.

Tenderness claimed his heart. He could look at them forever.

Only it wasn't going to be forever, was it?

The wind picked up, playing with Arianna's hair, and he tore his gaze away from her and loaded the rest of the food containers into the picnic basket. The air was growing more humid, and the fluffy white clouds were transforming into heavier grayer ones surprisingly fast.

He suppressed a grimace. "The forecast said there was only a twenty percent chance of rain, but we must be heading into that twenty percent. We'd better go home."

Isabella's lower lip stuck out again. "Do we hafta?"

"I'm afraid so." Arianna secured the girl's braids with tiny sparkly barrettes.

The girl's eyes grew round. "Will *buttaflies'* wings get wet? How they gonna fly, then?"

He pressed on her upturned nose playfully, then rose to his feet. "Don't worry, Cricket. They know how to hide from disasters."

"Unlike some humans," Arianna muttered under her breath.

What was she talking about?

He didn't have the time to ponder that because those clouds released a sudden downpour. Twenty percent his foot.

He scooped up his little girl and wrapped her in the picnic blanket. "Jackson, you're in charge of getting the picnic basket to the truck."

"I—what?" At least the teen looked up from his phone and shoved it in his pocket, but that might be because he didn't want to get his lifeline wet.

"Kieran needs to get your sister to the truck before she soaks through, and I'll help you carry the basket," Arianna said.

"On second thought, leave the basket where it is. No big deal," Kieran said.

Thunder struck in the distance, and Isabella shrieked and wiggled in his arms.

"We'll keep up. Please go." Arianna sent a worried gaze at her niece, likely concerned about the girl's nightmares and fearing the storm would add to them.

"It's going to be alright." Holding tight to Isabella, who thankfully stopped shrieking, he rushed to his truck. The footfalls behind him assured him Arianna and Jackson were keeping up.

Kieran made it to the vehicle first and tucked the girl into her booster seat, then unwrapped her from the blanket. His hair and T-shirt were soaking wet by then, but not even a strand of Isabella's wispy braids was damp.

"Are you okay?" He buckled her in.

Satisfied with her nod, he glanced back.

Arianna had dragged the picnic basket and her nephew to the truck, and her long wet hair clumped around her face.

Kieran frowned as he took the basket and hefted it into his truck bed. "I told you that you could've left it."

"I said the same," Jackson grumbled as he climbed into the back seat beside his sister.

"No food should be wasted." Her teeth rattled.

"Please get inside." He rushed into the driver's seat, turned on the engine, and cranked up the heat. "There are towels in a duffel bag in the back."

"Thanks." She twisted in her front passenger seat and accepted two white towels from her nephew. "Jackson, Isabella, are you okay?"

"Yes, Auntie," the girl said.

Jackson didn't say anything. You'd think the teen had to pay a hundred dollars every time a word left his mouth or something.

Kieran peeled out of the parking lot. He'd make hot tea or cocoa for everyone and get the fireplace going once they reached the lodge. The wipers worked furiously. Thunder rumbled in the distance again, but this time, the girl didn't shriek, his little butterfly probably feeling safe in a warm cocoon.

That trust touched him and made him want to be worthy of it. Would his wife deem him worthy of her trust one day and reveal things about herself? Not because of his curiosity, but because maybe then he could help her heal somehow.

Lord, please heal this family.

Arianna opened the air vent from her front passenger seat and rubbed her hair with a towel. Her wet black shirt clung to her, and he averted his gaze.

Heat spread through him despite his cold clothes. He concentrated on the road. "We should be at the lodge in a few minutes."

"I already turned on the heat there," Arianna said.

Sometimes he forgot how many gadgets were at that place. All the gadgets and numerous cameras made his skin itch. He preferred simplicity to high tech, though he used the truck for transportation more often than the horses. However, he'd been with his truck for nearly two decades. It lacked the fancy stuff modern vehicles sported, and it suited him just fine, thank you very much.

Growing up, his favorite pastimes were their Sunday family barbecues or their Friday night campfires or their time with the horses instead of being glued to the phone like Jackson now.

Of course, the cameras at the lodge served an important purpose, and anyway, it wasn't right to move the children again, especially to his small bachelor cabin that didn't have enough rooms for everyone. Arianna, Jackson, and Isabella took priority over his interests. Considering the threats she'd been receiving, it helped that the lodge had been renovated like a fortress.

His gut tightened over the possible danger to her.

"I must look like a wet chicken right now." Arianna snorted beside him.

That was what she worried about? Before he could say she looked more attractive than he could take, Isabella chimed in, "You don't look like a wet chicken, Auntie."

"Thanks." Arianna chuckled, more cheerfully this time.

"Chickens have that red thingy on their heads," Isabella said with authority.

After a moment of silence, Arianna started laughing. "Okay, I guess I look like a wet rat, then."

"You look beautiful," he said.

"How do you know? You're not even looking at me." Her voice was partly teasing and partly subdued.

"He's got to look at the road. You know, since he's the one driving," her nephew said, his voice dripping sarcasm more than the window was dripping rain.

In the rearview mirror, Kieran caught the teen rolling his eyes.

Minutes later, they dashed inside the blissfully warm house. He had umbrellas in the truck, though they hadn't bothered to take them to the field, only a twenty percent chance of rain and all.

He placed Isabella on the floor, having gotten used to the girl's pleasant weight in his arms. But she wasn't related to him. Getting attached wasn't a good idea. If—or rather *when*—Arianna left, Jackson and Isabella would leave with her. Just the thought made Kieran's rib cage constrict. But it wasn't the time to dwell on it.

"I'll get hot tea or hot chocolate started." He strode to the kitchen.

"Yay! Chocolate!" Isabella clapped.

Her brother shrugged as he folded his umbrella. "Chocolate for me, too."

A smile touched Arianna's eyes. "Same here. Jackson, please get changed into dry clothes."

"Seriously? I'm not a five-year-old. I know what to do." One more eye roll, and those things would stick in the back of the boy's head. But he did march to his room.

She touched Kieran's forearm, sending a trail of fire along his wet skin. "Thank you. It'll give me a chance to change and dry my hair. Even if I *don't* look like a wet rat."

He wanted to tell her she looked beautiful, but hadn't he said it already? He was so out of practice with this. Besides, how did one court his own wife?

He could buy her roses, but if she'd chosen maple leaves for her wedding bouquet, did she even like flowers? She was the most confusing, the most mysterious woman he'd ever met—most likely anyone in town had ever met. And he didn't exactly have extensive experience in the romance department to start with.

Maybe he should ask Declan for advice. He'd managed to have many girlfriends despite his constant travels.

Kieran didn't keep secrets from his family, and Arianna had agreed their arrangement should be shared with his parents and siblings. They all had supported his decision, though he'd spotted worry in a few pairs of eyes, especially his mother's.

Soon they all gathered around mugs with steaming chocolate. Isabella wanted lots of marshmallows in hers. Her blonde hair rested on her shoulders now and smelled of mango shampoo. Jackson's black hair was dry and combed, and for a few shocking minutes, his nose wasn't in his phone, though he took the hot chocolate into his room nearly immediately.

And once again, though technically it wasn't Kieran's family, he felt like they belonged together. He stifled the feeling. He shouldn't get his hopes up.

Later that evening, Isabella was finally asleep after *hours* of the bedtime routine, and Jackson stayed in his room, presumably to do his homework for Monday as Sunday was for fun. Hopefully, not just presumably, because Kieran and Arianna checked every day to make sure the boy didn't fall behind in his classes. If Jackson failed his grades, his phone time would be reduced, and the teen was attached to that thing—in many senses—as if it were a part of his limb.

He did put it in his pocket while helping at the ranch, so there was that. But so far, all of Kieran's attempts to talk to the teen resulted in nothing. Zilch. Nada.

How was he supposed to get through to him? He wasn't his father or even a relative.

But as puzzling as that was, Arianna puzzled him more. And captivated him at the same time.

He found her at the breakfast nook overlooking the yard. A peppermint aroma reached him from the cup she cradled. She acknowledged him with a nod but didn't look away from the grass and trees lit by lanterns in golden and pink hues. One of those mature oaks now held a swing thanks to his help. The extra work was more than worth it to hear Isabella squeal when he'd pushed her high in the air yesterday.

"I'm thinking of building a treehouse for her. Do you think Jackson would help?" One of his brothers would assist at the drop of a cowboy hat, but it would be more meaningful for their not-so-budding relationship if Kieran could get Jackson to help. On the other hand, the boy would probably only agree if he planned to drop a hammer on Kieran's foot. Good thing Kieran wore steel-toed work boots.

Arianna shrugged. "He might because it's for his sister. I'm not one to give advice here. I know them no better than you do." Ducking her head, she turned the cup in her hands, peering into it as if seeing more than her reflection—maybe a reflection of them as a family? "I do appreciate the intention."

He thought about pretending to want a cup of tea in order to join her. But he'd never been good at pretending for the lack of practice and wasn't about to start learning now.

So he simply asked "May I?" and pointed to the chair near her.

"Of course." She studied him as he took a seat. "Ask me."

Folding his long legs under the knotty pine table, he blinked. "Ask you what?"

"Anything. I mean, about my past. I don't promise I'll answer, but if it doesn't concern client confidentiality, I'll try." Her gaze clouded. "Unless you don't want to know."

"I do." He flattened his palms on the smooth table, the edge of one of those knots pinching against his skin, his heart beating faster. Millions of questions pummeled his brain, but he sensed a lot of them, especially pertaining to her childhood, would hurt her.

He asked what he hoped would be the least painful question. "Please tell me about your jobs. Not the current one, of course."

"Of course not." A half smile touched her lips as she lifted the cup and took a long, slow sip, hiding part of her face behind it. Was she buying time? "Thank you for sparing me."

"I didn't..." Well, he might as well admit it. "You're welcome."

She placed the cup on the table, and there was no longer a barrier between them—well, besides the table. "I'm sort of a tracker."

His eyes widened. Images of the Wild West, of men with coonskin hats kneeling by scat or tracing footprints in the dirt flashed through his head—heroes from his childhood games with his brothers. "A *tracker*? Like a... hunter?" But she was shaking her head, so he changed his question. "What do you track?"

"Whatever the client wants. Most of the time, it's something like a one-of-a-kind gift for someone special, and I'm the equivalent of an international shopper."

"People pay for that?" In his family, gifts were simple and often homemade.

"We had affluent clients. Their special ones already had everything at their fingertips, and it took something incredible, exotic, something nobody around them had and yet tailored to their tastes to wow them."

He rubbed his forehead. "Can't people just buy things like that online these days?"

"Yes, of course. Except when the buyer doesn't know what they are looking for. And not all things are available online. Sometimes the idea was to bring something unique and one of a kind. Sometimes clients wanted to add rare things to their own collections. I worked as a personal shopper when I discovered I had an intuition, an eye if you will, for things like that. I was also an employee available to travel to any part of the world at a moment's notice. It didn't hurt that I picked up on languages easily and blended in well."

Okay, so this wasn't that bad. But she'd said "most of the time."

"And the other times?"

"Let's say, valuables were stolen. I picked up a lot from my cop foster sister. I helped find them." She took another slow sip.

Was that even legal? He didn't dare to ask. There must be more to it, too. People didn't pay the kinds of fees she'd mentioned to get a one-of-a-kind gift or even to return stolen jewelry.

Her face grew sad, and she drained the rest of her tea. She smelled like peppermint now, and that was a distraction. "A few times, I'd be tracking people down."

His jaw slackened. "Like, disappeared people?"

"Or kidnapped. I served as part of a private extraction team. I'm skilled with firearms, trained in combat, and I can run miles. I'm also a good swimmer and have a high tolerance for cold. If people were taken away in a boat, I could be dropped in the middle of the ocean at night from a helicopter. I did that once, rescued someone who'd been kidnapped by her own brother and held for ransom."

His jaw nearly hit the table. Maybe it was a good thing he didn't drink tea, or he'd spit it out now.

"As you can imagine, I can't go into details of those cases." She studied him, her elbows braced on the table, her chin propped in one hand.

His gaze slid to the tattoo on her arm, and just like before, he wondered whether the letter *E* stood for the initial of a man she'd loved. The stab of jealousy was unwelcome.

Her gaze followed his, and her eyes softened. "It's the first initial of my grandmother's name. Besides my foster sisters, she was the only person who loved me unconditionally."

Then her features hardened again. "I cover the scars on my stomach and thighs with clothes, so I didn't need tattoos there. But the scars on my arm were too visible. I used to wear long-sleeved shirts and sweaters, but in hot climates, that wasn't an option. I decided to get a tattoo to cover the scars. I figured I'd get something to remind me of someone wonderful in my life."

He froze, compassion overtaking him. He should've guessed.

She chuckled without mirth. "You must be wondering, who did you just marry?"

Chapter Eleven

Had she told him too much?

Two days later, while Arianna cleaned up the ranch kitchen after lunch, the same question appeared again and again in her mind. The shock on Kieran's face still bothered her. She'd spared him the gruesome details of her life and only told him the good parts.

Well, he knew about the scars, due to her ridiculous, reckless, and oh-so-regrettable outburst in the principal's office, but she hadn't told him about their origin. Would he even believe her if she told him?

After all, nobody believed her. Nobody. Not even her mother.

Arianna's hand flew to her stomach, and she touched the smooth fabric as if she could smooth out the scars as well, make them disappear.

But no, they would always be there.

A reminder of what trusting people could cost. Even people who were supposed to love you. Especially people who were supposed to love you. People whom she loved dearly even after they hurt her again and again.

Her eyes burned, but she didn't shed tears. Her father would only hit her harder if she'd cried. Her tears irritated him, so she'd learned to hold them in. She'd learned to hold everything in, only sharing with two people. Grandmother had been aghast and insisted on Arianna staying with her, and it had been the best part of her childhood.

The sweet taste of her *pastel de tres leches*—literally cake of three milks—and empanadas. The pleasant warmth of walks in Grandma's flower garden with its amazing aroma and tender butterflies fluttering their wings so close. The dear comfort of Grandma's caring hands when she braided Arianna's long hair. Nostalgia tightened around her heart.

Then Grandma died, and Arianna returned to the place she'd dreaded. Only one person in the family truly seemed to care about her, and she'd leaned to that person like a flower to the sun.

Her foster sisters had never asked her about the scars, and she was grateful for it.

She was a mess, and no matter how hard she tried, she'd always be a mess. But for now, she was a functional mess. She breathed in the scents of barbecue.

The lunch cleanup was done, and plenty of leftovers waited in the gigantic refrigerator, in case anyone wanted to heat them for dinner.

Unlike the first day, Kieran didn't stay in the kitchen after lunch, and she missed him. Maybe she should pay him a visit. Well, not *him*. She needed to check on her nephew, and she might as well take him and Noah a peace offering. She placed a few sodas and a bottle of water in the cooler and added ice from the freezer.

She took off her abhorrently bright apron and hung it on the hook, then hefted the cooler. Kieran had volunteered to pick up her nephew and Noah from school for their community work at the ranch. She could imagine how excited the boys would be about that. Not.

As she hurried outside, the kitchen's heat changed to a fresh breeze that brought the scent of hay, reminding her of Kieran. Her heart shifted, and she increased her pace, but not because she wanted to see him. It was all about her nephew.

Despite speaking a bunch of languages, she still hadn't managed to find a common language with the teen. Would Kieran be able to?

At hearing his and Jackson's voices inside the stable, she stilled and placed the drink cooler on the ground.

Eavesdropping wasn't right, but then she didn't always do the right thing. Kieran and the boys wouldn't hear her, because she knew how to move without a noise. Horses neighed, though, feeling an intruder in their territory, and she nearly went forward.

But Kieran said something soothing and probably patted the horse's neck, and everything went back to normal. Based on his words, he'd been teaching the boys how to groom horses with much more patience than she ever would've had.

Then Jackson asked, "What breed is that?"

Huh. Could that be a good sign? Was he interested, instead of being dragged into something he didn't want to do, though there was that?

"Appaloosa."

"Is this the most popular breed?" Noah asked. None of his previous smugness coated his voice, probably because his father wasn't there.

"No. In the US, the most popular breed is the Quarter Horse. We have a few of those. As well as Thoroughbreds, the second most popular breed here. There are over six hundred breeds of horses." As if speaking to frightened horses, rather than obstinate teens, Kieran somehow kept his voice calming. "Now, take this brush instead."

Something in its timbre called to her, even without him meaning it. Her legs carried her forward without her realizing it.

Might as well. Once again, eavesdropping wasn't right. While she didn't want to change the group's dynamics and neither of the boys were fond of her, it was time to show herself. She picked up the cooler and marched forward.

Once she was inside the stable, the conversation silenced like she'd expected.

"I brought sodas and water." She clattered the cooler on the ground, staying far enough from the horses. She didn't know much about them, but she knew they were prey animals and easily spooked, and she had no desire to get a kick in the forehead.

"That's very nice of you. I'll have one." Kieran washed his hands and walked to her.

Jackson ignored her at first, but Noah followed Kieran.

Her fingers touched Kieran's when she handed him the cold bottle, sending a pleasant jolt through her. His breathing hitched while she struggled to keep hers even.

Usually, she could control her emotions. But not with him.

Their gazes met and held, and the heat in his melted her. How could he make her weak in the knees without even trying? She'd never had a thing for Wrangler's shirts, but when one was stretched across his muscular torso, she had the nearly irresistible urge to touch the fabric. To tip back that cowboy hat of his and run her fingers through his hair and bring him close so their lips could meet...

Her pulse skyrocketed.

But this wasn't the time or the place to show her attraction with two pairs of curious young eyes watching.

Maybe not ever?

No matter how much she'd wanted to. She slipped back. She'd need some of the ice in the cooler to cool off.

Then Noah grimaced as he drained his soda. "That horse looks at me funny."

Kieran chuckled as he took a swig from the water bottle. "Horses happen to have three-hundred-sixty-degree vision. Plus, they have some of the largest eyes of all mammals."

"Wow!" Noah's own eyes grew huge, and he forgot about his soda. "What else is interesting about horses?"

Jackson stayed near the horse, brushing its coat with a surprising gentleness. His eyes softened, too, while Kieran talked about a subject he seemed to love.

She didn't expect Jackson to fall in love with ranch animals and the ranch and magically heal, change, and adapt. But animosity didn't roll off the teen in waves now, and that was progress. She'd take what she could. She shouldn't let him see she was watching him, though.

She hid a smile and looked away from Jackson, back at Kieran, which she didn't mind in the least. However, she'd need to keep that primal call that drew her to him in check.

Her heart kept thumping in her chest. Easier said than done. As his fingers hugged the water bottle and his lips touched it, she found herself ridiculously, inexplicably envious of that bottle.

Unbelievable.

She took a deep breath of air that smelled of horses and hay and held it in her lungs before releasing it. She needed to appear calm. Giving in to her attraction would lead to nothing good. She'd paid a high price for learning that lesson.

He thanked her again.

One would think she made a grand gesture for how many times he thanked her. Interestingly, she'd done much more for her father, and every time, she'd only received grunts in return.

"You're welcome." She wanted to tell Kieran so many things.

How much she admired him, and not just his chiseled muscles but also his generous heart. How much she appreciated him for stepping up way more times than was expected. How much he invaded her thoughts and her dreams and how she had no clue what to do about it. But she had to hold that in, too.

"I've got to go." She collected the empty bottle with great care not to let their fingers meet and slid it back into the cooler. Her fingers touched ice. That's probably what touching her heart would feel like.

Or not anymore?

His eyes dimmed a fraction, and he returned to grooming horses. "You're welcome to stay."

She shook her head and forced herself to move. "I need to pick up Isabella and start on dinner."

Now that she knew the boys weren't going to kill each other or scare the horses, she had no reason to stay. The boys were much more comfortable with Kieran than with her. Like always, she was an outsider.

But then, she'd been an outsider in her own family even before she'd gone no contact with them.

Finally, Jackson walked to the cooler and took a soda bottle. "Thanks," he said through his teeth. But his entire demeanor changed for the better when he returned to Kieran and the horses.

Her stomach clenched as she lugged the nearly empty cooler. Kieran continued talking about interesting horse facts. Something about the tallest horse ever being over two yards or the longest-living horse having survived sixty-two years.

Noah asked when they could ride.

She didn't hear Kieran's reply because she already walked outside. She breathed in the scent of grass. The air wasn't as warm as this season was in Houston, so she walked faster to keep warm, the light breeze on her no-longer-heated skin.

She should be used to being an outsider. She'd designed her life that way. No attachments. Only connections and alliances. Her foster sisters were the exception, but no man had breached the security system around her heart. Well, Victor had been close, but then her moment's distraction had him shot. After that, she'd retreated to her usual lifestyle, fast.

Not letting anyone close.

Ever.

That was the way she'd survived.

Then why did it hurt so much now? Why, once Kieran and the children entered her life, did she have this longing in her heart?

One thing was clear. It would soon be time for Kieran to know her secret, and if that would push him away, so be it.

"Remember, you promised not to ever use your newly gained knowledge for harm," Arianna said the next day after a long lesson for her nephew.

Funny, how Jessie had first connected with Arianna—a surly teen who wanted nothing to do with her foster sisters—by teaching her self-defense moves and having Arianna work out with her. Now, Arianna was trying Jessie's move on Jackson. She'd had him join her in the basement room Jessie had converted into a state-of-the-art gym when she'd been staying here. It had been neglected once she'd moved out after marrying Ronan, but Arianna had breathed new life into it.

Speaking of breathing...

Breathing hard, Jackson rolled his eyes. Was that the hundredth or thousandth time? He took a swig from his water bottle. "Can we try this again tomorrow?"

"Maybe." She'd barely broken a sweat.

Meanwhile, he swiped a towel over the sweat dripping from his forehead. Strangely, he didn't complain about a rigorous workout she'd insisted he do first. "How come you know all this?"

"Hmm, those are the two longest sentences you've said to me lately. Besides 'you're not my mom.'" She started pounding the punching bag, her muscles straining. She used to imagine her father's face when she hit it and... someone else's. But not any longer. It used to be a good outlet for all her anger. Now it was just exercise equipment.

Might as well take advantage of some free time while Kieran was playing with her niece in the yard. Happy squeals reached her from outside. He must be pushing Isabella on the swing. Warmth spread inside Arianna. She'd never met a man like that. While she wasn't mother material, he'd make such a great dad.

Jackson collapsed on the bench, but his breathing got better. Good.

Huh. She never answered his question. She claimed a seat on the bench. Not too close, though. "My foster sister Jessie showed me some techniques. Later, I took courses and private lessons." She paused and drank from her water bottle, welcoming its fresh, cold taste. "By that time, I'd already developed good leg muscles. I was a runner." She flinched. In many senses. "I just needed to work on my biceps and triceps." She didn't say why she needed that for her job.

How could she explain the intricacy of her job? Talking about something he could relate to would be easier.

He grunted, but this time, it was probably not to respond to her words but because of the muscle strain.

She put the bottle back and went to lift weights. She didn't know yet if he'd accept her in his space if she stayed on the bench with him. "I used to get into fights at school when I was your age. But I didn't know how to fight, so I ended up with lots of bruises. Learning self-defense techniques was way overdue."

She could so easily remember her interest when Jessie offered to teach her—though Arianna had tried hard to hide it. How well she could relate to him! She worked out in silence, except for occasional grunts.

And then he said, "Why did you drag us here? Why not leave us in Houston and let our uncle adopt us?"

Her heart dropped together with the weight. Even people who were supposed to love and protect her didn't believe her. Why would a teen who could barely stand the sight of her?

She sipped the water and chose her words. "I wanted you and your sister to be safe and happy. It would be more possible here."

He snorted. "You didn't care about us. You didn't even know we existed."

"I do now," she said quietly. She'd hoped this could be a bonding experience, but it wasn't going well. Her heart constricted. "I had reasons to go no contact with my family."

"Fine, you might care about Isabella. Everyone loves that chirrupy little cricket." Jackson drummed his hands on his thighs, his shrug nonchalant. No envy tinged his words, no resentment, only brotherly affection. While Arianna had made a horrible mistake at twelve, she knew the difference between the two now. "But why would you care about me?"

"Because I see you as being so much the way I was at your age." She stumbled. "Well, not the girly parts, of course. But I was angry, confused, hurt, and lashing out at the wrong people." She shrugged, imitating his previous gesture. Mirroring someone's gestures, words, tone, and so on was a good way to establish rapport. She meant every word, though.

He stayed quiet. Then he shook his sweaty bangs away from his forehead, and his face contorted. "You don't know anything about me!"

"Then why don't you tell me?" When he didn't say anything, she continued. "Tell me about your favorite video games. What do you like the most in school? Tell me about your friends. Anything you want to tell me."

She'd done some research on her own, and Isabella had been a great voluntary source of information. But gaps remained in her knowledge about her nephew—lots of them. If she hadn't stayed away from her family for decades...

His eyes narrowed. "What I like the most in school is when it's over. I don't have any friends, thanks to you."

Fair enough.

Then a strange gleam appeared in his eyes. "Can Tommy hang out here sometime? He plays my favorite video game. He's in the program Mr. Kieran's family runs. Tommy was arrested a couple of times for theft."

Arianna swallowed hard. She did ask, didn't she? She'd request info on that boy from Kieran and Jessie. "I have to talk to Kieran first because we're a team here. But if you think it would be safe for Isabella, you have my vote."

Time to change the topic. She'd taken Isabella to the child psychologist, but he didn't find anything wrong with her—well, more than a normal child grieving her mother. He hadn't touched on the cause of her nightmares, either. "Why did your sister have to hide in the closet? Do you know who the bad guys she talked about were?"

He didn't say anything for some time and only drained his water bottle as if he were extremely thirsty. A delaying tactic.

He probably wasn't going to answer. She tipped her head toward the slim window high on the wall of the basement gym and reveled in more happy squeals from outside.

Finally, he spoke without looking at her. "Mom used to bring men home. If I was there, I'd take my sister for a walk. But if I was at school, Mom would tell her to hide in a closet or bad men would get her. Isabella needed to be very quiet so the bad man wouldn't hear her."

Anger surged in her veins. That was so wrong. But she could do nothing about it now. On the other hand, at least the little girl wasn't in danger.

"Thank you," she said and meant it.

Could the nightmares be connected to the bad man Isabella's mom talked about? Or were they a part of the grieving process? Madeline used to have nightmares too, although thankfully not any longer. For that matter, Arianna had, as well, only she hadn't screamed. She usually just woke up in a cold sweat, shivering.

"Mom was a good person, for the most part," he hurried to add. "She loved us. In her way. She could've left us if she wanted, and she didn't. I guess she just needed someone to love her." His voice turned bitter. "Isabella and I weren't enough."

Arianna moved toward him but stopped herself. She could relate to him way too much. "You're enough. Remember it. You. Are. Enough."

"This"— he raised his chin and waved around—"still doesn't mean we are good. You aren't my mom, and you'll never be."

A familiar knife sliced inside her. She didn't expect it to hurt as much as it did. "I'm not trying to replace your mom. But I hope we can be friends. I could use a friend, and I believe you might, too. Do you think you can get used to being here?"

"It's not so bad." He forked his fingers through his damp hair, then flung it back from his forehead again. His long hair was in a ponytail, but his bangs still fell on his forehead. "My sister likes it here. You don't like butterflies, do you?"

Whoa! Thrown off, she nearly dropped the weights again. "No."

Huh. He was more perceptive than she had realized.

"Yet you put butterfly cutouts in Cricket's room. And buy her butterfly-shaped barrettes."

"*She* enjoys butterflies, and I want to bring her joy. It's worth the discomfort for me. Besides, *it's not so bad.*" Yeah, she could use his own words. "Plus, one of my foster sisters loves butterflies. I'm used to having things with them around."

"Why do you hate them, then?"

She sighed. Her throat felt parched, so she drained the rest of her water bottle. "I don't hate them. They just remind me of someone who hurt me."

She tensed, expecting more questions, but he nodded. "Must be someone from the family, then. That's why no contact."

The kid was smart. There was way more than met the eye there.

"Mom used to take us to the beach. Cricket loved it there." He paused, then said through clenched teeth. "Mom had healed scars on her stomach. When I asked her about them, she said she used to be a cutter when she was a teen. She never liked butterflies, either. Weird, huh?"

Arianna froze. No. This couldn't be...

Could he handle the question she was about to ask? She'd bathed Isabella, knew there were no scars, but she had to know. She walked to him and pinned him with a stare. "Please tell me, have you ever heard your uncle Ric call Isabella 'mi mariposa bonita'?"

Chapter Twelve

The scream in the middle of the night threw Kieran out of his sleep. His pulse accelerating, he blinked in the darkness, trying to place where he was.

The spacious room didn't look like his cabin's small bedroom.

Right.

The guest room at the lodge. Even all these days after the wedding ceremony and moving in, the change was so surreal, it took him time to adjust. Was Isabella having nightmares again?

He leaped out of bed. He wore pants to sleep since moving in here. His stomach clenched from worry for the little girl. He and Arianna had agreed to trade nights attending to Isabella, him taking every other night. It was Arianna's night.

But how could he stay in bed when Isabella was screaming from fear? Well, Jackson apparently could. That boy could sleep through a tornado.

Kieran rushed out of his room into the hall. Or Arianna could be screaming? His insides went cold. Could they have an intruder? It'd be difficult for someone to break into the lodge with all the security layers here.

But not impossible. And Arianna did have those phone threats that kept him up at night sometimes, tossing and turning from worry. Ronan and Jessie had been trying to discover who was behind the threats, but so far, to no avail. Except for the fact that the texts had come from the area near Houston. Arianna had said she'd put out some feelers in her former circles and had asked Victor to do the same. But she hadn't gotten anything back yet.

Should Kieran retrieve a gun from the safe? But then, knowing Arianna the way he did now, she probably already—what did she call it?—*neutralized* the threat herself. That woman was amazing.

Another wail coming from Isabella's room confirmed his first suspicion. He hurried along the hall.

The first time he and Arianna had rushed to the girl because of her nightmares, they'd nearly bumped heads. Only her quick reaction prevented him from knocking her out.

This time, she was already in the girl's room by the time he made it there. He closed the door quietly and leaned against it, taking the scene in.

She held the wailing Isabella and rubbed small circles on the girl's back. "There. There. You're safe. You're okay. I'm here. Everything is going to be alright."

The words sank deeper in him, giving a meaning he hadn't pondered before. Everything was going to be alright. Not just alright. It was all going to be right *because* she was here.

For how long, though? He ignored the sharp warning inside.

She'd turned his world upside down, but she'd also made him realize what he was missing. He'd led a content life before he'd met her, but he'd never experienced the profound, overwhelming joy Arianna, Isabella, and even Jackson brought him.

Uncertainty wasn't a high price to pay for that. Kieran had no regrets about marrying Arianna. But did she? He was used to people who said what they thought, but her thoughts were a mystery to him.

The wails subsided.

"It was only a dream," Arianna whispered.

That caused a new flood of tears. "I saw the bad man come to take me away. I wasn't good. I didn't wanna take a bath. Mom always said, if I wasn't good, the bad man would take me."

His fists balled, but he unclenched them. No need for the girl to see his fury.

Isabella hiccupped. "I don't wanna leave! I wanna stay with you and Jackson and Mr. *Kiewan* and the ponies."

Wow. His name came up before the ponies. "And we want you to stay here."

"Of course, we do." Arianna swiped the girl's tears.

"*Weally*?" Isabella blinked, teardrops on her eyelashes catching the light from the night-light.

"Really." Arianna hugged the girl. "Besides, did you see all the locks we have here? It's like a fortress castle for the princess that you are. No bad man would make it through."

As if pondering that, Isabella tilted her head, her blonde hair adorably tousled on one side. "Okay," she said at last.

Minutes later, the girl's eyelids fluttered closed, and her breathing evened out. For some time, Kieran and Arianna watched the little girl sleep. Sharing this special moment with Arianna warmed everything inside him.

But it also made him want to reach for more than he had again. He wanted Arianna to love him. And he wanted Isabella to be his daughter. He wanted to be a father figure to Jackson.

Did he want the impossible?

Lord, please, help me. Is this the road You're guiding me on?

Peace soothed him after that question as if... as if this was his true family. Far from perfect, but he'd never striven for perfect. Waiting for Arianna to open her heart to him wasn't easy, and raising a traumatized child and a rebellious teenager wasn't going to be either. But they needed him, and he needed them way more than he'd ever realized.

Guilt stung him again. Arianna wasn't a believer, though she did listen to him when he'd talked about God. But he wasn't a great talker. Was he naïve to hope he could lead her to the Lord?

After they tiptoed out of the room, he blurted out. "I want to adopt Jackson and Isabella with you."

For a few moments, Arianna stared at him, her green eyes huge in the dim hall lights. Then something incredible happened.

Without any warning, she threw her arms around him. "I'm about to kiss you, so if you're not ready, tell me now."

His heartbeat became a gallop, and his breathing hitched. "I've been ready since the moment I met you."

Her mouth found his before he could say anything else or think anything else. Not that he could think of anything besides kissing her now.

Euphoria filling his every cell, he wove his arms around her waist to feel her close, to keep her close.

Oh how he wanted to keep her close for always! She'd molded against him as if she'd been made for him, as if they'd been made for each other, and he believed they had been.

A delightful wave swept him up, making everything around him disappear. He deepened the kiss tentatively, carefully, not wanting to push her too far. When she responded, waves of euphoria swept him even higher.

"Ew." Jackson's voice brought Kieran back to his senses.

Ironically, Jackson had slept through his sister's screams but just had to wake up for their kiss.

Arianna moved back, her sparkling eyes the brightest shade of emerald Kieran had ever seen. Her eyes had always turned the brightest at the height of emotion. For example, with anger when Jackson had been wrongfully accused in the principal's office. Or with tenderness when she braided Isabella's hair.

What was the emotion after their kiss?

Dare he hope...?

Isabella giggled at her brother as she stuck her head through her bedroom door. "They *mawwied*, silly. That's what mawwied people do. They kiss."

Arianna's cheeks pinked, and she walked to Isabella. "I thought you were asleep, princess. How about I read you a bedtime story again?"

Isabella grinned up at her, all traces of previous screams and tears gone. "About *buttaflies*?"

Arianna and Jackson glanced at each other as if some strange understanding passed between them, and a hint of a smile tugged at the teen's lips. Huh. What was that about?

"Mr. Kiewan, I wanna glass of milk."

"Sure." He nodded to Isabella's request.

Jackson disappeared into his room without a word, but instead of slamming the door and the telltale sound of the lock turning, he left it ajar.

Wide-eyed, Arianna stared at that door, obviously as surprised as Kieran was.

Then she gave him another surprise. She rushed to him and kissed his cheek, sending *buttaflies* of his own fluttering their wings in his stomach. "Thank you."

"You don't need to thank me. But would you ever leave the door to your *heart* ajar?" Had he said too much? Asked too much?

"I believe I already did," she whispered before disappearing into Isabella's room and leaving him with the goofiest smile ever on his face.

Two days later, Arianna still couldn't understand how the kiss with Kieran had happened.

She flushed as she turned the page of the children's book about a moth hiding away from the rain under a mushroom, reading it to Isabella for a bedtime story. Huh, on the new page, somehow a rabbit joined the moth under the said mushroom. She wasn't sure how that happened, either.

Okay, she knew *exactly* how the kiss had happened because she'd been the one to initiate it. But... but...

Ever since the cuts had started, she'd avoided physical contact with a guy. So, what had come into her the day before yesterday?

She smiled as she looked at Isabella, who slept peacefully now, and closed the colorful book that had quite a few animals under one mushroom by the end. Tenderness spread inside her as she tucked the blanket around the girl, then tiptoed outside the room after turning off the light.

Jackson was helping Brandon at the barn—voluntarily!—so she didn't need to check on him.

Okay, she'd kissed Kieran not just because she'd been drawn to him like the proverbial moth to the fire—or mushroom? She winced, though there was that. His broad shoulders and muscles chiseled by outdoor labor were attractive, of course, and could shelter anyone through a storm. And those Irish genes worked fantastically well in his handsome features.

But his kindness was what had made her forget everything her scarred body and soul had oh-so-painfully learned. Him wanting to adopt children he had no relation to had floored her. She'd given up hope that such men even existed a long time ago.

How was it possible that not only had he failed to disappoint her yet but she'd also been discovering better and better things about him? To her, kindness was exotic and as rare or unique as some of the items she'd brought from overseas.

Her heart fluttered, and her breathing quickened just at the memory of his mouth exploring hers. Since then, she'd spent every waking moment dreaming of another kiss.

Wow. She touched her lips. She hadn't daydreamed since her teenage years because shattered dreams cut deeper than even Ric's penknife. A shudder rushed through her, but it wasn't as strong as the ones before. At least, he'd disinfected that knife, but most likely, it was because she was a toy he didn't want to lose.

Enough.

After decades of suppressing memories and feelings, now she'd started seeing a therapist with Kieran's full support. Yes, it was just the beginning, and some of the damage done during so many years probably would be impossible to undo. But it was a start. And she wasn't going to spare Ric another thought when she could be in Kieran's company right now. She craved being beside him with such force that it shocked and scared her. It was as if the dam of her resistance had given in under a river of attraction that had burst and flooded with the rain of his affection.

He'd suggested watching a movie after Isabella had been tucked in for the night and before Jackson was home. She couldn't wait to snuggle up to him and found her lips tipping up again.

His humming reached her from the kitchen, off-key, but it was so endearing that it nearly made her laugh. Laugh! She didn't remember the last time she'd felt that elated, if ever. He was probably making some snack to munch on while they watched a movie. Though she'd rather taste his lips than a snack, and the idea sent a blaze of fire through her.

She hurried along the hall when the popping sound coming from the kitchen made her stop in her tracks.

Oh no. Nausea rose at the buttery scent.

Kieran stepped into the hall and grinned at her. "I'm making us some popcorn to go with the movie. I didn't know what kind you like, so I just got original. Hope you like it." Then the smile slipped from his face, replaced by worry, and he stepped to her. "Are you okay? Are you feeling unwell?"

"Yes. No." Her hand flew to her mouth as if that could help her control the gag reflex, but she couldn't stop everything she'd had for dinner from rising to meet her mouth again.

No, no, no!

She dashed to the nearest bathroom.

The only comforting thing about the whole ordeal was that she'd made it there in time instead of vomiting the contents of her stomach on his T-shirt.

So romantic! Not.

He held her hair while she threw up. Heat flushed through her. Now he'd never want to kiss her again. After everything she'd gone through, she didn't know why *that* broke her heart.

Her cheeks flaming, she avoided looking at him as she crawled back like a crawfish until her back met the bathroom wall. She didn't care that the tile was cold.

The popcorn scent was much fainter here yet still made her gag, but her stomach was empty. Her heart, too.

He wet a washcloth in the sink and gently wiped around her mouth. The fabric felt cool against her heated skin.

"Thanks." Her voice came out grouchier than she'd intended, and she pushed his hand away.

Gratitude mixed with anger at herself as she forced herself to get up and brush her teeth. Even the mint toothpaste didn't purge the horrible taste from her mouth. Or maybe it was her memories. After she'd pushed them away for decades, they'd returned with force.

"Would you like me to take you to a doctor?" His voice was worried.

"No. I know what's wrong with me." At least, when it pertained to popcorn.

"Was it something about the dinner I made?"

Would he drop it already? Why did he have to be this nice?

She whirled around, the wet toothbrush still in her hand like a weapon. "No. Dinner was great, and my... my sickness has nothing to do with it." Then it dawned on her what he might think. "Oh, in case you're wondering, there's no chance I'm pregnant."

Red blotches covered his neck. "I didn't... wonder that."

The innocent and sweet mango scent of Isabella's shampoo mocked Arianna's violent torrent of emotions. "I can't tolerate the scent of popcorn. My foster sisters know, but I should've warned you."

"I'm sorry. I'll air it out." He was about to leave the room.

She stopped him with a gesture. "Something bad happened to me when I was eating popcorn. I guess my subconscious still mixes up the cause and effect."

So much for a romantic evening together, something simple that other couples did all the time. But they weren't other couples. She wasn't other people.

Was she naïve to hope that their marriage could become real? That they could be happy together? That she could heal and make him happy?

Not to mention she still had those phone threats arriving regularly. Her past could hurt him. *She* could hurt him, no matter what she did.

She looked him square in the eye. "I might be too damaged to change. Too damaged to make you happy."

He held her penetrating gaze, which not a lot of men could do. "All I need to be happy is for you and our children to be with me."

The next night, Arianna closed her eyes as rain hit the glass door panels. Isabella was tucked in bed, and Jackson was playing video games in his room. Arianna and Kieran sat at the breakfast nook again. This time, they both cradled cups with peppermint tea neither of them were drinking. The mint aroma spread in the air.

But unlike the previous time, she'd asked him to come here. She didn't want to remember, to relive those horrible moments. Maybe it would be easier to tell him all this without looking at him, so she stared at the amber liquid swirling in her cup.

She couldn't bear to see pity swirling in his equally amber eyes. Though it would be better than the disbelief she'd found in her mother's. Yet it was time for him to know. "My parents bickered a lot, especially after Dad had a few shots of tequila. I do believe they loved each other and that's the reason Mom stayed, but it didn't stop them from throwing things at each other and yelling. Mom said their relationship was... passionate." She waited, gathering her thoughts. This was far from the worst part.

"That must've been terrible for you."

She shivered at the compassion warming his voice. Why did compassion always make her feel cold, left out? As if its comforting warmth could never cover her, never be given to her.

"There were good parts, too. The yummy taste of Mom's quesadillas with melted cheese, the aromas of fajitas with grilled peppers and onions on weekends, the excitement of loud fiestas with mariachis and potlucks when families gathered." She breathed in those memories, keeping them close to her heart.

He didn't say anything this time.

She appreciated that. "Mom worked late shifts, hostessing at my uncle's restaurant, so nights when she worked were quiet. Unless Dad took his anger out on me if I wasn't fast enough with his beef enchiladas and rice and beans or dropped a plate by accident. The man worked hard. He more than earned his food.

"Sometimes I'd end up with a black eye and had to skip school. I was too ashamed to show up like that. I was angry. But I couldn't talk back to him, or I'd get hit. I started talking back to my teachers and getting into fights at school with other children, instead. I'd have a legitimate way to explain my bruises, then. Of course, that only made things worse at home because I brought shame to his name." Even now, heat flushed through her.

"Could you talk to someone?" he asked quietly. "Maybe a teacher? A neighbor? A friend's parent? A relative?"

"We lived on the outskirts, so there were no close neighbors. I was getting a certain reputation at school, so I didn't think the teachers would believe me. I told my mom, but she preferred to believe my father, not me. Then I told my grandmother, and she took me in right away."

Her heart warmed for a moment, and she told him about the flower garden and sweet pastel de tres leches and her grandmother's kindness.

Then she suppressed a sob. "A year later, my dad showed up. He asked me to leave the room, so I don't know what they talked about. Only I heard my grandmother yell that she wasn't going to let him take me. I never heard Grandma scream before. Once he left, she had a heart attack."

Arianna had to stop talking because of a huge lump in her throat.

"I'm so sorry for your loss." Through the pain, Kieran's voice reached her, and she held onto it like a rope when she'd been hanging over the edge of a mountain.

"She died, and I had to go back. Dad said it was all my fault." Arianna managed to push the words past the lump in her throat.

"What?" Kieran leaped to his feet, then seemed to force himself to sit. "I hope you didn't believe him. If anything, it was his fault."

"Mom sided with him, and my uncle did, too. I didn't know what to believe. Then, just when I worked up enough courage to tell my close friend, Dad got laid off. Right before, he'd made some large debts. We had to sell the house and move to a cheaper place, and I had to change schools. I lost my friends. As for telling another relative, well, my uncle helped pay off my dad's debts."

"Maybe he could've helped. He sounds like a kind man." He stumbled. "Not that... that I'm trying to blame you for anything. I just wish you didn't have to go through all that. Did... did your father get so violent he started cutting you?"

She shook her head and took a careful sip of the liquid that went from warm to cold, just like her heart. She nearly wished it were that simple. "I have a large extended family, but I worried if I told them, the same might happen to them as to Grandma. Dad told me as much. Or they wouldn't believe me, the same as Mom didn't. At family fiestas and with friends and neighbors, Dad was so much fun and made everyone laugh.

"We lived off Mom's salary until Dad got hired as a trucker. I was relieved. My *kind* uncle didn't think I should stay home alone while Mom worked graveyard shifts. One of my cousins volunteered to babysit me. I was twelve by then and didn't think I needed a babysitter. But once again, nobody listened to me. I think the argument was that I would get myself in trouble if left alone at night. You see, boys had started to pay attention to me by then.

"I didn't argue much, though. Because, you see, that was my favorite cousin. One of the few people who always seemed to be nice to me." She paused as her throat went dry, and she had to take another long sip. "When I was little, he'd taken me trick-or-treating several times, and my tummy was happy with all the candies I got. Grandma made me a butterfly costume, but she was too frail then to walk for a long time. Ric was anything but frail. He was like the older, protective brother I never had, and I wished he'd been my brother and lived with us. I imagined he'd stand up to my dad. I almost told Ric about the abuse, but something stopped me."

Mi mariposa bonita.

The soft whisper in her mind made her shudder.

Why did two important people in her life have to love butterflies so much? Arianna would rather deal with scorpions.

But for Isabella and Paisley, she'd tolerate butterflies, even if the things made her nauseous. It had taken all her willpower not to scream when the monarch had landed on her nose the other day. Orange butterflies were easier to tolerate than blue ones, though, because they didn't bring the same memories.

The azure-blue wings had snapped into place as she was about to go trick-or-treating with her favorite cousin, her giggling from excitement. She was a beautiful butterfly, and it didn't matter that one wing was slightly larger than the other or that the wires the sheer fabric was stretched on were a bit crooked. She didn't have any siblings, and her mother had been working while her father's gait was unsteady by then and he smelled funny. So it was so nice of her older cousin to take her through the neighborhood. Maybe she'd get lots of her favorite chocolates oozing with caramel inside...

Since that day of trick-or-treating, he'd called her *mariposa*, Spanish for butterfly, and she loved it, thinking it a synonym for pretty. Until she'd learned that what he wanted was to dissect her first and then crush her under his boot like an insignificant insect.

She lifted her cup with trembling fingers. "Dad disliked Mom's cooking, so he usually flushed it down the toilet, and I spent evenings cooking dinners and serving him. Grandma taught me how to cook many dishes. My grades slipped, and I wasn't motivated to bring them up or to go to school at all. Dad said I wasn't too bright. Ric was the opposite of me, a straight A student with sights on a prestigious university. He set his mind on becoming a doctor, and nobody doubted he would. My family was ashamed of me, while his was proud of him. It was extremely *kind* of him to volunteer to look after the likes of me." She shuddered again, and the cup in her hands shook. She put it on the table.

The rain continued as if crying for her because she could no longer cry for herself.

Kieran searched her eyes, then reached for her hand in silent support.

She let her hand stay in his, needing the tangible connection to the present, to safety. "It was nice at first. He just studied while I went to sleep, enjoying the quiet. Getting a night of uninterrupted sleep was like heaven. A few times, he brought takeout. Yummy sweet-and-sour chicken with sesame seeds, and I didn't have to scrub pots and pans. I nearly worshiped the ground Ric walked on. I cooked for him sometimes too, and unlike Dad, he praised my food. He even helped me with my homework. Once, he suggested popcorn and a movie, and I gladly agreed." Her throat clogged up, and she moved her wrists as if to verify she could still move them. "The popcorn was salty and buttery, and I laughed around mouthfuls of it at a romantic comedy. Then he turned the sound higher."

She took a moment to find her voice again. "I don't know how it happened but the next moment, my hands were pinned above me. With his free hand, he took out a penknife from his pocket. He said if I screamed or told anyone, he'd slice my cat's throat."

From the corner of her eye, she saw Kieran's eyes darken. "Why?"

"I guess he liked to inflict pain. Or maybe the feeling of power. He never explained it to me. At first, I was too shocked to protest. My mind wasn't grown up enough to process what was happening. Eventually, I ran away, but the police found me and returned me home every time. My parents decided I was an ungrateful, disobedient teen and enlisted the help of my wonderful cousin to correct me."

"So you never told anyone." His voice, so understanding and incredulous, soothed her.

"I did, two years later. After my cat peacefully passed away from old age." Sadness still tightened her rib cage. That cat was one bright thing about her childhood. Someone who'd never hurt her. "I didn't want Ric to do the same thing he did to me to someone else."

"Did he get punished?"

She thought Kieran already knew the answer. Avoiding his gaze, she studied a knot on the pine table. "By that time, he'd created the rumor that I was a cutter. I couldn't contradict him because I wanted to save my cat." It didn't matter that he'd carved his initial onto her like other people carve them on a tree. "Nobody believed me when I exposed the truth. Even Mom thought I was trying to throw blame at someone else for my issues."

Mom and Dad had even accused her of carving those initials to frame a good boy.

"I can't believe this." Kieran sent her an apologetic glance. "I mean, of course, I believe *you*. I just can't comprehend... How could your parents do that to you?"

"I guess I was never the daughter they wanted. Dad wanted a son to start with, and then after complications during her pregnancy with me, Mom couldn't get pregnant again—couldn't give him the sons he so badly wanted. And even as a girl, I was too clumsy, too slow, too silly.... Not one of the perfect five children his brother had, all boys, by the way. Besides, often people believe what they want to believe. Remember, my cousin's father helped them financially. Several times. Plus, Mom worked for him. Believing me would put my parents in a tough situation."

"How... how did you survive?" He squeezed her fingers gently.

"Thankfully, one of the nights when Dad was at home and Mom was at work, he got too much tequila, or I was too slow with getting his quesadillas. Or both. He started shouting, and I dropped his dinner on the floor. He lost it. I just remember screaming and pain... everywhere. A neighbor walking their dog found him pummeling me and me in a pool of blood. I ended up in foster care, and Dad went to jail. The neighbor was too elderly to take me in. My aunts, who lived in Arizona, considered it.

"But my *kind* uncle made it clear that anyone in the family who took in the brat who unfairly accused his son of horrible things would attract my uncle's anger. Mom took Dad's side and said I was no longer a daughter of hers. She said I must've provoked him. I was always a troublemaker. I brought shame to her family. She wished she had children like her brother-in-law." Despite all the years that passed, Arianna's gut still twisted, and it was difficult to swallow around the lump in her throat.

"You're amazing to have gone through all that and turned out as incredible as you did."

His sincere words melted the lump in her throat a bit, filling her starved lungs with fresh air. The rain stopped, and the silence was nearly deafening. "When I showed up for my father's funeral, hoping for reconciliation with Mom, she told me to leave. I didn't bother going to my uncle's funeral."

"What happened to Ric? Did he get caught for his violent behavior?"

She nearly choked on a mirthless chuckle. "He went to medical school just like he'd planned. He became a successful surgeon. I hear he's dedicated to his job and often takes on surgeries other doctors refuse. I can only hope he's used sublimation to channel his violent outbursts into something healthier. Oh, and he married the wonderful girl next door, and they had children as perfect as they are. Three boys. Straight A students in a private school."

"You don't think..." He didn't finish the sentence.

She didn't need him to. "After years with my foster sisters and already working on my own, I took two weeks off and spent them trailing him. I befriended several of his friends. Then I asked..." She nearly said Paisley's name but stopped herself. "Asked a friend to hack into the camera feed of his house."

She wasn't proud of the latter, but she wasn't ashamed of it, either. "I found nothing suspicious. I've kept tabs on him from then on."

And after hearing about the scars on her half-sister's stomach, she'd arranged for extra checks.

Breathing in the scent of peppermint, she waited to exhale. It was one of the scents of her grandmother's garden. Together with flowers, Grandma had grown herbs she'd made teas with, teas she'd said helped people. Peppermint was the most vivid scent, but there were many others. Chamomile was supposed to have a calming effect, for example. Arianna exhaled and breathed in again.

At that time, she could name the plants by their aroma, and Arianna had started developing a sense of scent good enough that it had helped her in her travels later. Recipes and knowledge about herbs were passed through generations, and Grandma had asked Arianna to write them down. Arianna had done so gladly, but she hadn't touched those handwritten notes in many years. She'd tried so hard to stay in the moment that she'd pushed all memories away, good and bad.

She needed to remember, to know the great parts about her heritage, her childhood, her family. She needed to find her way back, if not to her biological family, then to the parts of herself she was missing. If not for her own sake, then for Jackson and Isabella who deserved to know more about their heritage, to cherish where they'd come from.

And maybe, eventually, Arianna could start making her grandmother's quesadillas and empanadas.

"Was it enough?" he whispered. Not judging but wondering.

"Not to me." She kept quiet, then let out a long breath. "After I got trained in combat and became skilled with weapons, I visited Ric at night. His security system was good, but I knew, um, people who were better. I tied him up when he was asleep." Again, she wasn't proud of it, but she wasn't ashamed, either. When he'd wielded that penknife on her, Ric had carved out the forgiving, soft parts out of her, leaving only a hard shell.

He gasped. "Did you cut him?"

"I was tempted, yes. Instead, I promised that, if he ever cut someone else—except for surgeries, of course—I'd do the same thing to him that he promised to do to my cat. I had a feeling he believed me."

"Wow."

Was that it? She didn't know what reaction to expect. She just hoped he wouldn't see in her what her parents had seen, a nuisance, a troublemaker unworthy of love.

Chapter Thirteen

Two weeks later...

Excitement bubbled under Arianna's skin as she looked over Isabella's blonde head and out of the airplane window at the clouds beneath them. The simple fact that she could be above the clouds had never ceased to amaze Arianna. Though, of course, she no longer had the awe of her first time flying.

Isabella did. "Wow!" She glanced up at Arianna, the girl's blue eyes huge. "I wanna touch the clouds. Would they be soft like cotton?"

Arianna laughed. "I don't think they'd be, sweetie. The temps are too cold outside to survive."

"Awwww." Isabella's lower lip stuck out adorably, and she glued herself to the window again.

Yes, the softness of clouds was an illusion. So many illusions had passed through Arianna's life until she'd decided no more. That her father would stop being angry. That her mother would love her. That her cousin would stop hurting her. That her family would believe her...

Was her hope that one day she could have a real family with Kieran an illusion, as well? Longing squeezed her heart. She'd thought she'd stopped hoping for things that couldn't be, and yet...

The idea of having an extended weekend at the ocean was a spontaneous one.

Isabella had missed family trips to the ocean, so Arianna had suggested a family weekend at the beach to Kieran in a one-on-one conversation. She hadn't expected a homebody like him, who'd never left the Show Me State before, to agree to it.

To her surprise, he'd liked the idea and claimed his friends from the nearby ranch owned a bungalow on the beach in South Texas they rarely used themselves.

She searched her mind. Had she used the little girl's request to her advantage because Arianna wanted a change of scenery? Unsure, she nearly cringed.

But really, she wanted to give her niece the gift of positive memories and also reexperience a good part of her childhood. Isabella had been ecstatic about the idea and jumped up and down. While Arianna still had difficulty reading Jackson's reactions, joy had seemed to flash in his eyes at the news before he rearranged his features into his practiced indifference. He'd just nodded and strode into his room.

Currently, he was sitting in the row ahead with Kieran. While Arianna would prefer Kieran sat with her, she understood that arrangement. And while she still couldn't get through to her nephew despite their daily combat lessons, he'd been warming up to Kieran much faster.

She had another sting, this time of jealousy, but she reminded herself to be grateful. It would've been much worse if none of them could reach through to Jackson.

"You're missing out on beautiful scenery," Kieran said in front of her.

"Uh-huh," her nephew replied, probably glued to his phone screen again.

He hadn't gotten in trouble at school and had shown up for his community service all the time. He'd made two friends—Tommy, who'd been hanging out sometimes at their place, and a teen girl from a neighboring ranch who dressed surprisingly similar to Arianna. Jackson had even admitted guys at school thought Arianna was *cool*.

Especially after Arianna had shown up to collect Jackson in Madeline's Ferrari while Arianna's car was getting tuned up.

She hid a smile, then worry twisted her stomach again. Had she been too harsh on him in the beginning? Or not harsh enough? How did parents manage to do this every day and figure out what was right and wrong?

Was she too judgmental of him? *Teenaging* wasn't easy under the best circumstances. Her nephew's world had come crashing down on him. He'd lost his family as he knew it and his home. Then she'd made him lose friends by dragging him into a different state. He'd had to earn respect in a new place, and that hadn't started well.

She'd spent most of her life as an outsider and had gotten used to it. But, as a teen, it'd been heartbreaking. Then changing schools and losing her friends had left her further adrift. She'd later found out Ric had helped create a bad reputation for her at her new school, as if she hadn't been doing an efficient enough job of it on her own.

Now she twisted her hands in her lap, clenching her fingers. *Had* she done the right thing by taking in her nephew and niece and moving them far away? The answer to that question could easily be no.

If not for the alternative.

Ric could not be allowed to have access to Isabella.

The pilot announced landing, and she handed Isabella a peppermint chewing gum stick so her little ears hopefully wouldn't get clogged up. "Here, sweetie. Chew on this, but remember, don't swallow the gum." The change in the atmosphere and its effect on the ears was one of the parts of travel Arianna liked the least.

"I know, Auntie. Thanks." Isabella popped the gum into her mouth, and the peppermint scent in the air reminded Arianna of her grandmother. Only now, her heart filled with love instead of the usual guilt and regret.

Just a few days ago, Isabella had had tantrums in the night because she didn't want to sleep, and then in the morning because she didn't want to wake up. Then more fits before bath time because she didn't want to get *in* a bathtub, during it because the water was too wet, and after it because she didn't want to get *out* of the tub. The tantrums seemed to subside now, especially once Kieran explained how much those rubber butterflies loved bath time.

Oh, and who knew children could scream and cry if *they* weren't allowed to drive to the grocery store?

Arianna had braced herself for more tantrums and judging gazes of people on the plane. But so far, the girl had behaved on the trip. And there were no more nightmares, for which she was immensely grateful. Her words about no bad man getting behind the gates had seemed to work.

"Auntie, I'm thirsty." Isabella turned to her again.

Arianna unscrewed the top on a small orange juice bottle and handed it over.

Isabella scrunched her nose. "I don't wanna orange juice. I wanna mango juice."

"Sorry, sweetie. It's all I have for you to drink right now. But aren't you excited to see the ocean soon? And look out the window. Do you see the ocean and the city at the shore?"

The girl's baby blues brightened, and she turned to the window again, draining the juice bottle fast. Arianna was experienced enough now to know they'd be looking for the restroom soon, but hopefully not *before* landing.

How did people manage road trips with children? They probably had to map out all the rest areas on the route first.

As they left the airport, the sun outside was as bright as Kieran's and Isabella's smiles, such a difference from the gloomy days in the Show Me State and Jackson's frown.

Did that boy ever smile? Then Arianna chastised herself as they all walked to the rental, Isabella's tiny trusting hand in Arianna's and a skip in the girl's step. Arianna shouldn't judge him. He'd gone through a lot of hardships. Besides, she wasn't a smiling person, either.

Except when she was with Kieran and Isabella. What was it about this guy that lifted Arianna's spirits and nearly put a skip in her step, too?

Oh, right, there was a long list. From the kindness in his warm amber eyes to the caring in his nature to the amazing way he treated children. *Her* children! And fine, she wouldn't complain about those broad shoulders either that were shadowed by his signature brown cowboy hat.

Or the long legs and trim waist cinched by a leather belt with a buckle sporting his family's ranch brand.

She fanned herself as he opened the car door for her after buckling Isabella in the back seat. Thankfully, he'd thought to bring the booster seat.

"Hot? I'll put the air conditioner on in a moment." He hurried around to the driver's seat.

"Yeah, very hot," she whispered to herself before sliding inside the car. Then she turned back. "Everyone okay?"

"Yeah!" Isabella grinned at her and clapped. "We're goin' to the beach! We're goin' to the beach. Are we gonna see *shaaaaks*?"

I hope not.

Out loud, Arianna said, "Maybe, but I'll be right nearby."

Jackson didn't say anything, his nose in his phone already. But then, it had been that way even when he'd walked to the car. How he managed not to bump into anything was beyond her.

The rental car smelled of leather inside, but the scent weakened when cool air appeared from the vents.

"Grandma used to bring me to the ocean once in a while," she blurted out as Kieran drove off.

Just like the scents of flowers in Grandma's garden and empanadas in Grandma's kitchen, the salty ocean breeze was the best memory of Arianna's childhood. But all kitchens and cooking had become tainted because of her spending so much time there to keep her dad happy—in vain. And the garden, well, because of the butterflies.

But the ocean memory remained as clear and clean as its sparkling waters. She still carried a necklace with seashells she'd found on the beach. It was one of her most prized possessions.

Her hand flew to her T-shirt, and she touched the necklace through the fabric. She kept the necklace hidden from curious glances, just like so many other things in her life. Her throat clogged up, and she turned away and pretended to pay attention to the streets outside the window.

While walking along the beach and holding Arianna's hand, Grandma had talked about *islas bonitas*—or beautiful islands—far away with tropical flowers and lots of food where everyone was happy and the sun shone all year round. Did Arianna choose a profession that included lots of travel because subconsciously she'd been looking for those islas bonitas without realizing it? She touched the necklace through the smooth fabric again.

Another prized possession, if only she had it, would be Grandma's heirloom ring. In her will, Grandma had left it to Arianna. But Mom had said she'd take it for safekeeping so Arianna wouldn't lose it. She'd get the ring on her eighteenth birthday.

By then, her parents had long since lost parental rights, and she'd gone no contact with them. Regret clouded her eyes. It wasn't so much about the ring's value, but about the memory. About feeling a connection to the generations before her.

Linking herself to her roots.

Sure, her father and cousin had been a bad part of her family—rotting produce she wanted to cut out of her life—but a few bad sprouts didn't mean the roots were bad. Those roots had given life to a beautiful prosperous garden, so rich in culture. One she'd left behind and needed to find a path back to again.

Maybe seeing the new generation in Jackson and Isabella made Arianna crave a connection to the previous ones.

Kieran's hand found hers and gave her a different—but just as much needed—connection. "Your grandmother sounds wonderful. Is that why you wanted to come here?"

"Yes. Well, because of Isabella, too. If this is a happy memory for her, I want her to experience it again and again." She winced from a fresh stab of guilt. Giving this mini beach vacation to Isabella and Jackson was insignificant compared to taking them away from places and friends they'd loved.

Children needed stability. But what choice did Arianna have? She'd needed to take them away from that family. While Isabella looked nothing like Arianna, she had some of the same naïveté and openness Arianna used to have. And it might sound silly, but Arianna still shivered thinking Ric had gifted Isabella toy butterflies. He had three children, all boys, and several nephews. Isabella was the only girl in the family, since Arianna had long left and Isabella's mother had died. And Jackson had mentioned his mom had scars, too.

But Ronan and Jessie hadn't found anything suspicious in Arianna's half sister's accident or in her life. New probes into Ric's life showed he was a perfect family man and a community pillar.

Was Arianna reading too much into it, trying to be the protective mother her own had never been and projecting her fears onto the girl?

Once they settled and unpacked at the bungalow, Arianna and the rest of the family let Isabella drag them to the beach. Well, they didn't resist too much.

With a navy-blue dress swirling around her ankles above her surprising choice of flip-flops, Arianna filled her lungs to the fullest and smiled at the seagulls' distant greeting. Of all her travel assignments, she'd most loved the ones near the sea or the ocean.

Jackson didn't seem to have the same fascination as he sat on the sand, his fingers flicking fast on his phone screen.

Kieran picked up two large seashells and handed one to Arianna and the other to Isabella. "Put it to your ear, and you'll be able to hear the ocean talk to you," he told the girl. "Even when we get home, the ocean will speak to you."

"Wow." Isabella's eyes went round as she placed the seashell to her ear, then moved her blonde hair out of the way to hear better. "I hear the ocean!"

And something about Kieran spoke to Arianna's heart. Who was she kidding? *Everything* about him spoke to her heart. At first, it had been a whisper she'd nearly missed. But now it was loud and clear. She was falling for the man.

The bright sky with azure waters reflected in Isabella's wonder-filled baby blues. Something fierce stirred inside Arianna and grew fast like an incoming tide that could sweep her off her feet if she wasn't careful. She didn't know many things, but she knew she'd protect this little girl with her life. Did she have a maternal instinct, after all?

She even wanted to protect Jackson, but mostly from himself. In part, because nobody had protected her, and it wasn't right. Only now, she could think about it without the familiar guilt and shame. It wasn't her fault. Even if she had to repeat it to herself a million times. The conversation with Kieran had helped her realize what she should've known all along.

And the memories of Grandma now warmed her instead of slicing her with guilt. Maybe Arianna would even grow a flower garden next spring. Isabella would be thrilled with all the butterflies it would bring.

Arianna stared far away as she'd done when she'd visited the ocean with Grandma, hoping to see those magical islas bonitas. She'd stopped looking years ago, sure beautiful islands that made people happy didn't exist.

She knew now they existed. Back then, in Grandma's heart. And now in Arianna's own and in Isabella's, too.

"Auntie, more seashells! More ocean to *bwing* home!" Little legs hurried across the shore.

Arianna chuckled. "Great! Be careful! Don't run too fast!"

He reached for her hand again. "That. I could listen to that sound all day. Every day."

Her lips tugged up as she laced her fingers through his, a luxury for her, and lifted her face toward the sun and its warm, gentle rays. "What sound? The whisper of the ocean?"

"That, too. But I meant the sound of your laughter. It's so rare." He stopped. "I'm happy you're happy here."

So was she. She was truly happy at that moment. But it wasn't just because of the ocean. It was because people dear to her shared this experience. She wanted to tell him all that, but something stopped her. Maybe the memories of her father's shouts and slaps on her face or Ric's painful cuts. So once again, she said nothing.

Kieran's fingers caressed her face, and they were even gentler than the sun's rays.

Instead of jerking away like she'd normally do from physical contact with a man, she leaned into his touch. A pleasant wave swept her up, and she cherished the incredible moment.

From the corner of her eye, she watched Isabella and Jackson, who finally slipped the phone into his pocket and joined his sister.

"You miss your grandmother, don't you?" Like the sun's rays, Kieran's amber eyes softened and warmed her.

"Yes. Besides my foster sisters, she was the only person who loved me. Her love was endless like this ocean. Nobody ever loved me that way before or after." Even all these years later, it still hurt.

But now, after blaming herself for decades, Arianna knew she didn't need to blame herself for what had happened to Grandma. She'd been drowning in an ocean of guilt, and it had taken Kieran throwing her a life preserver to reach for the surface and breathe the fresh air.

"You never know. Someone's love for you might be as endless as the ocean already," he said quietly, his gaze probing.

Her heart skipped a beat.

Did she dare to hope...?

Probably best not to ask. Hope was much better than disappointment, and she knew it all too well.

She spotted a jagged shard of a broken beer bottle, and though she was reluctant to move away from Kieran's touch, she picked it up. "I'll throw it away later. Someone could be walking barefoot and get cut on it." She was grateful Isabella had kept her shoes on, but Arianna suspected it wouldn't be for long.

The sun caught in the glass, and through it, the sky looked brown instead of blue. Things changed unrecognizably depending on the prism one used to look at it. Why had it taken her so long to look at herself through the prism of acceptance and forgiveness?

He cupped her face again. "You're much kinder than you're willing to admit. Why do you hide that kindness?"

Because it had been taken advantage of.

"You know why," she said instead. Her gaze traveled to make sure Isabella was okay and with her brother. "I don't remember someone ever calling me kind in the last decade—probably far longer."

"You're kind. And gorgeous. I don't know all the beautiful, fancy words to tell you how I feel. But you make my head spin. In a good way." He glanced at the children as if to make sure they were all right, as well, then tipped her chin, and leaned forward slowly, giving her time to change her mind.

She rose on her tiptoes and met him halfway. His lips tasted of the ocean and hope, and she responded with all the fervor that was in her. Elation filled every atom in her body.

But she had to withdraw, way before she wanted. "Jackson and Isabella could be watching."

"Right. They could." Kieran was out of breath, and she liked it.

Jackson started teaching Isabella how to throw pebbles, so Arianna and Kieran joined him. She threw a pebble the furthest, which seemed to impress the boy. Well, whatever it took to make it past his guarded attitude.

"Auntie, look what I found!" Isabella picked something from the sand.

Arianna winced. Hopefully, it wasn't another shard. "Let me see, please. There are some glass shards around, so please don't touch them. I don't want you to cut yourself."

"Yes, Auntie." Isabella surrendered the little piece.

It turned out to be a glass piece indeed, but sea glass with its edges smoothed out by the ocean waves for a long time.

"It's emerald green. Just like your eyes," Kieran whispered.

Her heart stuttered again from the admiration in his gaze. Did she dare hope that maybe God could smooth out her sharp edges and make something as beautiful from her? "Isabella, may I keep this one, please?"

"Sure, Auntie. I'll find more." The girl skipped ahead, her pink dress with blue butterflies ruffled by the breeze.

Jackson followed her with a shrug.

Arianna spotted driftwood further away. "How long has it been floating in the ocean before drifting ashore?"

"Are you talking about driftwood or yourself?" Then Kieran grimaced. "Sorry. I hope that didn't sound offensive."

"Not at all. You understand me better than I do." She moved closer to him as they walked.

Closer.

Instead of distancing herself. Huh.

"I don't want to drift any longer," she surprised herself by saying.

His face lit up. "Dare I hope you'll choose to stay at my shore?"

"I love life with you at the ranch." Was she saying too much? "But I don't mean just that. I have an extended family in another state I want to contact again. I want to tell Grandma's stories and sing the songs she taught me. I want to come back to my heritage. We have such a rich culture. I want to study our history, read books. How do you feel about mariachi music playing in the house together with country songs?"

He smiled. "I'd love that."

"I should start cooking fajitas again." She perked up. She'd rediscovered her love of cooking again at the ranch kitchen because her cooking was praised instead of criticized. "Grandma left me some great recipes. Her empanadas were amazing."

"I love seeing this light in your eyes." He brought her hand to his lips and kissed every finger, sending delicious shivers through her body.

"I wanna build sandcastles!" Isabella landed on the sand.

Jackson perched on a boulder nearby, and Kieran and Arianna sat on the sand close to them but still out of their earshot.

The breeze played with her hair, but she liked it more when Kieran ran his fingers through it. "Your family knows and cherishes your Irish heritage. It's high time for me to do the same about mine. And I want Jackson and Isabella to know about their ancestors. I'm going to learn more about their mother, too. I'll need to talk to them about her. I'm not trying to take her place in their lives, but I should've explained it better to them."

"I'll help in any way I can." He sounded sincere, and she knew he was.

"You asked me how I survived," Arianna said quietly as she looked at Isabella, then at the sparkling waters. "It took me a long time to learn to pay attention to people to stop concentrating on my pain. In a lot of countries I went to, I met people on the streets who didn't have much. But they were smiling.

"One of our customers wanted a unique handmade blanket. I delivered it, of course. It had azure and turquoise hues flowing into each other. Kinda like the ocean. It could be worn as a shawl, too, and was exquisite. The softness and the feel of the fabric was amazing. I told that client about the village where women were making them. They could make way more and provide for their families. He started a small company selling their handiwork around the world. Each blanket is unique, hand-signed, and made with lots of love. It made me feel good, you know. I started a similar project with a different client. Then I joined Paisley's project helping abused people." She squared her shoulders. "I finally had a purpose. I could do something. I wasn't a useless brat any longer."

"You were never a useless brat." His eyes shadowed.

True, but when somebody she'd trusted and loved unconditionally had branded her soul with those words, just like another person she'd trusted and loved had branded her body with cuts, it took the patience and kindness of someone like Kieran to teach her otherwise. "Ric carved roads of pain on my skin and in my heart, but I'm not letting what he did define me any longer."

"Not any longer," Kieran echoed. "You have no idea how much I admire you. How much you mean to me."

"Ditto," she whispered.

Arianna wanted—*needed*—to stay. But with the phone threats and the past that could come to haunt her, would it be safe for Kieran, Isabella, and Jackson if she stayed?

Chapter Fourteen

Premonition squeezed Arianna's heart. She didn't understand the reason for it. It should be the other way around. The mini ocean vacation had gone wonderfully, much better than her expectations, which were just for nobody to drown. Isabella didn't have nightmares any longer. Jackson was tolerating her presence. And—a miracle—Kieran had kissed her!

The phone threats had stopped for two whole days. Was it because that person gave up? Or was this the calm before the storm?

"So tell me about your vacation—and why you were in Texas and didn't visit us?" Genevieve's warm voice came from the speaker on the marbled gray countertop.

Keeping her hands busy lining a tray with bacon, Arianna laughed. "We weren't *that* near you—Texas is bigger than many of the countries I've visited, you know."

The sounds of a hammer hitting wood reached her from outside and edged out the uneasy feeling in her stomach. Or rather, that was a duet of hammers—Kieran and Jackson at work, and just the thought warmed her, chasing away the previous chills that drove her to call Genevieve for impromptu counseling. Arianna talked to very few people. Genevieve was one of them.

"Things couldn't be better, so I don't know why I am feeling this.... Is it because I still can't trust things to stay pleasant? Always waiting for someone to erupt in anger like my father, or..." She wouldn't mention her cousin's supposed kindness turning to cruel violence.

"It's understandable. You went through a lot." Genevieve's voice was soft.

Still, Arianna's fingers separating bacon slices quivered. And as she laid out the last one, a sting of guilt reminded her she'd made the conversation all about herself. There was so much kindness and openness about Genevieve that it invited other people to come to her, even closed-off people like Arianna. A blast of superheated air slammed her as she slid the tray of bacon into the preheated stove.

Once again, a kitchen had become a happy place instead of the one that had made her shudder with fear.

She trapped the air back inside and set the timer for twenty minutes, then scooted across the kitchen and leaned over the speaker. "Anything new in *your* life?"

Genevieve paused. "Well, I've been spending quite some time with a new coworker."

Hope unraveled tender shoots in Arianna. Yes, she believed a person could be totally happy on their own and had practiced it for decades. But since she'd experienced a taste of love through her feelings for Kieran, a part of her ached for Genevieve to find a love as amazing as she was dreaming of.

Only one that could be real, not just a dream like Kieran was for Arianna. Was he her islas bonitas, beautiful islands of happiness and love beyond the horizon? "And?"

"And nothing." A sigh traveled down the line from Genevieve. "Men always only see a friend in me. A cuddly, sweet, always-ready-to-help friend. It. Happens. All the time. Well, since the time my daughter grew up enough for me to consider dating again, anyway."

"I'm sorry." Arianna grimaced.

She suspected people sometimes took advantage of kind Genevieve. Even Arianna and her foster sisters had done it in some way. They'd gone to Genevieve when they'd needed help with homework or when they'd been upset or when they'd been hungry. Pretty much, any time they needed something. She'd practically raised a large family when she was a child herself and way before she'd given birth amid a tragedy that still made Arianna shudder.

Not only had Genevieve survived in circumstances that would've destroyed another person but also she'd helped others.

But when would it be Genevieve's turn to experience all that life had to offer? Once Arianna could untangle herself from the web of her issues, she needed to talk to the girls about doing something special for Genevieve. It might have to wait for school break, the long summer vacation, but they had to come up with something.

It was high time Genevieve received kindness from others.

"It's for the better." Genevieve's voice broke, then grew stronger again. "You know my story. It's not easy for me to trust again. I have Gold to brighten my day, all of you foster sisters to cheer on, your children, our sisters' future children to nanny, and my school and my students. I'm blessed."

As Arianna peeled carrots, she marveled at her friend's optimism. Genevieve had been damaged, too, but unlike Arianna, Genevieve had never shown cracks in her foundation. "We're blessed to have you in our lives. We should've said it more often. And we should've shown you. Once this hoopla with the threats is over and things seem safe, bring Gold to Cowboy Crossing. Let us pamper you."

"Pamper me, huh?" Genevieve's laugh bubbled up. "That'd be... unusual. But my daughter has school to study at, and I have school to teach at. I'll talk to her. Maybe Gold and I can stay for some time at the lodge next summer."

"I'll hold you to it." After a few more words, Arianna disconnected and pondered an idea as she walked to the stove. Maybe she could even introduce Genevieve to some cowboy here who'd see what a treasure she was.

Hmm. Her foster sisters seemed to have started the tradition of marrying O'Neill brothers. But only two brothers remained single, Declan and Sean—well, maybe Kieran, too. Though Arianna couldn't yet allow herself to think of letting him go.

Could it be Declan? As much as she liked him—he was probably her favorite brother, aside from Kieran, though to be fair to Sean, she hardly knew him—Arianna nearly snorted as she washed vegetables for the stew, then started peeling them. She'd gotten the recipe from Kieran's mother and wanted to surprise him.

A giggle escaped her lips. A giggle!

So unlike her. And the anticipation building inside her was unlike her, as well. She couldn't wait to see his smile, to hug him, and to breathe his scent of cedarwood and hay. Her pulse spiked. She cut peeled potatoes and placed them in the steaming pot, then moved on to cut the carrots. She shifted her mindset back from tempting thoughts about Kieran to thoughts about Genevieve.

Even if Arianna tried her hand at matchmaking, would it make sense to set her friend up with Declan?

Of course not. Yes, Declan was charming and easygoing, but he was the opposite of Genevieve and never stayed in one place or relationship for long. Genevieve didn't need to get her heart broken. Arianna shook her head in response to her thoughts as she dumped the carrots into the pot and started on the onions. Her eyes prickled as the punchy scent stung her nostrils and tear ducts.

If anything, Declan would fit Arianna much better, as they could be united by their love of travel and their dislike of getting close to people. Yes, if she connected to any of Kieran's brothers as a friend, it would be Declan. They loved to discuss the countries they'd visited and different cultures. But she'd never felt attracted to him and had plenty of attraction to Kieran, who was, in turn, her complete opposite.

Go figure.

Her affection for Kieran was as overflowing as the pot was going to be. She reduced the heat under the burner.

Why did her thoughts keep returning to him? Okay, she knew why. Her heart fluttered. She cut onions fast before tears could start rolling.

Back to Genevieve. Declan and Genevieve could become friends. But she'd been friend-zoned too many times already. Not that there was anything wrong with having a lot of friends. It was like having lots of stars in the sky. But she deserved to have someone for whom she'd be the entire world and the center of the universe.

Arianna's lips tugged up as she dumped the onions in the pot and slid the bacon from the oven—Kieran had taught her the trick of cooking bacon in the oven, rather than frying it.

Who knew it could be so easy that way? No smoky kitchen, no grease-splattered stove, either. Just fold up the foil lining the tray and you're done. Perfect for making large breakfasts for the ranch crew. She returned to the counter, slathered slices of toast in mayo, and added bacon strips, then tomato slices and lettuce. The bacon scent still hung with the onion aroma in the kitchen.

Then she took plates with BLT sandwiches to the yard to her hardworking men. The tree house was supposed to be a surprise for Isabella, so Arianna had planned to take the girl for ice cream while the guys built it. But then her mother-in-law had volunteered for the ice-cream outing.

As Arianna stepped outside, she breathed in the scents of fresh-cut grass and fresh-cut wood. She'd always considered herself a city girl, but she found the scents endearing.

But even more endearing was the sound of Jackson's laughter. Another exotic and unique thing to her because, so far, she hadn't even been able to coax a smile out of the sulky teen, much less laughter.

Kieran had been able to connect to her hurting, rebellious nephew way better than she could. She now chose to be grateful for it instead of being envious. Kieran had a way with people. Animals, too.

He'd even managed to get her out of her cocoon. Cocoon. She winced at the word but held onto the plates, and that was another miracle. Her heart shifted as from the porch she watched his large frame among the gold-tinted foliage.

She yelled, "Time for a break! I've got BLT sandwiches!"

Then she climbed down the porch while the guys climbed down the sprawling tree sturdy enough to support them and the tree house.

They all sat on a wooden bench he'd brought from the ranch, one she suspected he made himself. She stroked the white surface of his handiwork and found herself longing for his touch.

Shocking, really. Her heart fluttered. Since she'd learned she'd rather be independent than tortured, she'd avoided leaning on others. She'd avoided being touched. Yet her body shifted toward him on its own.

He had no idea what effect he had on her, and it was probably better to leave it that way. Regret mixed with the scent of grass. Her nose distinguished a few familiar plant scents now.

He took the simple sandwich with such words of gratitude as if it were an elaborate feast over which she'd slaved for hours. When Jackson snatched his without a word, Kieran gave the teen a pointed look.

"Thanks," her nephew grunted as he gobbled down the sandwich with a surprising appetite. Then he looked up and met her gaze. "*Gracias.*"

Huh. She'd taught him a few Spanish words during their combat lessons, but she didn't think he'd remember. "*De nada.* Thank you for building the tree house. Isabella will be thrilled."

She still couldn't comprehend Kieran's motivation.

Could he be that kind? Okay, she understood he'd worked himself to the bone for his family. But she and the children were nothing to him. His wanting to adopt them was still shocking. She'd promised him a marriage in name only and couldn't go back on that promise.

Even if she wanted to.

A vise tightened around her heart and wrenched tight.

Maybe he *was* a kind man, something extremely rare but possible. "I didn't know men like you existed," she blurted out as she took the empty plate and scooted out of the way of a butterfly. Thankfully, it was a monarch and didn't carry as many painful memories of her trick-or-treat outfit with its blue wings. "I guess you're like a stripeless tiger. They exist, though I never met one."

The tips of Kieran's ears pinked, and he stopped chewing. "I'm just an ordinary guy."

"You're extraordinary to me."

Jackson snorted. "Stripeless tiger? Like you saw a *regular* one."

She grinned. "Actually, I had to bring a tiger cub for a client."

Her nephew's jaw slackened. "What?"

"A lot of exotic animals are illegal to keep as pets in the US, and the list varies from state to state. But tigers are not one of them."

"You're kidding me." Jackson wiped crumbs off his pants. At least, these weren't excessively ripped or baggy and hanging on his hips, probably to avoid getting snagged on a tree limb.

Was he curious?

Huh. Maybe some perks from her previous job could be useful. "I heard there are now more tigers in legal captivity than in the wild, though the number in the wild is thankfully increasing. Of course, it's a challenge to keep them as pets. They require up to eighty-eight pounds of meat in one meal and at least forty miles of enclosure to roam."

"Not to mention one can eat you if it gets angry or hungry," Kieran added, probably in case Jackson decided to ask for a pet tiger.

She nodded. "Just like an alligator. One of our clients wanted to gift his twenty-year-old daughter an alligator. It was legal to own them in their state. She just fell in love with baby alligators and wanted one. After all, baby alligators are cute and harmless. I tried to explain that, once grown, that cute pet would weigh over one thousand pounds and could live up to fifty years. And they become dangerous. You never know when you might turn into"—she pointed at the rest of the sandwich on Kieran's plate—"a snack."

Jackson rolled his eyes. "No thank you. Alligators aren't for me." His eyes softened then—or did she imagine it? "Though I'd love to have a horse one day."

"Sometimes we have bottle babies," Kieran said. "When the mother refuses to give them milk and we have to bottle-feed them. We had one earlier in the year. If we get another in the future, care to help? It could be your horse then. But remember, they require lots of care, and you won't be able to ride it for years. We'll get you riding other horses in the meantime."

Jackson's brown eyes lit up. "Deal! I bet Isabella would be thrilled to help, too."

Arianna's insides softened, too. Jackson was a city slicker just like she was, but he seemed to be adapting to life on the ranch. To a new lifestyle. In a large part, thanks to Kieran. Paisley helped, too, even if long distance.

Considering Jackson's love for his phone and the computer, Arianna had connected him with her computer geek foster sister, and Paisley was teaching him programming. To the point that even the principal was impressed when he'd helped remove a bug from the school computer. Arianna wasn't convinced he hadn't introduced that bug to start with, but she kept that tidbit to herself.

She'd been concerned that now Jackson could be teased for being a computer geek, but knowing how to fight and having a *cool aunt* seemed to prevent that.

To Arianna's huge relief, Isabella slept through most nights now. She did still throw tantrums sometimes, trying Arianna's patience, but Kieran had seemed to navigate them fine, being strict when needed and gentle at other times. He was a native in the land of good parenthood. Meanwhile, she'd only crossed its border and was trying to find her way with GPS and directions and still getting lost.

"It's like with this tree house. Seeing the joy on Isabella's face makes the work more than worth it." Kieran nudged Jackson. "Right?"

"Right," Jackson grumbled, but a hint of a smile twitched up his lips.

And the entire scene tugged at Arianna's heart. It was domestic, simple, so unlike her, and yet somehow pure bliss. Birds sang somewhere in the trees, and Kieran's gaze lingered on her face. She wished it were his fingers.

How far she'd come already from jerking away from a man's touch and staying a mile away from any emotional intimacy!

The wind whipped hair into her face, and he reached out and brushed her hair aside. The back of his palm touched her skin, sending delicious tingles over it, and she wanted to close her eyes and cherish the feeling. She could be a tiger out in the wild, but in Kieran's arms, she nearly purred like a kitten.

Could she embrace this new reality instead of pushing it away, or was it too late? And did the threats on her phone mean she was a liability to whoever was around her?

While she didn't know the answer to those questions, it wasn't fair to let Kieran close. She pushed to her feet. "I need to get back. Kieran's mom might bring Isabella soon."

Jackson rolled his eyes. "Oh please. If you want to kiss, don't mind me."

Just the idea sent a jolt of pleasure through her. But as it was, she'd been sending Kieran mixed signals. She'd pushed him away, then kissed him after Isabella's nightmare and his willingness to adopt the children, then shifted away after vomiting her guts out in his presence, then kissed him back at the beach.

All this emotional roller coaster wasn't fair to him. Yet the disappointment in his eyes sliced through her.

He took the last bite of his sandwich and handed her the plate. "That was yummy. Thank you very much. I guess we'd better get to the tree house."

A lump formed in her throat, but she squared her shoulders and walked back inside the lodge.

The moment she put the plates in the dishwasher, her phone rang. She tensed, then straightened out, and fished it out of her pocket.

Relief whooshed out of her lungs at Jessie's phone number. Arianna swiped the screen to answer. "Hi, Jessie."

"I have some news." Jessie didn't waste time on pleasantries, and Arianna liked it that way. "There was an accident in Springfield. I was called to it. The driver is dead. The passenger walked away with a few scratches and bruises."

"I'm so sorry to hear about the driver." It had to concern Arianna somehow, or Jessie wouldn't have passed along the information. Her heart dropped. "Oh no. It wasn't Victor, was it?"

"No. It was Richard Montemayor. Your cousin."

Going weak in the knees, Arianna sank onto the nearest chair. She hated herself for the wave of relief. She didn't wish him harm—okay, maybe a little, but she didn't wish him dead.

Nearly her entire life she'd been afraid he'd come for her. She could admit it now. He had, several times when she'd lived with her foster sisters, but Jessie had none-too-gently insisted on him leaving because Arianna had wanted him to leave.

In a way, he'd marked her as his territory with those cuts. No matter how much time had passed, she couldn't be sure he wouldn't one day try to torture her again. Or that he wouldn't do it to someone else, and it would be her fault because she hadn't done more to prevent it.

So yes, she felt relieved now—and empty.

"Are you okay?" Jessie's worried voice filtered through Arianna's mental fog. The pause stretched too far, apparently.

"Yes." Then Arianna froze. Her friend didn't say whether Ric was the driver. "Was the driver...?"

"Yes. His wife was the passenger. I thought you needed to know."

Gratitude pierced Arianna's mental haze. She'd never told her foster sisters everything, but maybe they'd pieced it all together from what little information she had provided.

"Thank you." Arianna forced herself to think. She needed to pull herself together. Isabella would be here soon, and Arianna shouldn't show any sign of distress. "Do you know why they were in Springfield?"

"They rented a car to go to Cowboy Crossing. That tells us something, right?"

Arianna clenched her teeth. "It sure does."

Did Ric come here for the children? Or did he have something more sinister in mind? She'd never know.

Unless... unless she talked to his wife. Arianna stared at the phone in her hand. She didn't know the phone number, but it wouldn't be difficult to get it.

No.

It was time to move on. Enough of unanswered questions and painful memories.

Then her phone rang, and she flinched and nearly dropped it. The unfamiliar number on the screen made her hold her breath. It could be a bot selling a warranty, right? Hopefully?

She answered it, nearly wishing it was a bot. "Hello."

"My name is Tanya. I'm Ric's wife." A sob muffled the last word. "His *widow* now. I think we should meet."

Arianna wasn't happy with herself as she paced in the park near the pond the next day.

Her shift at the ranch house had ended, but Madeline had stayed with Isabella because Arianna had decided to go to this meeting. Arianna drew a shaky breath as she breathed in the pure scents of earth and foliage to calm her racing heart.

Why had she made this call? Yesterday, she'd told Tanya meeting up wasn't a good idea. Even after Tanya had said she'd wanted to apologize for all the harm her husband had done, Arianna had stood firm.

Then she'd tossed and turned the entire night and gotten up with her head pounding. She'd needed... What, closure, maybe? Tanya had also said she'd wanted to return something that belonged to Arianna, and that piqued her curiosity. As a child, she'd given him dried flowers from Abuela's garden—she'd started using the Spanish word from her grandmother, now—as a clumsy gift. But surely, he'd thrown those away.

It wasn't just about her curiosity. It seemed unkind to refuse someone who was suffering, and Arianna wanted to be kind. Compassion for Tanya squeezed her heart. And she could've suffered at her husband's hands, too. Maybe Kieran's good-naturedness was rubbing off on Arianna.

Even if she remained suspicious of the woman.

Kieran... He was part of the reason Arianna was here. She wanted to start a new chapter of her life, the life that could include him, but she couldn't do it while being stuck on the previous pages.

Her heart was beating fast. Her life was about to change, and she knew it.

Footsteps made her tense, but she visibly relaxed her shoulders and stretched her lips in what she hoped looked like a compassionate half smile. Intently, she watched the direction the footsteps came from, and her hand moved to her purse where she kept her gun, but more out of habit than because of the threat.

Tanya walked briskly, dressed in sneakers and a dark-gray loose coat with a hood that hid her hair and part of her face. Though Arianna had never met her, she'd done her research a long time ago and recognized Tanya from the photos online. Dark circles under her eyes and a puffy nose told of a sleepless night and lots of crying.

Guilt stung Arianna. If the doctors hadn't allowed Tanya to travel home yet, Arianna was likely the only person Tanya knew here, at such a difficult time of loss and grief.

Once close, Tanya looked up and threw the hood off. Her uncombed hair was cut short, though not as short as Jessie's. Mascara caked under her eyes, but she didn't seem to care. She still wore her wedding ring, and Arianna had a feeling Tanya wasn't going to take it off any time soon.

"Thank you for coming." Tanya's voice sounded hollow as if all life had been drained out of her.

Arianna gestured to the bench further away, but Tanya shook her head, so they remained standing. A distant bird cried in the sky, and the breeze from the pond brought cold air.

A few voices reached them, and Tanya frowned. "Is there any place where we could talk without interruption?"

"Sure." Arianna gestured toward the least frequented part of the park, and they walked there together without talking. Once there, she stopped. "I'm sorry for your loss." It seemed insignificant, but what else could she say?

Tanya's eyes narrowed. "Are you, really?"

What had Ric told his wife? Most likely, not the truth. But it was in the past now. "I knew him differently from how you did. But I can't even imagine your loss—"

"He loved those children, you know. The nephew and niece you never even bothered to meet."

Loved them? Or pretended to love, to get access to Isabella? Just like he'd pretended to love Arianna.

But it wasn't Tanya's fault.

"I had my reasons to stop contact with my family." Arianna wanted to pace or, even better, to run, but she rooted her feet in the ground and remained standing. "But I do love Jackson and Isabella now. I'll do everything to give them the best life I can."

"Are you even capable of love?" Tanya scoffed. "The only reason you decided to take in Jackson and Isabella was because they mattered to Ric. Just to make him suffer."

Arianna's limbs hung heavy as though filled with lead. Suddenly extremely tired, she struggled to keep her head up. How could she reverse all the years Ric had fed Tanya lies? Plus, she was grieving the very man Arianna had issues with. "I never wanted to make him suffer. It was the other way around."

"Oh yeah? Everyone in the family knows the lies you spread about him cutting you. You wanted to ruin him, his future, and you failed. But you never forgot. With those children, you took your chance for revenge." A glow sparked in the woman's eyes—pure hatred.

Whoa. Arianna lifted her hands in a placating gesture as she stepped back. "It's not true."

Her stomach clenched. Nothing she was saying would change this woman's mind. Coming here was a mistake. She needed to put distance between them and fast.

"You know why we came here? He was desperate to talk some sense into you." Tanya's face twisted.

Or threaten her with harming the children. Arianna wouldn't put it past him.

Then it clicked.

"The phone threats—*you* sent them to me, not your husband."

Tanya raised her chin, not a hint of remorse in her eyes. "He loved Jackson and Isabella. And I loved my husband. I had to stand by him and do whatever I could to make him happy."

Really? She saw nothing wrong with what she'd done? And how far would she go?

Arianna's heart dropped into the frosted yellow grass, and a shiver, having nothing to do with the strengthening wind, ran down her spine. She made a few more careful steps back.

Then Tanya's expression crumpled. "Now he's gone. All because of you. If we didn't come here to make you change your mind, he'd still be alive."

Just how twisted was that?

Arianna measured the distance to the nearest tree because she could guess what was going to happen.

The next moment, she was staring down the barrel of a gun in Tanya's hands.

Tanya's eyes were just as menacing. "I told you that you were going to pay with your life. I'm going to keep my promise."

Fear squeezed Arianna's heart with its ghastly fingers. She'd risked her life plenty of times before, but how different it was now when she had something—someones—to live for.

She licked her dry lips. "You don't want to do this. Think about your children."

Tanya's hands shook, but she didn't put down the weapon. "We're alone here. Nobody will know."

"Freeze!"

Arianna dropped to the ground at Jessie's voice, and a split second later, a shot thundered. Her heart beating wildly, Arianna rolled behind the nearest tree. She didn't know its name, and all she cared about was that it had a wide trunk she could hide behind.

"Police! Drop your weapon and put your hands up in the air!" Ronan's voice didn't leave room for argument.

She didn't peep out of her hiding place. But the wind brought the click of handcuffs closing and then Ronan repeating the Miranda rights.

Then Kieran scooped her up. "You know how much you scared me? How difficult it was to stay still?"

"I figured it was best to leave all this to the professionals. And if my suspicions were right, I wouldn't want her to harm the children just to get back at me."

She let herself savor his embrace, the comforting scents of cedarwood and hay that smelled like home now. She wanted to stay alive for this man, for Jackson and Isabella. Despite all Arianna's resistance, she'd fallen in love with him. With her own husband.

Could the road to happiness finally be open? Or was there another obstacle on the way she didn't know about yet?

Chapter Fifteen

"Are you sure you want to do this? Do you really want to go for a new assignment?"

"No." Arianna responded to Madeline's question and glared at the half-empty—or half-full?—suitcase on the bed, then dropped herself on the plush rug where a moose stepped through trees in the moonlight, and she drew her knees to her chin. A rip on the knee of her black jeans glared at her. She stuck a finger through the hole and twisted the strings around her fingertip. "But I need to. And look at the mess I created. I could've put the children in danger!"

In the three days since the incident at the park, Arianna still hadn't resolved that issue in her mind, her terror of bringing danger to those she cared about.

Madeline lowered herself onto the floor near her and tucked her long legs clad in elegant white slacks under her. "First of all, *you* didn't put them in danger. You've done everything to keep them safe. Even by drawing danger to yourself."

Tears stung Arianna's eyes, but she didn't let them drop. "Listen, I'm not abandoning Isabella and Jackson. I'll be gone for three days, hopefully less. The kids will barely notice that I'm gone. Isabella already adores Kieran, you, and Mrs. O'Neill. Jackson spends all his spare time with his phone, the horses, his friends, and Kieran. I'm not like Genevieve or Paisley who'd make perfect moms for them."

Something flashed in Madeline's eyes. "Do you think I wouldn't be a fit mom, either?"

Arianna gasped, then swatted at her friend playfully. "No! I'd never say that. What even makes you say that?"

"I was also damaged. It's difficult for me to show affection." Madeline brightened. "Except affection for my hubby. And even him I hurt badly at first. But he wants a child so much."

"You're showing plenty of compassion and affection to me right now." Which wasn't usual for Madeline, who used to hold her emotions in, just like Arianna. Often, Genevieve or Paisley comforted their foster sisters while Jessie did her best to protect them and Madeline used her modeling to help provide for them. What Arianna had done for them, she hadn't a clue. Of course, she wouldn't mention that or hers and Madeline's lack of maternal instincts. Instead, Arianna studied her friend. "Do *you* want a child?"

"I do." Madeline nodded without hesitation. "But with our history, we don't have great mother role models. Well, I did, more than the rest of us. Still, I was little when I ended up in foster care, and my memories of her are fading."

"If you'll love that child, the rest will come."

Madeline looked at her pointedly.

"Okay, I see it applies to my situation, too." Arianna covered her face with her hands. "I do love Jackson and Isabella. But I feel like they deserve better than me. Kieran deserves better." This time, she couldn't keep her tears at bay, and one of them slid down her cheek, bringing a salty taste. "A wife who is softer than I am. Who knows how to communicate. Who can show her love for him. Who doesn't have people coming to shoot at her."

Even if just the thought of being apart from Kieran and her children for a few days crushed Arianna's heart already. She'd gotten attached. Too much.

Madeline groaned and shifted closer, which Arianna felt by the movement in the air and the lavender scent getting stronger. "Arianna, seriously? You provided a home and care for those children. And I'm sure Kieran would say there's nobody better than you for him."

"He'll forget about me with time—"

Madeline squealed. "Hold on. Hold on! Did you just say 'who can show her *love* for him'? Are you in love with Kieran?"

Did Arianna let that slip?

"Does it change anything?" She peeped through her fingers at her friend. Before meeting Brandon, Madeline would never squeal. She'd been that composed. Only her foster sisters guessed how many undercurrents had run under that iceberg.

"It changes *everything*." Madeline clapped. Not much composure anymore. "Why would you walk away from the man you love and the children you care about?"

Precisely because of that. Arianna moved her hands away from her face, and Madeline's smile slipped away from hers as if she felt the chill in the air.

"You're not telling me something," Madeline said quietly.

Arianna sprang to her feet and started pacing. Movement helped her think. Movement used to help her stay alive. "It might be nothing. But remember how the information about Paisley leaked and a price was put on her head?"

"Did information about *you* leak? From one of your assignments you say you have no right to talk about?" Madeline's crimson lips set in a grim line, and her head moved back and forth following Arianna's steps, the thick rug softening her stomps.

Well, either way, Arianna knew how to move without creating any noise. Being able to fade into the background had saved her plenty of times. Just right now, she wanted to stomp, to shout, to express her frustration somehow. "I don't know any details yet. Victor said he'd been working on it. He heard some rumors. Information is an extremely valuable commodity. It can be bought and sold for the right price. If someone offered a high enough price for information about me, it could be sold to them."

She rubbed the sharp pangs over her stomach. Her profession had kept her sane and given her a sense of purpose for years. Putting her life on the line had seemed a fair trade-off then. She hadn't cared that much about staying alive in the first place, and the constant necessity to be on guard distracted her from her memories, from her emptiness inside.

"I need to go on this assignment. It's not only about this gig Victor received for us. I'd refuse it then. But I need leverage with the higher-ups to find out who might've bought information about me and why. I need a large favor I can call in. The days away can also give me more opportunities to do my research in the field. I can't bring danger to the very people I love with all my heart. I nearly did it once already."

"I understand now." Madeline frowned. "What about the custody arrangements?"

"It's just a short trip." Arianna closed her eyes, and another tear escaped her eyelids. What was going on with her? She didn't remember the last time she'd cried. And now she couldn't stop the tears. "Okay, fine, Jackson and Isabella might be upset, but I must ensure they stay alive. If it's safe for them, I'll be back in three days."

"And if not?"

Madeline's question hit Arianna like a brick, and she opened her eyes. She didn't answer. Instead, she asked, "Will you help take care of them?"

"Of course. I'm sure Jessie will help. Genevieve will be here, too, if needed." Madeline wiped away her own tears. "You can always stay with Brandon and me. You know Jessie and her husband will offer their place and protection to you, as well. Come back to *us* then. We'll keep you safe."

Gratitude swelled Arianna's heart. She was beyond blessed to have her foster sisters. She'd never want to put them in danger, either, but Ronan and Jessie were cops, so there was that.

How was Arianna going to explain all this to Kieran? He'd go into protective mode. She couldn't allow that. And if something happened to her, she wouldn't want him to be devastated.

Another tear slipped out before she could stop it. For the first time in decades.

"I've never seen you cry." Madeline leaped to her feet and took Arianna's hands in hers.

After Arianna turned fourteen, she'd stopped crying. It had seemed her tears only spurred her cousin on when he'd cut the lines on her stomach. A satisfied smile had spread over his face at the sight of her tears, and he'd scooped them up and tasted them. Her mother had called her tears crocodile tears when Arianna had eventually shared what had been done to her. Her father had hit her harder if she'd cried.

To survive, she'd become a woman of steel. Women of steel didn't cry.

So why was she crying now?

"When are you leaving?" Madeline passed her tissues from the nightstand.

Arianna dabbed at her eyes, the lump in her throat growing. This moment of weakness better pass. She sank onto the bed near her suitcase. Where she was going, weakness wouldn't be forgiven. "Tomorrow morning." She closed her eyes and opened them again. "Kieran and I already filed the adoption papers. If something happens to me..."

Jackson and Isabella's lives were tumultuous already. Arianna couldn't add another tragedy to it. She'd have to be careful. Very careful. She'd never had a thirst for life until now. She'd been good at her job partly because she wasn't afraid to die. She swallowed around the lump in her throat.

Now, she was afraid. Her famed courage, so appreciated by her superiors, wasn't courage at all. It was the lack of appreciation for her life.

Madeline's eyes hardened, and she hugged Arianna, though neither one of them was a hugger. "Nothing will happen to you. Either way, I, as well as the rest of our foster sisters and our husbands, will help Jackson and Isabella. When are you going to tell Kieran?"

Arianna's heart squeezed. "It's going to be a difficult conversation. I won't be able to tell him the whole reason." The real reason. This assignment was a dangerous one, hence the possibility to earn a valuable favor. "Plus, I might have a target on my back again if Victor's suspicions are true."

She needed to release Kieran from any obligations. To allow him to move on if something happened to her.

He deserved nothing less.

For that, he'd need to think she was a selfish, even reckless person capable of abandoning her niece and nephew after all they'd gone through. She dared not let him guess she loved him, or it would make things difficult for him if something happened to her.

Her gut twisted at the thought of hurting him. But then he'd have a lifetime ahead of him. She shouldn't have dragged him into the mess of her life to start with, and—now that her cousin was no longer around for her to protect the children from—she needed to correct that mistake for Kieran's sake. She'd even give him a divorce if he wanted it.

And Jackson and Isabella... Why did doing the right thing bring so much pain, especially to the people who didn't deserve it?

"Tonight," Arianna finally said. "I'll talk to him tonight."

Everything in Kieran lit up when Arianna entered the kitchen. "Dinner will be ready soon." He covered the pan with a lid and turned off the stove.

Arianna groaned. "Really? Can you be any more perfect?"

Perfect. What a word to have applied to yourself. He almost rolled his eyes like Jackson had a habit of doing. Instead, Kieran played it up with a wink.

"I never considered myself perfect—after all, I *do* forget to put the cap on the toothpaste sometimes." He wiped his hands on the kitchen towel. His joy dimmed at the sadness dulling her eyes to swamp-water color. "What happened? Are you okay?"

"We need to talk." She gestured to the breakfast nook.

His heart dropped as he followed. Nothing good usually came after those words. "O–okay."

She must still be traumatized after the shoot-out. *He* certainly was. His insides trembled just at the thought of how close he'd come to losing her. He should be more understanding.

Once they sat, he reached for her hand. "What happened must've been horrible for you. But you know I'm here for you." He wanted to say how much she meant to him, but her carefully blanked expression stopped him.

He'd never seen her like this, even at the beginning of their relationship, and her green eyes had been carefully blank a lot then. Then those eyes brightened and got misty. But she blinked fast, and they cleared. "I need to leave for three days. Can you... can you take care of the children?"

"Of course. You don't have to ask. Now Sean is back, I'm not so busy with ranch work." Was *that* what she'd worried about? His heart shifted. He didn't like her going on unsafe assignments, but he wouldn't try to control her. Hopefully, it was just one of those shopping-for-a-unique-gift gigs.

He'd fallen in love with her just the way she was. He wouldn't change a thing. Well, he'd love to remove all the suffering in her life.

Because yes, he'd fallen in love with her. Did he dare to tell her? Considering the heavy look in her eyes, now probably wasn't the time.

"I'll miss you." He couldn't imagine a day apart, much less three, but he wouldn't influence her decision. What would he do if someone had told him to leave the ranch? She was obviously good at her job and enjoyed it. Even if he'd miss her like a limb, he wanted her to be happy.

However, he wouldn't be the only one who'd miss her, who needed her presence badly.

"Have you told Jackson and Isabella yet?"

Her lower lip trembled, though only for a moment. She met his gaze. "Isabella is already tucked in for the night. I'll tell her in the morning. I'll tell Jackson after I speak to you." She removed her hand from his. "That's not all."

His stomach clenched. This wasn't going to end well, was it? He couldn't have been mistaken about that affection in her eyes. And the kisses they'd shared... Heat pooled in his belly at the memory. She'd told him she cared about him very much, and he believed her. But now, she appeared a different person.

Usually, her green eyes looked to him like a forest lake reflecting bright foliage. Now, they were like swamps where he was about to drown if he braved the next step.

"Okay. Tell me." Somehow, he managed to give her an encouraging smile.

She didn't smile back. She looked like a monument made of steel, unmovable. "If you want, I can give you a divorce earlier than we discussed."

What?

His heart plummeted again, and he gaped at her, unable to say a word. How... how could this happen? When he'd thought they were growing closer, apparently they'd been growing apart. Had the signs of her affection for him been his wishful thinking and nothing but gratitude on her part?

He knew he couldn't—wouldn't—tie her down. He'd worried she wouldn't stay. Maybe she'd remained on the ranch for as long as she had not because of him but because of the children. Maybe she cared about him, but not enough to change her lifestyle. She hadn't deceived him about who she was, but he'd thought... He'd hoped...

Everything inside him shook.

Then things started to fall into place. An angry rush of heat surged through his chest and out to his limbs. "This new assignment. Is it with Victor?"

She nodded.

It fit then. He nearly gnashed his teeth. She wasn't just returning to her old job but also to her old flame. The dashing man who led an exciting life instead of a boring one like Kieran had. Did she consider Kieran himself boring, too?

She'd loved that man once, and apparently, those feelings had returned. Or never left. Maybe it didn't matter to Victor that he'd gotten shot because of her. That made sense. Kieran would've gladly taken a bullet for her.

Her leaving now... It crushed him. His lungs screamed for air, and yet the simple task of drawing another breath seemed like an insurmountable one.

Her gaze turned pleading, so unlike her. "Jackson and Isabella..."

"I'll take care of them. I'm not going to stop the adoption process. I'll do everything so they won't go back to that family or into the system." Speaking around the giant lump in his throat was a struggle, but he had to push the words out. "I'll sign whatever papers you want me to sign. I hope your trip is great."

Hurt glazed her eyes. But why? Wasn't that what she'd wanted? To be free to live the life she wanted with Victor? The expression disappeared so fast he wasn't sure he'd seen it.

He couldn't imagine his life without her. "Are you going to return?"

"I don't know," she whispered.

That answered his question, and his heart shattered. Her eyes glistened, but it couldn't be from tears. She'd told him she never cried.

Chapter Sixteen

The conversation with Jackson and Isabella had been gut wrenching.

Arianna would change her mind if she didn't believe her very presence might get them killed. She had a habit of bringing danger to people.

Then Kieran had offered to drive her to the airport, and she'd refused. The look in his eyes had almost shattered her. He wanted to carry her duffel bag out to her car, but she shook her head. Tears burned her eyelids, but she couldn't allow herself to fall apart. She'd need every ounce of concentration. Attending to her broken heart would have to be postponed.

She hugged her niece, though her nephew would never let her, and she couldn't bring herself to hug Kieran. Even though she'd give up her life to be able to crawl into his arms again and feel the tenderness of his embrace.

Well, if Victor's suspicions proved to be true, she might not have much life left to give up.

Her hands shook as she clicked on the fob, and the keys rattled into the yellowed grass. So much for being concentrated.

Isabella rushed forward, picked up the keys, and handed them to her. "Come back soon, Auntie. We'll miss you." She hugged Arianna's legs and held on tight.

It took all Arianna's willpower not to break down right there. "I love you. I'll miss you." She couldn't say she'd return soon. She wouldn't make a false promise.

Kieran's amber eyes hardened like resin when their gazes met. She didn't blame him for being angry. She'd upended his life. Somehow, she'd need to change all that chaos into a peaceful existence. If Victor was wrong, she'd return to the kids, and she'd figure out how to co-parent with Kieran.

Maybe?

Or had she lost him already? Trying to breathe around the unbearable sense of loss, she leaned to Isabella and kissed the top of her head where a butterfly barrette—Arianna's gift—had perched. The scent of mango shampoo made something squeeze her heart. She'd miss them more than she could ever imagine. She'd be leaving her heart behind at the lodge.

Jackson walked to them and peeled his sister away from her. "Come on, Cricket. Our *tía has to work.*" The latter phrase dripped with sarcasm, and his glance cut with accusation.

She had to lean against her car because her legs went weak.

A few moments flashed in front of her. Isabella dancing with the butterflies. Kieran touching Arianna's neck when untying her apron strings and leaving a blaze of fire in the wake of those fingers. Jackson high-fiving her after a lesson. Kieran's admiring glance she'd caught so many times across the dinner table. Him handing her a mug of hot cocoa after they'd gotten drenched in the rain and his fingers staying on hers for much longer than necessary. The longing in his eyes that tangoed with her longing as he leaned to kiss her.

Such simple and such precious things that she might not have again. She'd spent the happiest times of her life with this family....

Squealing tires made her look in their direction. Only a few people knew the gate code.

Jessie and Madeline leaped out of Jessie's car. Without a word, Madeline snatched Arianna's duffel bag while Jessie took Arianna's elbow and led her to the still-running car.

"What are you doing?" Arianna could've jerked out of that hold, but for some reason, she followed her friends on noodle legs.

"Driving you to the airport." Jessie opened the front passenger door and pretty much folded Arianna inside like an arrested criminal.

"Did I ask you to?"

Madeline snorted unladylike when she slid into the back seat with the duffel bag. "We're your friends. We don't have to be asked."

Arianna opened her mouth to protest, but Jessie already jumped into the driver's seat and took off. Of course, Arianna could make a run for it when they stopped to wait for the gate to reopen. But a large part of her was grateful for her friends' supportive presence.

So she just said thanks.

Jessie tapped on the steering wheel as they left the gate. "I spent the night thinking about what Victor told you and doing research."

Arianna cringed. "You shouldn't have."

"I was careful." Jessie made a turn from the country road to the freeway. "Did it occur to you that he has a stake in the game? The reasons he might want to have you back?"

Did Jessie hint he could've twisted the information he'd provided? Doubt had crawled into Arianna's mind before, but she couldn't risk Kieran and the children's safety in case Victor was right. Their safety was a priority.

Arianna rolled her eyes, just like Jackson had many times. It must be rubbing off on her. "Did I ask you to interfere?"

Jessie waved her off. "Didn't you hear Madeline? We're your friends. We don't have to be asked."

"That's right," Madeline chimed from the backseat. "By the way, Genevieve is flying in from Houston to help with Jackson and Isabella. She's got lots of experience with children. She'll also try to talk some sense into you."

Arianna groaned over the motor's growl. "I don't need anyone to talk sense into me! Besides, what reasons could Victor have to lie to me?"

"Revenge, greed, even love. Revenge because you caused him to get wounded. Greed because it's a lucrative assignment and the client requested you again. Love because he might still be carrying a torch for you."

"Yeah," Arianna grumbled. "I'm *that* lovable."

"Yes, you are." Madeline leaned forward in the rear passenger seat and gripped Arianna's shoulder. "We adore you, in a sister kind of way. And plenty of guys wanted to get to know you better. You never gave them a chance."

Jessie passed a truck the color of Kieran's eyes. "I'm glad you gave Kieran a chance."

Right. Talk about giving him a chance. Arianna ducked her head and swallowed hard. "I offered him a divorce, and he agreed to sign the papers."

Jessie threw her hands up in the air, then slammed them back to the steering wheel. "Are you kidding me? Why would you do that?"

"Um, so he wouldn't suffer if something happens to me, obviously. And to give him freedom if it doesn't. After all, I emotionally blackmailed him into marrying me."

Jessie shook her head as if in disbelief. "We'll sort out that mess when we're back."

Arianna's gaze swept over the sprawling hills spotted with cows and trees majestic with autumn color. Soon the trees would be bare like her soul. But did it have to be that way, at least for her?

The increasing longing in her heart told her she'd gotten attached to this place and to the hardworking, honest, caring people of this land. Especially to one particular man.

Her heart fluttered just at the thought of him. Could she and her children put down roots here?

Because they were *her* children. She nearly told Jessie to turn the car around.

No. First, she needed to get to the bottom of this. As a teen, she'd spent years tolerating pain and hoping things would get better on their own. They hadn't.

There were times for patience and times for action. She knew which one this was now.

Mission accomplished.

Three days later, adrenaline still pumped through Arianna's veins as she picked up her worn-out duffel bag, but not at as high a rate as during the trip. She stroked its lumpy charcoal-gray surface with affection, then slung the strap over her shoulder, and marched toward the car rental place. The bag had a couple of leather patches she'd put there out of necessity and not for fashion purposes.

She could've bought much newer, fancier luggage that she could just roll. But this bag had accompanied her on so many travels that the only way she'd abandon it was if it became so threadbare things started falling out of it. And that wouldn't do, considering that a taken-apart gun would be one of those things. The worn-out look also told a passerby there was nothing valuable in the bag, and she wanted it that way.

Flipping back her blonde wig, she pushed her clear-lensed glasses up on her nose as she studied her surroundings. All clear so far. She disliked the nauseatingly sweet scent of her perfume, generously splattered on her leopard-print jacket, but it needed to be done. People often remembered scents more vividly than they remembered appearances, even if they didn't realize it.

As she wove among people, the scents of perfumes, coffee, hamburgers, and some other food filled her nostrils while a conversational buzz purred into her ears. She used to like it, especially when the words and scents were unfamiliar.

Why had a loner like her sought out crowds? Was it because it was easier to disappear among strangers? Because they'd distracted her from her memories? Because no one could hurt her in a crowd?

Or because no strangers could know just *how* broken she was?

Watching her surroundings from time to time, she texted Victor and Jessie that she'd landed and everything had gone great. Jessie would let the rest of the foster sisters know.

Then Arianna filled out the rental car forms fast. Her sisters would gladly pick her up, but she'd forced herself to rely only on herself and avoided asking for favors, even from her siblings.

Sadly, her research had netted zero results, but she'd called in the newly earned favor with the necessary people. She'd hear something back soon.

Her fingers wrapped around the sparkling keys, and she walked to the nearest restroom that was thankfully empty. Her movements rapid and precise from years of experience, she unlocked the bag's zipper, then pulled her gun parts from the check-in baggage, and assembled it fast. She discarded the jacket in the trash and slipped into a stall. Sparkly shoes were exchanged for high combat boots, and she added the much-needed accessory of the ankle holster and the gun hidden inside the boot. The blonde wig went into the duffel bag, and the clear glasses did, as well. A black cap and sunglasses took their place. Jeans were such a widespread staple that they could stay.

She hurried outside the restroom and outside the building, after making a quick sweep that nothing was suspicious, of course. The air was much colder than where she'd come from, nearly crisp, and it energized her as she rushed to the car. Even the sky, gray and cloudy, didn't dampen her mood or smother her anticipation of seeing Kieran and the children soon.

Her rib cage constricted.

Why oh why had she asked him for a divorce? *What* was she thinking? She'd wanted to give him back his freedom if he wanted it, but there had to have been a better way to do it. She hadn't asked what he wanted, what *he* felt before uttering those fateful words. Her communication skills were truly nonexistent.

She slipped inside the nondescript car and placed the duffel bag in the back, then turned the key in the ignition. The motor revved to life. A yellow-hued vanilla air freshener danced in the air, and the scent reminded her of Genevieve who loved to bake. Maybe Arianna and Isabella could bake some cookies tonight. But even if people said that the way to a man's heart was through his stomach, it would take way more than a few batches of cookies to find her way back to Kieran's heart.

As her fingers tightened around the smooth steering wheel, she studied her simple wedding ring without a single diamond.

Her heart squeezed as she drove from the parking lot. She didn't want to give the ring back. Not because of the ring, of course, but because she didn't want to leave him. She'd done her job well, was proud of it, but the entire trip she'd been miserable without him, Isabella, and Jackson.

Maybe the reason she'd loved crowds of strangers was that the people close to her had hurt her. Being with strangers felt safer. At the time, she hadn't found *her people* yet, except for her foster sisters, of course. Now she had found them.

As she pulled onto the freeway, she grimaced, her frown deepening at the heavy traffic. She'd messed up with Kieran, but would she still have an opportunity to correct her mistake?

She studied the rearview mirror for any tail, then changed lanes several times and glanced in the mirror again to check if anyone followed. So far so good, and her shoulders relaxed a bit.

This trip felt different from the previous ones. She couldn't wait for it to end. She'd known she'd miss Kieran and the children, but the sheer force of overwhelming longing surprised her.

That man had her heart in the wide palm of his callused hand, and he didn't even know it. That heart stuttered.

A luxury white car cut her off, dashing in front of her and almost skimming her bumper. Mindful of the cars behind her, she tapped on the brakes, but her reaction was slower than she liked. She rolled her eyes. She'd gotten spoiled at the ranch where there were way more cows than people and life was hard but peaceful.

Except when Tanya had shown up to shoot her.

Did Arianna have the right to disrupt that peace? Was it selfish to go to the ranch just because she craved to see Kieran, Jackson, and Isabella? Should she stay with Ronan and Jessie, who were both cops, until things cleared?

She'd better decide before she got closer to town.

Completing this assignment so well had given her a much-needed opportunity to ask her higher-ups a favor. They'd promised they'd find out whether any leak with her information had happened, and if so, when and how as well as from whom and to whom and what info had been leaked.

With renewed hope, she glided between vehicles and glanced in the mirror again, then nodded to herself. She knew how to spot a tail, be it in the car, on foot, or even on the back of a camel.

Her heart skipped a beat. How would Kieran meet her? Really, how could she expect him to welcome her back after what she'd done? She didn't, but she'd do whatever she could to correct it—*if* it wasn't too late. Was it?

Something cold gripped her heart again as she changed lanes to take the exit she needed. Another car followed, and she tensed, but the apple-red SUV didn't stay behind her long.

Paranoid, much? Or not enough?

She wasn't sure about many things, but one thing was crystal clear. She needed Kieran, Jackson, and Isabella in her life more than she needed to breathe. But did they still want or need her in theirs?

Her nerves getting taut already, she swallowed hard. One good thing that happened on this trip had been with Victor. She smiled as she paid attention to the road signs. If someone had told her years ago that she'd be this exhilarated to learn he'd fallen in love, she wouldn't have believed that person. Yet when Victor had asked her for advice about an engagement ring and any tips on how to propose to the amazing woman he'd met, she'd been thrilled.

And now, when she knew what true love felt like, she knew what she'd once felt for him didn't come close. She'd persuaded herself they should be together because they shared the same interests, but she'd been wrong.

There was only one man in the world for her, and there was no doubt in her mind. She just wished she hadn't pushed that man away forever.

A vise wrapped around her heart and clenched. All her life, she'd avoided this kind of commitment and love and the uncertainty and pain that came with it. But she didn't want to avoid it any longer. Kieran, Isabella, and Jackson were worth it. She even missed the ranch, its endless sky and rolling hills and multitude of animals. She hadn't approached a cow yet—it was great she didn't have to milk them—but she'd patted a horse, so there was that.

Ha. She missed cooking for a bunch of people—who'd think?

She missed Isabella squealing when Arianna suggested a new butterfly barrette and tiny arms hugging her, missed tucking the girl in bed. Difficult to believe, but she missed Jackson, as well, because she knew now that, just like with her, vulnerability hid behind the outward indifference laced with arrogance.

And oh how much she missed Kieran, the way his eyes lit up when he'd enter the front door and see her in the house. The way he held her when she'd been hurt. The way he ignited a fire in her belly when he kissed her. The way he was always, always there for her, including the times she wasn't nice to him. Everything in her craved his gentle touch, his calm voice, his scent of cedarwood and hay that enveloped her like a soft blanket and his very presence...

He was the glue that brought her broken pieces together and made something new.

Maybe God had done this? Was Kieran right, and God *did* care for Arianna, had cared all along?

She still had a lot of healing to do, but she now knew healing was possible. She could be a different, better person. She didn't want to run anymore. She wanted to stay and build a life brick by brick and kind word by kind word, and she knew where she wanted to stay and with whom. She could open her heart to God and to faith.

Hope unraveled inside her, swelling her chest.

Then she pulled herself out of her daydreaming and scanned the road behind her. The closer she was to the small town, the slower traffic was becoming. Several raindrops hit the windshield, but nothing major yet.

Then she zoomed in on a car with emergency lights on the roadside far ahead. Did they have a flat tire or a mechanical issue? She tapped on the brake. Should she stop?

Stopping and asking if they needed help was the right thing to do. What Kieran would've done. But Victor's warning flashed in her mind, and her eyes narrowed. Could this be a trap? Guilt stabbed her as she was about to drive by.

Then a man stepped from behind the side of the car, carrying a baby bundle. Her rib cage constricted as he gestured with his phone.

Did his phone battery die? She couldn't leave someone with an innocent baby to suffer, especially with a storm about to start and the temperature outside dropping. Besides, she was armed. How could she be a better person if she left a father and a tiny child stranded?

Decided, she pulled to the side and turned off the engine. The maternal instinct she didn't know she had before meeting her niece and nephew called to her. Then she pulled out her phone to call for road assistance if the guy had been unable to do so. Premonition almost overpowered her, but she shook it off. Usually, she paid attention to her intuition, but she'd been paranoid since Victor had told her about the possible danger, constantly looking over her shoulder.

She slipped out of her car and rushed to the guy with the child. "You can use my phone if you need to..."

Then she realized she couldn't see the baby's face in that bundle with a pink ribbon, and he hid his behind it, as well. And *why* would a man remove the child from a warm and dry car in the first place?

She threw herself on the ground a split second too late as he pulled out a gun from the baby blanket bundle and fired at her. The gunshot thundered, echoing with the rumble in the sky far away. Sharp pain erupted in her chest.

What... How...

She didn't want to die! She hadn't even told Kieran how much she loved him. And Jackson and Isabella...

A crimson fog already started filling her brain, and she didn't think she could breathe any longer. But the second bullet would kill her for sure.

He threw away the baby bundle for the decoy it was and lifted his gun again.

Gathering all her remaining strength, she managed to pull out her gun and squeeze the trigger, trying to aim at his center mass but firing blindly. Her consciousness was slipping away like a red-tinted mist she couldn't hold onto any longer.

At least, she hadn't brought danger to Kieran and the children. She'd been right to leave them. Now she'd be the only one hurt. She needed to fire again. But the gun rolled from her weak fingers, and her eyes closed as her face hit the asphalt. She didn't have the strength even to open her eyelids, much less lift her head or move her fingers.

Rain poured down, but she barely felt it. Was this going to be it?

As the world disappeared, her last thought was about Kieran.

Chapter Seventeen

Kieran tensed. He loved his family, but he needed to be alone right now.

Anger surged as he glared at Declan in the field close to a cluster of oaks and maples, their bright foliage underscoring Kieran's mood.

Was it so hard to understand? And if there was a pressing issue needing his attention while Sean was in Springfield getting tractor parts, he'd take care of it in a few minutes, when he pulled himself together.

Besides, if he wanted to talk to someone in the family, it wouldn't be Declan.

Loud, flighty, and nomadic, not steady and quiet like the rest of the family, Declan got along well with Arianna because they were alike in the sense of never staying in one place and nearly scoffing at the value of family.

He'd thought Arianna started to value him and his family, that she'd searched for her place in the world and that place could be at the ranch with the children and him. He'd been wrong.

He grimaced instead of offering his usual smile, but Declan didn't take a hint. Without a word, Declan sat nearby on the grass and stared beyond the horizon, probably thinking about the faraway places that always tempted him.

Just like Arianna.

Kieran clenched his jaw. He had nothing against traveling, would go with Arianna again if she'd ever asked, and wouldn't change who she was. But he didn't want to lose her, even to someone who could be more adventurous, who understood her better, and who would help her keep running from her memories.

"She'll come back soon. You'll see," Declan said in a voice unusually quiet for him.

Was Kieran that transparent?

"How do you know?" He slid down the oak trunk to be on his brother's level, crisp, vibrant leaves crunching beneath him.

Declan picked up an acorn and studied it as if it were some kind of treasure. In a way, it was. One day it might become a large oak and give shade and oxygen to people and animals and homes to birds and squirrels.

It was interesting how it worked. Something small and, at first glance, insignificant could become something so large and important.

Just like his love for Arianna grew from a kernel of attraction to something huge that still overshadowed his world, rooted deep in his soul.

"Come on! I saw you interact with Arianna. It was clear how much you love each other." Was that envy raising Declan's voice?

Nah, couldn't be. Declan was content traveling the world in search of a new newsworthy sensation, attracting women fast and leaving them just as fast. Unlike the rest of the family, he'd never had any interest in staying at the ranch—or in a steady relationship, for that matter. Well, except in high school, but that had happened decades ago.

Unless that story had affected him more than he'd let on. Kieran studied his brother. Declan had always been easygoing, an antidote to his brothers' seriousness. Everything seemed to roll off him like spring runoff to the creeks. But was it really that way?

"Everything will be fine." Declan patted Kieran on the shoulder as if projecting his own happy-go-lucky attitude.

That attitude that glossed over Kieran's pain to give him a false hope rubbed him the wrong way. Something rebelled.

"This isn't right." He slammed a hand against the soft earth, pummeling something that was faultless, not to mention as steady and giving as he was. "I've always played by the rules—always worked hard and taken responsibility for myself and others. I gave Arianna my everything, all my love and devotion."

What had he gotten in return? A cavity deep in his soul, his body hurting as if his insides were ripped out.

Yet Declan didn't seem to have a care in the world, and it worked great for him.

Kieran stood and straightened to his full height. "That love you thought you saw was one-sided. It doesn't look like Arianna ever cared about me."

The air grew more humid, and the wind picked up, whispering something in the bright foliage above them. They needed to go back before the storm started, but Kieran wasn't ready to face people yet.

Thunder rumbled, reminding him of the time he, Arianna, Jackson, and Isabella ended up in the rain. Long, wet strands of mahogany-hued hair had hung around her face, but it had only made her more beautiful. Her green eyes had sparkled, and so had the raindrops on her skin. He'd wanted to kiss every tiny drop away, including the ones on her eyelashes, and his pulse picked up speed at the thought.

When their gazes had met that amazing day over their mugs, attraction swirled in hers, sweetness mixed just like in their mugs, sending jolts of astounding joy through him. Her resistance to love had seemed to be melting together with marshmallows, and so had his heart.

How could he have been so mistaken about all of that? The said heart ached now. "I want to be alone."

Declan got up, as well, and brushed straw and leaf debris from his pants. "Understood. But if you ever need to talk, you know that... well, I might not be around all the time, but I'm here now."

"I know. I mean, I know I can come to you if I need to talk." Kieran stumbled. "We should head back."

Declan nodded, looking relieved.

Great. Kieran stifled a groan as they strode toward the distant ranch house. Declan had shown compassion and understanding, and Kieran had nearly pushed his brother away, yes, because he'd been hurting but also because in some way his lifestyle and mentality were different from Declan's.

Had he been internally judgmental in the same way toward Arianna and she'd noticed it?

Drops splatted on Kieran's forehead when Declan's phone rang.

Not the best time to answer, but of course, he did. His life seemed tied to the phone and social media where he'd posted his travel adventures. Unlike Declan, Kieran knew when to put his phone on silent, which he did most of the time.

Ouch. He slowed his pace for his brother. Again, he was being judgmental.

Wait—Declan's eyes went huge. Something was wrong. More raindrops plopped on Kieran, but he didn't care as premonition overtook him.

Declan went pale like snow. "Thank you for letting me know. Kieran is right here with me. We'll meet you in front of the house." He slipped the phone into his pocket, more compassion than usual filling his gaze as he raised it. "We've got to run."

"Because of the rain?"

"Because Arianna was shot." Declan took off in a sprint.

For a moment, Kieran's mind refused to process his brother's words because he must've misheard.

Because it couldn't be the truth, right?

Then he had to get out of his stupor and force his legs, which seemed to be made from cotton, to move and keep up with Declan. "Is she alive? Is she okay?" Though how could she be okay if she was shot?

If he'd previously thought his heart had been shredded, the pain had been nothing compared with now. He'd give her freedom and anything else she wanted, he'd let her go if only he could know she was alive and happy... somewhere. Even if it wasn't with him.

The thought of her not existing... He couldn't bear it.

"I don't know much." Declan spoke over his shoulder, his voice apologetic. "Jessie told me all she knew. Arianna is in the hospital in Springfield. Her sisters are heading there right now. They called you, but you weren't picking up. So then they called the rest of us, starting with their husbands."

Right. Because Kieran's phone was on silent mode. His cheeks heated as his feet beat the grass. Then his heart went cold while they rounded the house. "What about Isabella and Jackson?"

"Madeline brought Isabella to Mom, and Mom will watch the girl. I'll pick Jackson up from school. Between myself and the rest of us, we'll take care of the children. And Sean should be home soon."

Kieran had always known he could rely on his family. But he didn't expect the brother he'd considered the least reliable to come through for him. If worry for Arianna didn't overwhelm him already, gratitude would mix with this guilt. "Thanks, bro."

"That's what family is for."

Kieran knew that. He just hadn't known Declan knew it, as well.

A rumbling motor alerted them to the car's arrival. Madeline waited by the front porch. She and Kieran jumped inside the moment the police car stopped. It smelled of lavender and citrus, and it felt... too normal for the situation.

Jessie glanced back at him from the driver's seat and nodded in acknowledgment without a single word. With her face ashen and her gray eyes dark, she looked like the storm clouds. If she could create thunder, she would. Instead, she took off, burning rubber.

Madeline twisted in her front passenger seat, her face ghostly, her blue eyes shiny. "I can't even imagine... if Arianna doesn't make it."

His heart about stopped beating.

"We've got to pray. And we've got to keep ourselves together. For Arianna's sake," Genevieve said near him, her lips in a grim line.

He turned to her as if she were a life raft and he were drowning. "What happened? How? And how serious? Was it on her assignment?" Should he have stopped Arianna from going? But he could never forbid her to do things. He'd respected her too much.

He'd already decided he'd sign the divorce papers if she wanted him to. So she could be with that guy. Kieran's entire universe right now revolved around her next heartbeat. He just wanted her to survive. He prayed like he'd never prayed before, each thought, each word a desperate plea.

"We don't know yet how serious it is." Genevieve gripped his hand as if she could hold him together—or maybe she needed something to hold onto as much as he did. Kindness shone in her hazel eyes as they reflected the worry everyone in the car grappled with. "No, it wasn't on Arianna's assignment. She texted Jessie that the assignment went without a hitch and she landed in Springfield. You probably know she took this assignment only because she needed to call in a favor with the higher-ups."

He blinked. "No, I didn't know that. I thought she took it because she wanted to—because it was the kind of work she loved." And because of Victor, but Kieran didn't want to sound bitter. Arianna's life mattered way more than his jealousy and heartbreak.

"Seriously?" Jessie said from the driver's seat, passing one car after another. She didn't put on the siren, but she must've been tempted to by the way her fingers tightened on the steering wheel and she leaned forward as if it would make the car go faster. "In case you didn't notice, she loved being with you and the children and the ranch. We've never seen her blossom like that."

The thought would've put so much joy in his heart if Arianna's life weren't slipping away second by breathless second.

"Victor feared her information might've been leaked and others beside her cousin's wife could be after her. So she needed leverage to find out if that was true. Until then, she could be a danger to you and the children. She needed to neutralize any threats before she could let herself be near you. No matter how much she wanted to be." Genevieve's full lips flattened into a thin line, her fingers tightening around his.

Arianna... *what*? He usually understood things fast, but this time, he felt like trying to see through a thick mental fog. "Hold on. I thought she left me for Victor."

Jessie groaned as she weaved between traffic. "You guys really need to communicate better."

Madeline twisted in her seat again. "Why would she do that if she loved you?" Then her hand flew to her mouth, smudging crimson lipstick.

"She said she wanted to divorce!" His mind spun, and his hand jerked free from Genevieve's grip to wave in the air. Then everything stilled. The fog cleared. "Wait a moment! Did you say she *loved* me?"

"I said too much." Madeline clammed up as she turned back in her seat, and he couldn't even try to read her facial features.

Wow.

Okay.

Okay.

This couldn't be real.

Arianna... loved him?

But the main thing was for her to survive. He turned to Genevieve, who seemed the most understanding of all the foster sisters, so it was astonishing she was still single. "Please tell me how..." He had to force the words out. "How she was shot. And if... if there's any hope."

"There's always hope." Her hazel eyes dimmed. "While she's still alive."

He winced at the latter part.

Someone honked as Jessie passed more cars, but she didn't seem to pay attention, her back rigid.

Genevieve drew a deep breath. "She landed safely back in Springfield and rented a car. I wish she'd called us to pick her up, but she can be way too independent for her own good." Affection coated her words, despite the huff that followed them.

Jessie spoke next. "On the way back, she stopped for an apparently stranded car and was ambushed. I only know what the duty officer told me, reported to them by another driver who saw it all. Sean also stopped to help, not realizing at first that one of the victims was Arianna, but didn't see the shooting."

His heart plummeted. "It was a setup."

"Yes." Genevieve nodded.

"But who else wanted to kill her?" His heart squeezed. After the other attempted shooting, now this.

She had to live. She had to.

"That's what she took the assignment to find out. Victor found out, but too late to prevent the shooting." Genevieve released a sigh. "He called Jessie to pass on the information he'd uncovered, since he couldn't reach Arianna and it was urgent. Eleven years ago, she rescued a kidnapping victim, a woman who married a rich guy and was held for ransom by her own brother.

"The kidnapper was recently released from jail, festering with resentment. Somehow, he managed to finagle information about Arianna's location. Victor discovered the guy was headed for Missouri and out to get revenge."

Kieran wasn't a man of violence, but he hoped he'd never meet the man who'd shot Arianna because he'd choke that person with his bare hands. "What happened next?"

"Seems he pretended to have broken down on the Springfield road and was standing beside his car with a baby in his arms. There was no child, of course, just a decoy. When Arianna stopped to help, he shot her. She managed to reach her ankle holster and shot back when she was already on the ground. Another woman driving past saw everything, stopped, and called 911. Good thing there's a witness to report he shot first, because there'll have to be a police investigation. When the ambulance arrived, the man who shot Arianna was dead."

Chapter Eighteen

Kieran sank into an uncomfortable chair in the hospital hall in Springfield, flanked by Jessie and Madeline.

With Arianna in surgery, all they could do now was wait. Jessie's stoic face could be carved from stone. Madeline sobbed on Genevieve's shoulder who patted her friend on the back, her own tearful eyes brimming.

Maybe it was because of the condition he was in, but every molecule of the air seemed to be bursting with despair and worry. The overbearing, scalpel-sharp scents of antiseptics. The tired scent of the plastic from the gray chairs, ripped in some parts and exposing yellow stuffing like pus on infected wounds.

He hid his face in his palms. A huge lump lodged in his throat, and tears burned behind his eyes, begging for release.

What could he tell Jackson and Isabella if Arianna didn't make it? Isabella hadn't stopped asking for her auntie and counting the days and then the hours until her return. He shuddered. He couldn't think like that. He wouldn't think like that.

No, Arianna had to make it. She had to!

Heavy footfalls against the tile didn't make him lift his head. He didn't want to move, and every breath came at a cost. He couldn't even pray any longer. Why was this happening? Why?

The foster sisters had suffered so much in childhood. And even as adults, they'd seemed to attract danger—and bullets. Of all the sisters, Arianna had seemed to take on most of it. If he could give his own life so she lived, he wouldn't hesitate for a second.

A heavy hand landed on his shoulder. "Hey, bro."

He looked up at Brandon. Concern twisted his brother's features. Of all his brothers, Kieran had felt closest to Brandon because they'd been the most alike.

Madeline ran to her husband, still sobbing, and he hugged her with one hand as she cried into his chest but didn't step away. Ronan nodded to Kieran, then sat in the chair near his wife without a single word and drew her close. Jessie seemed to go limp in her husband's arms. Compassion mingled with awkwardness. Few men knew what to say to comfort brokenhearted women.

Kieran forced himself to think about the things that needed to be done. "How are Isabella and Jackson?"

"Blissfully ignorant for now. Mom is with Isabella. Declan is playing video games with Jackson. Jackson warmed up to Declan way faster than to the rest of us."

"Declan always had great people skills," Ronan said.

A tiny part of Kieran was relieved, but he couldn't imagine having Jackson and Isabella's world explode again when they learned the news. Should he have brought them here, just in case they needed to say... goodbye?

He couldn't think that! A shiver ran down his spine that had nothing to do with the cold, though they sure kept hospitals nearly like refrigerators for humans. The rain kept hitting on the windows as if asking to be let in.

He'd dreamed of Arianna letting him into her heart, but now that she had—possibly, if Madeline was right—he could lose her forever. He couldn't accept that. Ever.

His brothers didn't say everything was going to be alright, and he was grateful for that.

Brandon led Madeline to the vacant chair and sat her down gently, then lowered himself to the chair nearby. She hid her face in his shoulder, and her sobs became more like hiccups.

Ten minutes later, Sean arrived, face tight and pale. He'd seen—no, Kieran couldn't let himself think what his brother might have seen on the roadside.

"Any news?" Sean's firm hand gripped Kieran's shoulder.

"Not yet." The passing seconds stretched his taut nerves, ready to snap.

Sean slumped into a hard plastic chair beside the others. Ronan's lips were moving, and so were Brandon's. Sean's now, too. Were they praying? Kieran managed to join in the chorus of silent prayers, though everything inside him shattered.

When a doctor in forest-green scrubs entered the room, everyone leaped to their feet. The guy was young, much younger than Kieran was used to, and unfamiliar. The doctor looked around as if reluctant to start, and Kieran's stomach dropped onto the grayish tile.

No!

No, no, no. Feeling as if he were suffocating, he pulled on his Wrangler's shirt and ripped the upper button out to be able to breathe.

The doctor looked around. "Are you the family of Arianna Montemayor-O'Neill?"

"Yes, all of us," Kieran said. That was true. Whether Arianna realized it or not, they were her family.

"We extracted the bullet," the doctor continued. "By some miracle, it didn't hit any major organs or arteries. It did damage some tissues, and she lost a lot of blood. We've given her blood transfusions and repaired the damage the best we could."

Kieran froze, afraid to believe the good news. It... it *was* good news, right? It was as if his entire life was hanging on a thin thread of the doctor's next words. "Does that mean she'll live?"

"Yes." The doctor nodded.

Madeline would've fallen to the floor if her husband hadn't caught her. Everyone brightened but stilled as if afraid to believe the words yet because anything could still happen. Infection, fever, other complications.

Kieran went light with relief and hope and nearly sank to the floor, too. It was as if all sounds and scents disappeared. His entire world concentrated on two words.

She'll live.

The doctor sent Madeline a worried gaze, but she stood straighter, her posture more determined now, so he continued. "Could be worse, but the person who stopped to help also significantly reduced the bleeding by applying pressure to the wound."

Kieran didn't even know that woman's name to thank her, but he thanked God for her, with his whole heart.

"The road to full recovery will be long, but there's much more hope than before the surgery. Once the anesthesia wears off, a nurse will allow one of you in the room." The doctor turned to Kieran. "You're the husband?"

Kieran nodded as his mouth went dry and he couldn't utter a word.

"Unless there's a good reason for someone else to, you'll see her first. Correct?"

A chorus of voices said yes.

Thank You, Lord!

The doctor probably figured Kieran was the husband because he was the only man in the room with a wedding ring on his finger but without a woman by his side. But then, there might be another reason for the quick guess.

Tears were running down his face.

Arianna was floating in the ocean.

It was peaceful and calm and friendly, and she was drifting away from the shore where she'd left worry, pain, and all attachments. Only eternal sunshine awaited her now.

All she had to do was to surrender to it.

What was that? A weird scent that didn't belong to the ocean. Something citrusy? How could it have carried over many miles from the shore? But the scent was comforting, so she stopped questioning it.

Then another scent reached her and called to her. Cedarwood and hay. Weird. It belonged here even less than the previous ones. It tugged at her memory and hugged her like a warm blanket. She'd welcome it, but it pulled her back to the shore.

A place she didn't want to go because she needed to escape. Escape something... Something horrible. Pain, so much pain.

Disappearing into the sea, becoming as light as the foam was what she wanted to do. She'd struggled for a long time. She'd given her best. But maybe her best wasn't enough.

There were hushed voices, vaguely familiar, but she couldn't place them. No, it couldn't be voices. Must be birds in the sky. One of them seemed to dive into the ocean as if spotting fish, but it was too far to say for sure. Everything was a blur.

The ocean stroked over her arms oh so gently. She needed to remember something, and her exhausted mind struggled. But it was escaping her like water through her fingers. Soon it wouldn't matter, anyway.

It was time, wasn't it?

Someone screamed at her from the beach, but she was too far to see who that was. She must be imagining that tiny dot, because the shore was a thin line on the horizon and soon would disappear completely.

"Sir, you have to leave." A nurse tugged at Kieran's sleeve.

Machines beeped furiously as more people in scrubs rushed inside Arianna's room.

He followed the orders, but he couldn't understand this. Just moments earlier, he'd been by Arianna's side, stroking her arm while avoiding all the IVs. She was asleep, her expression more peaceful than he'd ever seen it.

He and Jessie had been allowed into her room, even though the anesthesia hadn't worn off yet, and he was grateful to be with Arianna already. Madeline, along with his brothers and Genevieve, had left to get some coffee or sandwiches after hanging around outside for some time.

What was going on? It couldn't be what he'd suspected. Horror crushed him as if he'd slipped from a horse and the horse was falling on him. It became difficult to breathe, even to think.

Jessie followed him into the hall, her eyes wild. "They are using a defibrillator. That means her heart stopped."

His own heart nearly did the same. He refused to believe his ears. "It can't be. She was doing fine. I mean, wasn't she? The most dangerous part was behind her. They extracted the bullet. It didn't hit major organs or arteries. She was going to be fine."

He was blabbering.

Jessie's gray eyes turned into giant pools of compassion. "I'm sure the medical personnel are doing everything to bring her back."

Bring her back? But she hadn't left. She was right there.

Alive.

Just asleep.

That was all.

Asleep.

He hadn't realized he was screaming until a burly male nurse with a beard was hanging on him from one side and Jessie was tugging him from the other side while trying to explain something to the nurse. Kieran couldn't hear a word, could only see their lips moving. Then the sounds came back, including his own scream that he needed to stop if he didn't want to be kicked out of the hospital.

Yet he couldn't stop the words from escaping his lungs in one more desperate plea.

"Arianna, please come back to me!"

Arianna was sinking in the wonderful calming waters when she heard the scream. It wasn't the words that somehow pulled her back. She couldn't distinguish them, anyway, except for her name as if someone was calling for her. Needing her.

It was the voice. She couldn't place it, but it was someone who mattered to her. Someone she didn't want to leave behind. Something else tugged at the edges of her consciousness, something as slippery as ice.

Her entire body shook, and some already distant part of her started struggling to get back to the surface.

To the ones she loved. Was it too late?

Another voice was counting. *One, two, three.*

Why?

Then her body shook again. Violently, ruthlessly. She broke onto the surface, but instead of the sunlight she'd hoped for, an onslaught of pain slammed her. Where was the voice that had pulled her back like a rope?

Then the reality hit. She wasn't at the ocean. It wasn't warm.

And it was going to hurt.

Someone unfamiliar spoke, the voice clear and relieved. "She's back."

At this point, Kieran was afraid to believe it.

The emotional roller coaster had left him drained and empty.

Slowly, molecule by invisible molecule, he gathered hope as he held Arianna's warm hand in his, the pulse on her wrist syncing with his own. His heart kept beating because hers had—well, after the most terrifying moments of his life.

He needed this tangible connection, was desperate for it. He'd known how fragile life was, of course, but he'd never experienced it this way.

Her long, slim fingers laced through his. "It's okay. Don't be sad. I'm fine."

Great. She was comforting him instead of the other way around. He groaned.

Then he straightened his back as he gazed into the eyes he'd be happy to look into for the rest of his life. Grateful to.

What was wrong with him? He'd received the most precious gift possible, and still, he'd been harping about how he'd nearly lost her?

"You have no idea how much you mean to me." Joy filled him, tentatively at first as if tiptoeing into a room where everyone was asleep.

"And you to me." She grimaced as she shifted in the hospital bed. "Well, I'm not exactly *fine* yet. But I hope to be. Eventually." She searched his eyes. "I didn't mean it about the divorce papers. Unless you want to—"

"I want you to marry me." Okay, oops, they were already married. But it was a hasty marriage for the children's sake, at least on her part. He wanted Arianna to know she was his world, and this was his way to do it. "I mean, how about renewing our vows?"

Her eyes widened.

His stomach sank. Was Madeline wrong about Arianna loving him? Arianna had never told him she loved him.

But then, he'd never told her, either. Jessie was right. He and Arianna were two people who didn't communicate well at all. He'd thought he'd shown her how much he'd loved her by kissing her, by helping her in any way he could, even by building that tree house with Jackson.

But Kieran had never said the actual words, and maybe he should have. "I love you."

Her face lit up against the pillow. Her eyes turned bright like emeralds, but they were still a tad guarded. "Even if I'm different from everything and everyone you know?"

"That's actually refreshing. I wouldn't change a thing about you. I love how caring you are and how you'd do anything for the people you love, even risk your life. I love your adventurous streak and your thirst for new experiences.

"I love every strand of your luscious mahogany hair, every tiny dot in your striking green eyes, and every one of your freckles. Well, the birthmark on your neck drives me particularly crazy. I love your rare courage and your dedication to everything you do." He stroked her fingers while her affection-filled gaze stroked his soul. "The list is so long that I can talk about everything I love about you forever and never run out of things to say."

She stared at him, making him worry he'd gone too far. "Wow. I knew you were a great man, husband, dad, son, and brother. But I didn't realize you could do so much to make a woman swoon. Not that I can swoon properly while in a hospital bed."

"I wish I could do this in a more romantic way for you. To have this confession in a field filled with flowers or in a forest with golden and burgundy foliage. With roses in my hands. Maybe a dinner with candles hidden behind a tree."

She chuckled. "No, candles in a forest wouldn't be a good idea. It could cause a fire."

He loved seeing her smile. He loved seeing her. Period. "Yeah. And wild animals would probably get to the dinner before we did. See, I'm so not good at it."

She chuckled again. "I think you're amazing."

"I was yours for life since the moment I met you. You had my heart long before the day you married me. It's yours if you still want it."

"I do." The words echoed their marriage vows. Her fingers twitched in his grip, then squeezed as if they would never let go. Oh how he wanted to believe she'd never let go of him. "I was scared to love you, scared to get hurt again. I thought broken people like me didn't belong with wholesome people like you. I was afraid my damaged parts would cut you. Maybe it's selfish to love you, but I do."

Elation filled his every cell. "True love is never selfish."

"I can't live without you." She paused and muttered, "Apparently, literally. I love you too much. Nothing would make me happier than spending the rest of my life with you. And Jackson and Isabella."

"Of course." Oops! He should've thought Jackson and Isabella might think he abandoned them. Declan had called him with the children on the line just minutes ago, and Kieran had explained the situation, but still...

"Are they all right?" Worry shadowed her eyes.

"Yes. Would you like to talk to them?"

She thought for a moment. "I sound too weak. I don't want to scare them."

Jessie and Madeline whooped as they entered the room. "Finally! You're communicating."

Arianna snorted. "Yeah, it just took me getting shot for us to express our feelings and start communicating."

Kieran's fingers tightened around hers, and the lump in his throat prevented him from speaking. He could've lost her. More than once.

Madeline sighed. "And it only took me getting a hit on the head to show my true self to Brandon. I'm trying to do better now."

Kieran couldn't blame the sisters. With their childhood and teen years so hard, no wonder they'd learned to hide their tender, bruised hearts to prevent them from getting hurt.

Arianna beamed at her friend. "We're going to do a vow renewal ceremony. It might take some time because I want to *walk* down the aisle."

"I'll do everything I can to help you get better. And while you recover, I'll be happy to carry you everywhere." He kissed her fingers.

She smiled up at him. "There's only one place where I want to be, and that's with you."

Chapter Nineteen

Several weeks later, Arianna entered the lodge leaning on Kieran's arm.

Isabella ran forward, then jumped up and down. "Auntie, Auntie, Auntie, welcome home!" She thought for a moment and grinned. "*Bienvenida.* Jackson taught me that word."

Kieran had brought Jackson and Isabella often to visit Arianna in the hospital and then rehab. But they were much happier at home, and she didn't blame them.

"Thank you, sweetie." She adjusted the girl's slipping pigtails, then leaned down, and kissed her on the top of her head, the sweet scent of mango shampoo comforting like the child's innocence.

"We missed you!" Isabella hugged Arianna's legs tightly as if she never wanted to let go.

Arianna didn't want to let go, either.

Jackson didn't hug her, but as he brought her trusted duffel bag with clothes from the car, a half smile tugged at his lips. Arianna had told him what had happened, but the three of them unanimously decided Isabella had been traumatized enough in her life. All the little girl knew was that Arianna was sick for a while, which was true.

For the first time in many years, Arianna truly felt at home. The sense of belonging enveloped her. She liked the lodge, but she'd felt like a guest here before. She'd felt like a guest even in her apartment in Houston because she'd never stayed there for long, always on the go, ready for the next assignment.

The lodge seemed to greet her differently, as well. It was always kept clean, but now it was sparkling.

Her foster sisters and Kieran's family had wanted to do a welcome-back party. She'd asked them not to. Even after weeks in the hospital and then the rehabilitation center, she was still weak, and she didn't know whether the trip from the rehab center in Springfield to the lodge near Cowboy Crossing would wear her out. She didn't want them to take the strain on her face for displeasure.

"Welcome home, my love," Kieran whispered into her ear, his warm breath sending a delicious shiver over her skin. "*Bienvenida a la casa, mi amor.*"

Appreciating the fact he'd made an effort to learn the phrase, she leaned into him and drank in his strength and affection.

"Jackson, you glad Auntie is home, too?" Isabella glanced back at her brother when she finally released Arianna.

He shrugged, but his eyes softened. "I guess it's all right."

Arianna would take that.

"Auntie, look at my new doll Dad bought me!" Squealing, Isabella tugged at Arianna's hand and led her to the living room.

Kieran had been amazing through the entire ordeal. Arianna had been right. She couldn't have chosen a better man to marry—a better man for her children to adopt as their father—and hearing Isabella call him *Dad* was precious. Arianna had already made it clear she never wanted to take their mother's place. She was happy being their aunt, even though her heart had taken them in fully as her own children. It was right that they should remember their mother. But they'd never had a father figure, so they needed Kieran as their dad.

Right now, their dad, her husband—gulp!—placed her luggage on the floor and helped her to the sofa in the living room where she was grateful to lower herself because her legs were weak.

Her breathing was shaky. At least, the room didn't spin like it used to at the hospital. She promised herself she'd be running her daily miles again. Some day. Just not today. Or tomorrow, either.

The comfy sofa with its cuddly pink and blue throw pillows left by Paisley, the fireplace with their family—yes!—photos, even the chandelier that seemed to wink at her, everything looked more inviting now because this was home.

Home.

The word, so familiar to other people since birth, felt foreign to her, but she already liked it. When Arianna took in her niece and nephew, Paisley had offered to gift the house and its surrounding land to Arianna. She and her husband didn't need the lodge, anyway, while they'd lived at the military base in Germany, and when they returned to the Show Me State after her husband finished his enlistment, they intended to build their own home on a particular parcel of the ranch that meant the most to her husband.

Kieran and Arianna had thanked Paisley for her generosity and decided to pitch in equally and buy the lodge from her. Now, when they came home to the land they loved, Paisley and her husband planned to live in Kieran's cabin on the ranch while they broke the ground for their new home.

Isabella plopped herself on the plush rug in front of the sofa, another splash of color in azure blue. "Auntie, *bwaid* my *haiya*, please." She still couldn't roll her *R*, and the familiar and endearing sound tugged at Arianna's heart.

Kieran spread his arms. "I never learned how to braid hair well."

Arianna's lips tugged up. How nice that at some parental things she could be better than he was. "It's okay. I enjoy doing it."

Tenderness spread through her like when her grandmother had braided Arianna's hair. It had been thoughtful of Kieran to make wood frames for many family photos, including one where little Arianna was with Abuela in a flower garden. He'd carved the word *Grandma* into the frame. She and Kieran had explained to the children about Arianna's grandmother, their great-grandmother. It was important to Arianna for her grandmother to live in their memories, and even more important to her for them to have that knowledge of someone great in the family, even if they'd never met her.

To Arianna, Abuela was the true representative of their culture, carrying out lots of traditions, the most important of them the tradition of kindness. Now when she looked back, in her travels, she'd met a lot of people of their heritage who shared that type of kindness and love.

In a similar photo in a similar frame, Kieran's mother spun Isabella in a field of flowers. It said Grandma on the frame there, too. Isabella had started calling Mrs. O'Neill grandma while Arianna had been away, and Kieran had asked Arianna if she was okay with it. She was more than okay. She was grateful. She'd wanted to give the children a generational structure, *la familia* that in some way she'd taken away from them.

"I'll go start on dinner." Jackson placed the duffel bag with the rest of Arianna's clothes on the rug and strode to the kitchen.

Arianna blinked at Kieran. "Does Jackson cook now?"

Kieran shrugged. "Real men cook."

Her father had the opposite opinion, making Arianna cook for him as a tween and punishing her if it wasn't to his taste. He'd yelled that, while she was in his house, she'd better earn her keep.

She shivered, but then she dismissed the unpleasant memories. She could make her own memories with her own family in her own house now. Well, the house that would become her own soon.

She'd never had to do anything to earn Kieran's love and approval. For many years, she'd been conditioned that she didn't have enough to earn love. That she hadn't been enough. She'd simply given up trying.

Her heart swelled as he hugged her. Thanks to him, she knew now that not only was she worthy of love but also, if crumbs of what seemed like love came with many strings attached, it wasn't love at all.

"You made a miracle with Jackson," she whispered as she secured one braid while Isabella clumsily braided her new doll's hair.

"Nah. He's a good kid at heart." Kieran leaned to her. "What would you like? Tea, coffee, cocoa, something to eat? To take a shower? To start unpacking? Or for me to get lost because I'm fussing too much?"

All she wanted was to be near him. "I'm good. Just... just stay with me." The words came out vulnerable. Something she'd avoided being for decades, but she didn't mind now.

His gaze softened. "Of course. Gladly." He slid his arm around her shoulders and drew her close to his side. "I never want to let you go. Ever."

She rejoiced in his embrace. The main reason this place started feeling like home was because Kieran and the children were there.

She started on the second braid, glad she could do this simple yet so meaningful-to-her task. Her mother had stopped braiding Arianna's hair when Arianna was little, claiming she was too busy, but it had felt like punishment. She'd missed those times of bonding until she finally realized there was no bonding to be had with her mother. Abuela, even when she clearly hadn't felt well, had never refused to braid Arianna's hair. Even the day she died. That was also the last day Arianna had worn a braid.

For many years, she'd worked hard on being independent. Never again did she want to feel weak and unprotected the way she'd felt in her birth family. Yet she knew now that there was no weakness in admitting she needed him.

Because she meant what she'd said. All she wanted was to have Kieran by her side.

Kieran and Arianna were great on their own, but they were much better together.

As she finished the second braid, she kissed the top of the girl's head again, tenderness nearly overwhelming her. If someone tried to harm her little girl, Arianna would go full mama-bear mode on them.

Then why hadn't her own mother? The woman who was so good to others? Was it because she'd loved the wrong man so much?

Kieran's touch and then Isabella's affectionate embrace as she spun and hugged Arianna reminded her to concentrate on the things she had in her life instead of those she didn't. It was high time to stop questioning what had happened to her. She couldn't make her past better, but she could make her attitude toward it better.

Delicious aromas reached her from the kitchen. Was it a vegetable stew?

Was she a bad mother by allowing Jackson to cook instead of cooking herself?

Kieran seemed to read her mind. "Jackson told me he enjoys cooking. Seriously. Helping someone gives him a sense of purpose and direction, and you know how he needed one. Please let him help you. Please let *me* help you."

"I can help, too!" Isabella grinned. "What do you wanna me to do, Auntie?"

"To be happy." The words slipped from Arianna's tongue. She meant them, but she needed to remember Isabella was her own person and not a chance for a do-over of Arianna's unhappy childhood.

Isabella tried to climb onto the sofa, and Kieran helped her up. "I'm happy with you and my brother. And Daddy, of course."

Kieran stiffened. Their gazes met over the top of the girl's head, and a hint of guilt flashed in his. The girl had fully embraced him as a parental figure while still calling Arianna "auntie."

"I didn't ask her to call me that," he mouthed to Arianna.

She rolled her eyes. Of course, he didn't. Plus, during her recovery, he was both dad and mom to the children. She had no intention of replacing their mother and could only be grateful they took a shine to him and finally had a father figure. And that he'd stepped up and embraced the parenthood thrown at him.

"I know." She mouthed back. "I'm glad she does. And thank you."

"I hope you know I'll never cut your wings." He flinched. "Maybe not a good comparison. What I meant is, if you'd like to travel later, that's okay. I want you to be happy."

"I already am. I don't have wanderlust any longer. But maybe in a few years, we could go somewhere we both like. Something the children would enjoy, too. Ireland maybe?" She'd heard so much about it during family dinners. He embraced his heritage. Maybe later, they could expand their travels. It was high time for her to embrace her roots instead of trying to cut free of them, and the children needed to know the beauty of their heritage.

His face lit up. "I'd love that. But what about your unique talents? About the excitement?"

"I had enough excitement recently to last me a lifetime." She grimaced. "As for my talents, I've been receiving requests for translations. I enjoy cooking for cowboys. Besides, Declan talked to me about his travel videos. I could help him with video editing and adding some of my own material." She paused, hoping she could say this right. "The enormous, fascinating world that we've never fully explored is not only around us. It's inside us, as well."

He kissed her on the cheek, leaving a blaze of fire. "Just when I think I can't love you more, you prove me wrong."

"Ditto." She glanced back at Isabella as she didn't want the girl to feel neglected. "Sweetie, would you like me to read you a book?" She couldn't run around with Isabella like she used to, but she could still do some things to make the little girl happy.

"Yes, Auntie!" She jumped from the sofa and brought over a large colorful book. "Daddy bought it for me. Daddy bought me lots of books. And lots of toys."

Kieran lifted Isabella on the sofa again, and snuggling against one of the pink throw pillows, she settled between him and Arianna.

Smiling, Arianna opened the book and started reading about—of course!—a family of butterflies.

He was spoiling Isabella, but Arianna couldn't blame him. She wanted to give Jackson and Isabella the world. She wanted to give Kieran the world, but she had no clue how. She'd never thought she'd make a good wife and mother and wouldn't have started a family if she hadn't been thrown into it. She was still learning.

"Arianna, you complete my world," he said out loud.

Her chest swelled. "Ditto." It was she who apparently didn't know beautiful words and just said that one back again and again. She turned the page but couldn't stop her heart from singing.

"And me, Daddy?" Isabella turned her adorable face up to him.

"And you and your brother, of course." He pressed on her upturned nose.

Her chest swelling, Arianna cherished the moment and tucked it away, then continued reading. She'd once sought happiness in foreign lands, then thought it could be found in being accomplished in her specialist field and earning a lot.

Now she knew happiness was in having her husband care about her, in reading a book to a little girl, and in a surly teenager accepting her and—wow!—even cooking for her. Happiness was in moments like this, and she felt like the most accomplished person ever.

"I'm going to go check on Jackson and see if he needs help." Kieran got up from the sofa. "Is it okay?"

"Of course." She looked after him before returning to the book. It was all so simple, wasn't it?

She could give Kieran the world just by being in it.

Chapter Twenty

Three weeks later...

Seated in a tack room they'd cleared in the barn, Arianna smiled and breathed in deeply the scent of hay. Barn weddings were supposed to be all the rage, but everything about this one was real—no rented venue or props for ambiance. And no marriage of convenience for her and her genuine cowboy.

This day was so different from that one months ago. At that time, she'd been filled with doubts about whether she'd scar Kieran for life, though in a different way than she'd been scarred. She'd been anxious about what the future would bring, whether she'd be able to keep Jackson and Isabella and whether she'd been the right person to keep them to start with. How out of place she'd been at a ranch in the Show Me State where life was too peaceful for her restless soul.

Immense joy spread through her as Madeline brushed her hair. Arianna had decided to try a French braid, and Madeline had volunteered for the job. Her gentle fingers tugged through Arianna's hair, the sensation bringing a tingle to Arianna's eyes as she remembered Abuela. Arianna reached up to squeeze Madeline's hand, knowing Madeline couldn't realize everything this moment meant to her.

Still, as their gazes met in the cheval mirror before them and such softness melted Madeline's former ice-queen persona, Arianna suspected maybe her friend did realize it. Opening herself up to become vulnerable again, Arianna felt closer than ever to her foster sisters. Particularly to Madeline, who'd cut herself off from everyone almost, if not more than, Arianna had until love had freed her, too.

No doubts lingered in Arianna now. She was done being scattered by the wind across the globe. She was done running away from her past hurts, in search of adrenaline and new experiences to help her forget the horrible things.

Sadness lingered, but only for a moment, dissipating like a morning mist. As she looked at herself in the freestanding mirror Kieran's mother had brought into the tack room, she liked her reflection now. Wasn't it amazing how much could change if one looked at it through the prism of love?

Kieran had helped her accept herself the way she was, scarred, damaged, yes, but so worthy of love.

"Why did it take me so long to accept that I wasn't to blame for what was done to me?" she whispered.

Madeline stilled, then continued brushing Arianna's hair. "The main thing is that you realized it." She paused for a while, then started braiding again. "I hope our other foster sisters and I didn't fail you. Maybe we should have…"

Arianna flinched. "No. I wasn't ready then yet. It was too… too raw. I would've pushed you away, and then it would've been so much worse for me. As it was, I knew I could trust you all and rely on you. I needed that more than you can imagine."

Madeline secured Arianna's braid and leaned to her. "I hope you know we'll *always* be there for you."

Gratitude swelled Arianna's chest. "I do know. And the same for you. I mean, I'm there for you all whenever you need it."

"We do know." Tenderness filled Madeline's gorgeous blue eyes. "You're going to have your hands full for a while, though."

Arianna laughed as she got up from the chair and turned to her friend. "Me, living in domestic bliss? Who'd think? Kieran and I even discussed my being a stay-at-home mom if we add a little one to the mix. Alternatively, he said he could be a stay-at-home dad if I decided to keep working."

"Hey, it's the most important job in the world." Something in Madeline's expression changed when Arianna said "little one."

Arianna picked up on it, and her eyes widened. "Are you… are you expecting?"

"We just found out yesterday." Madeline's cheeks pinked. "I–I didn't want to say anything because I don't want to steal your thunder and—"

Arianna squealed and threw her arms around her matron of honor. "Please steal my thunder! Congratulations! I'm so happy for you." She withdrew for a brief second and searched Madeline's eyes. "You're happy, right? Or…"

She'd said she'd wanted a child, but things could change.

"I'm ecstatic." She beamed, glowing already. "And we all know Brandon will be the best dad in the world."

Arianna tsked, then hugged her friend again before releasing her. "Well, I believe *my* husband holds that title."

Madeline chuckled as she rearranged Arianna's pearl-hued dress, a dress she had gone shopping with Arianna for because, well, no one could have chosen Arianna's dress better than Madeline. She'd even approved the buttery-soft tan cowboy boots Arianna had traded her combat boots for—especially when Arianna paired them with a matching belt sporting the O'Neill ranch brand. "He's a great dad for sure. To love children he's not related to this much..."

She picked up the bouquet with dried wildflowers her mother-in-law had picked in the field months ago and Arianna had helped her preserve. Just like Abuela had done before. "We both know family is about so much more than shared blood."

It was best not to mention that people with shared blood were who'd hurt Arianna and shredded her into pieces. Then the people who *weren't* related to her had picked up those sharp pieces, even if the edges had cut them, and patiently put her together like a dangerous puzzle.

Madeline looked at her wedding ring with a shiny diamond. "Yes, it's about love and care and honesty and devotion and..." She stopped, and her eyes clouded. "Do you think God sent us this happiness to compensate for our terrible childhoods?"

"I don't think God needs to compensate for anything. But I'm new to faith. I'm still trying to figure out so many things. I'll grow in faith as I grow in love. Well, one thing I'm sure about. I'll be forever grateful to God for sending people like you and our other sisters, Kieran, and my children into my life."

Saying "my children" felt good. And the decision to adopt them felt right. Just like the decision to marry Kieran felt right. What once had been a desperate last resort had turned out to be the best decision of her life.

"Auntie!" Isabella burst through the door.

Jessie followed the girl and sent Arianna a guilty glance. "I tried to stop her. But she wanted to see you."

"Auntie, you look *pwetty*!" Isabella giggled. She wore a matching French braid and large wings similar to the ones she'd worn to the wedding, but this time in blue. She held a little basket, and it looked like she'd managed to spread half of the petals already.

Arianna leaned to her daughter and adjusted her sparkly tiara. "You look pretty, too. Ready, sweetie?"

Isabella nodded, then rushed out as fast as she'd rushed in, nearly running into Paisley. Paisley had finally gotten to go on an extended "honeymoon" in Europe since her husband's enlistment ended. They hadn't had time for one when they married last spring, but they'd flown in two days ago for Arianna's vow renewal. Now Paisley met Isabella outside and gestured to Arianna that she'd watch the girl.

Should it bother Arianna that, while she considered Isabella her daughter now, the girl still called her "auntie"?

Arianna lifted her chin. It was fine by her. It wasn't about the word or the name but about what she felt for them and what they felt for her. Love and devotion were in her heart, and that was what mattered. And after all, didn't the woman whom she'd called mom fail to care about Arianna?

Arianna had sent her mother an invitation. If she could forgive her cousin, she could forgive her mother. Maybe.

Genevieve entered the small room. "It's time."

She looked at Genevieve. "Did you see my mother among the guests?" She'd reached out to her extended family on her mother's side, and they'd started talking over the phone. She'd sent them invitations. To her surprise and joy, three cousins she'd never met had shown up with their children. But she hadn't seen her mother.

Then she realized none of her foster sisters had met her mother. None of the people in her life now had, and a small, selfish part of her was grateful for that. "I'm her mirror image—well, with the black mascara and eyeliner."

"And a conscience?" Madeline muttered under her breath. Her sisters knew her story now, and apparently, none were fond of Arianna's family.

Genevieve studied her shoes, then looked up, and shook her head.

A chill squeezed Arianna's heart, but she kept her head high. She'd found the people she loved and who loved her and celebrated her, scars and all. Maybe her mother had given Arianna a huge gift by not being present in her life any longer, and Arianna should take it as such and appreciate it.

"I'm sorry." Madeline squeezed Arianna's hand, which was surprising. Madeline wasn't usually one to show affection, but marriage did wonders for her. "It's not easy, and we have to grieve our losses. Then cherish what we have." Her gaze slid to her still-flat stomach. "Now, let's go get your vows renewed to one of the most wonderful men in the world."

Arianna grinned, feeling better already. "*One of* is because the other most wonderful men in the world are standing right beside him, right?"

"And two of them are still single." Jessie nudged Genevieve while walking to the door. "You know, Genevieve, all those wonderful qualities run in the family. You've been hanging out with Declan a lot lately, haven't you?"

"I believe we're running late." Genevieve blushed. "Ready, Arianna?"

And Arianna was. Maybe she'd waited all her life for this man without realizing it.

She followed Jessie, flanked by Madeline and Genevieve, and the new cowboy boots she'd worn beneath her creamy dress thudded on the barn floor.

The open space had been cleared of tractors and hay and filled with chairs the family set up, the season being too cold for a backyard get-together. Like every wedding on the ranch this year, the chairs were mismatched again, just like the outfits, from tuxedos to jeans and parkas. And the mishmash of people filling those chairs had become dear to her, from her husband's family to the crew she fed on his ranch, her dear sisters, her cousins she wanted to get to know better, and even her hardcore former coworkers. Were those tears in Victor's eyes? The petite and lovely blonde beside him gazed at him with adoration.

Arianna had never imagined her heart could contain so much love.

Maybe it couldn't. The moment she saw Kieran, shining with happiness at her mere sight, her heart nearly stopped. Then it started beating with a wild force as she walked toward him, and she felt ready to burst, her emotions being stretched beyond anything she'd thought existed. How was it even possible that this man was her husband?

Would it always be like this? While she didn't have a suicide wish, she hadn't expected to live long before. Her life had been a trade to offer to the highest bidder in the riskiest assignments.

Now she could imagine growing old with Kieran, even spoiling grandchildren when the time came.

Would he always take her breath away? Did they have what it took to stay in the marriage for life like his parents? Did she? She took her place beside him, smiling up at him.

The answer was yes. She'd spent many nights trying to write her vows and still had no clue what she was about to say. But as she'd taken a leap of faith by marrying him for the children's sake, she was going to do the same for her own sake.

When the time came for her to renew her vows, emotions clogged her throat so much that she couldn't utter a sound. He just smiled at her and squeezed her hand. She looked at their intertwined fingers and was grateful their roads would be like that now, as well—intertwined.

"Auntie, just tell Daddy you'll love him always," Isabella chimed in.

A few nervous chuckles erupted in the audience.

Her throat cleared, and her head did, too. "I will. I mean, I'll love you forever, Kieran. You're the type of man I never knew even existed. Your kindness and your love have no limit. I can easily imagine you with distinguished gray hair. And twenty, thirty years from now, however long my heart will be beating and probably longer, I'll love you just as much, probably more. Because every day I spend with you, I fall for you more and more. I'd walk after you to the other side of the earth and back. But staying at your family ranch is even better."

A few more chuckles sounded from the people who'd come to share this event, people who had come to share her life despite her attempts to keep them out.

Tears glistened in his eyes. "It's *your* ranch now, too. I'd follow you to the other side of the earth, too. But I'm grateful you and our children decided to stay here."

Jackson's chest puffed a little when Kieran said "our children." And unlike at the wedding before, he wasn't glaring. His hair was pulled back in a ponytail, and he was—a miracle!—wearing a suit.

Then Kieran cleared his throat. "I'm the happiest man alive. But you said everything so beautifully that I don't even know what to say."

"Isabella gave a good hint. Say you'll love me always, and if you keep that promise, that's more than enough."

He beamed at her. "I'll love you always. My heart belongs to you, but you know it already."

Men. They didn't realize women wanted to hear things like that again and again. Preferably accompanied by lots of chocolates. But she loved him even without chocolates, and if that wasn't a true kind of love, she didn't know what was.

Epilogue

Summer...

The thought of the upcoming birth caused excitement to bubble under Genevieve's skin.

It didn't matter that it was tinged on the sides with wistfulness like a sweet pie with a crust slightly burned. She was happy for Madeline, who was due this month. The impending birth had prompted Genevieve and Gold to pack their bags and arrive in Cowboy Crossing for a month or two. Well, besides Arianna incessantly inviting them and other reasons.

A wave of tenderness swept over Genevieve as she folded adorable tiny onesies, bootees, and socks in her guest room in the lodge. Her fingers traveled over the soft fabric. She'd pushed those thoughts away for years, but all these baby clothes brought them to the surface. She wanted her own bundle of joy. Yes, she had Gold, who was her life, but Genevieve ached to repeat the experience when she wasn't a young single mother, hurt and terrified out of her mind.

But falling in love, getting married, and having another child wasn't meant to be for her, so she'd poured all her motherly love into her students. That had to be enough, right?

How ironic was it that Arianna, who'd always said she lacked motherly instincts, had adopted two children? That Madeline, who'd never seemed to want a child, was about to have one.

Guilt sliced Genevieve as she arranged all the gifts in boxes with ribbons for the baby shower—the baby shower Madeline had postponed until Genevieve and Gold were here. Genevieve wasn't envious of the happiness her foster sisters had found in an unexpected place. She couldn't be more thrilled for them.

She'd just wanted... What *did* she want? Yes, to give love to a baby, but there was more to it. She wanted to be loved—to experience the kind of all-encompassing romantic love her sisters were experiencing.

She'd never had that, and regret constricted her rib cage. Yes, she'd caught male attention occasionally, but she didn't feel attracted to those men. And for the first twelve years of raising Gold, Genevieve had avoided any romantic relationships after being traumatized by Gold's father so much.

When she'd eventually met men she'd liked, they'd only wanted to be friends. Some of her female colleagues had advised her to lose weight to have more success on the dating scene. She'd scoffed at that. People came in all shapes and sizes, and there was just more of her to love. Right?

Children's laughter drew her to the bulletproof window that overlooked the fenced-in backyard. That sound made her smile as it always did. One of the perks of her job was hearing it relatively often. She looked out the window.

Isabella and her little friend from the neighboring ranch, dressed in blue and green socks and blue and green shoes—the shoes did *not* match the socks—played catch with Madeline's German shepherd. Kieran and Declan played with them, and their laughter joined in.

Heat rose inside her, and her heart started beating faster as she watched Declan. She'd hidden her crush well so far, hadn't she? She'd even become friends with him. It was easier that way. She loved spending time with her sisters and their families, and since Declan had been spending his summer vacation at the ranch, he'd joined in.

She hadn't noticed how she'd started looking forward to those meetings. He had the deepest brown eyes she'd ever seen and could put everyone at ease and make them laugh in less than a minute. Especially the few times when he'd picked up the guitar at the campfire and sang country songs. The words had spoken to her, and his voice had caressed her skin like fine velvet.

A longing stirred inside her.

He yelled something, then lifted Isabella onto his shoulders, and the little girl giggled, clearly delighted.

Genevieve could relate.

This crush didn't make sense, and she was a sensible woman or had to be. While other children had played with dolls, she'd had to grow up fast. While other teens had gone out, she'd had to cook and mother her sisters. While other young women had dated, she'd been raising her child alone. She needed a sensible, responsible, stable partner and husband.

On the contrary, Declan was a player. His relationships never lasted. He was also a wanderer. He'd never stayed in the same place for long.

Falling for a guy like that was setting herself up for heartbreak. Yet... She touched the smooth glass, wishing she could reach out and touch him.

Not to mention she had a history, a secret she'd kept hidden from everyone except her sisters. Gold was an heiress, but the family she should inherit from didn't know about it. Genevieve was determined to keep it that way. Even if the death of the previous heir, Hayden, seemed to be a hiking accident, Genevieve wasn't so sure.

A shiver traveled down her back, ruining the beautiful moment.

What was she going to tell Declan if he asked about Gold's father? Okay, maybe he wouldn't ask, but how could she hide something that huge? Something that could put at risk anyone close to her if the truth ever became known?

The knock on the door made her flinch and jerk back as if she were nearly caught doing something wrong.

"May I come in?" Arianna's voice filtered through the door.

"Sure." Genevieve's voice sounded strange, almost husky. That wouldn't do. "Of course," she said again, this time sounding much more like herself.

Arianna opened the door and walked in. A newfound peacefulness about her softened her serrated edginess, making Genevieve's lips tug up as if she were a proud parent of a child who'd excelled. Arianna still wore black clothes most of the time—jeans and a T-shirt today—but a bright marmalade-hued apron was wrapped around her waist and her feet drowned in pink slippers with bunny ears.

She must've caught Genevieve's gaze. "The slippers are Isabella and Jackson's Mother's Day gift for their auntie." She wiggled them, showing off the floppy ears. "I think it was a challenge on his part."

Genevieve hid a smile.

Since Arianna had met Kieran, her prickliness smoothed out, making her unusual beauty much more approachable. Happiness suited Arianna, and Genevieve was grateful. Of all her foster sisters, Arianna had worried Genevieve the most.

But not any longer.

"Dinner is ready." Arianna took off her apron. "Of course, it's not as awesome as anything you cook."

"You think my food is awesome because most of the time you all were hungry by the time it was ready. Your food is great. Besides, I'm not spoiled."

Genevieve chuckled, pleased, however, that Arianna liked her cooking. "Sorry I didn't help make dinner."

Arianna's gaze was unreadable, but then it always was. Though marriage and motherhood had made her more open and sociable, a lot of times she was still the proverbial closed book, even to someone who read as much as Genevieve.

"Maybe you should be." Arianna turned around and stepped into the hall.

Genevieve blinked and followed. "Should be what?"

"Spoiled. So don't be sorry you didn't help with dinner. You're the guest, and I want to pamper you. Not that we can ever repay what you've done for us."

Seriously? "I never expected or wanted any of you to repay me."

Genevieve caught up with Arianna as they stepped into the kitchen. She let Arianna go first. It wasn't just out of politeness. Genevieve had learned the hard way that if she didn't, the situation could get very awkward, and she could get stuck. Literally.

Heat rose inside. It wasn't a great pedagogical moment when she'd been stuck in the doorframe with another teacher, a guy she'd liked, of all people. After they'd managed to wiggle through, he'd blamed the incident on her size.

Argh.

Arianna started laying the table, and Genevieve reached for utensils when Arianna shook her head. "How about you let everyone in the yard know dinner is ready, please? Oh, and invite Declan to dinner, will you?"

Genevieve froze. Did Arianna suspect Genevieve's secret crush? While Arianna didn't speak much, she'd always been observant.

"Are you okay with inviting Declan to dinner?" Arianna searched her face.

Genevieve swallowed hard. "Of course. We're friends. Best friends." Her phone rang, and she perked up, glad to be saved by the bell.

No, she shouldn't use this as an excuse not to talk to Declan. Besides, nothing would happen if she invited him to dinner. She flushed. It wasn't like she'd be inviting him to dinner with just two of them.

"Sure. I'll do that." She walked to the door leading to the backyard.

She considered letting the call go to voicemail. Seeing Jessie's name on the screen, she changed her mind and answered before stepping outside. Jessie was always fast and to the point, and if she called, it was usually something important. "Hello, Jessie."

"I have new information about what happened to Hayden."

THE END

From Alexa: Thank you so much for reading! Did you enjoy Kieran and Arianna's story? I hope you'd like to read about Declan and Genevieve's chance at happiness. If so, please click here[1] to purchase the next book.

.

Are you curious about the person who saved Arianna's life when she was shot? Here's the link[2] to download the bonus scene from Courtney's perspective for FREE. By downloading, you'll sign up for my newsletter, but you can unsubscribe at any time.

.

If my readers become curious about Courtney, she might get her own book, too!

---

1. https://books2read.com/u/bONrOK

2. https://dl.bookfunnel.com/5tukl47wgf

Other books by Alexa Verde

To see an updated list of all my other books or subscribe to my weekly reader newsletter (and get a free ebook as your welcome gift!) click here[1].

1. https://www.subscribepage.com/alexaverdepublishedbooks

Acknowledgments

First of all, thank You to God for putting up with me, and for all the blessings!

A million thanks to you, my readers, for reading my books, for sending me encouragement, and for supporting me.

Many thanks to my street team, Alexa's Amazing Readers, and to my beta readers, whom I love to pieces. Special thanks to Terry, Trudy, Priscilla, Mary Jane, MaryEllen, Julie, Carol, Michaela, Margaret, Debbie, and Kim for their feedback and help with typo-spotting!

Heartfelt thanks to author Jessie Gussman for coming up with the idea for the Cowboy Crossing series and for helping me so much on the way. Jessie, you make me laugh, you make me smile, and you make the world a better place.

I also thank my wonderful editor, Deirdre, for coming through for me every time.

www.ingramcontent.com/pod-product-compliance
Lightning Source LLC
Chambersburg PA
CBHW021527150726
47990CB00006B/2127